NARWHAL AND JELLY

SUPER POD PARTY PACK!

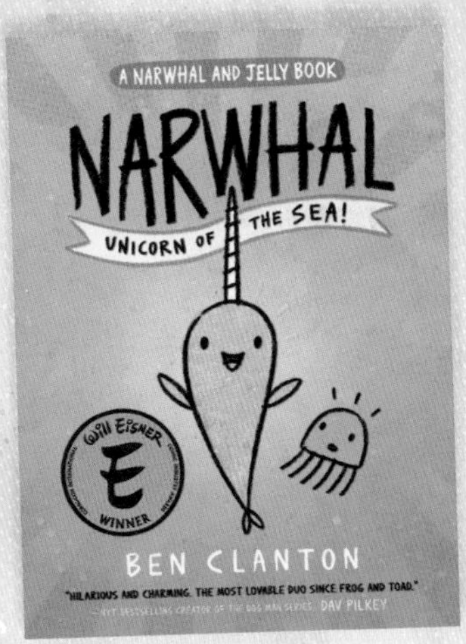
A NARWHAL AND JELLY BOOK
NARWHAL
UNICORN OF THE SEA!
Will Eisner WINNER
BEN CLANTON
"HILARIOUS AND CHARMING. THE MOST LOVABLE DUO SINCE FROG AND TOAD."
—NYT BESTSELLING CREATOR OF THE DOG MAN SERIES, DAV PILKEY

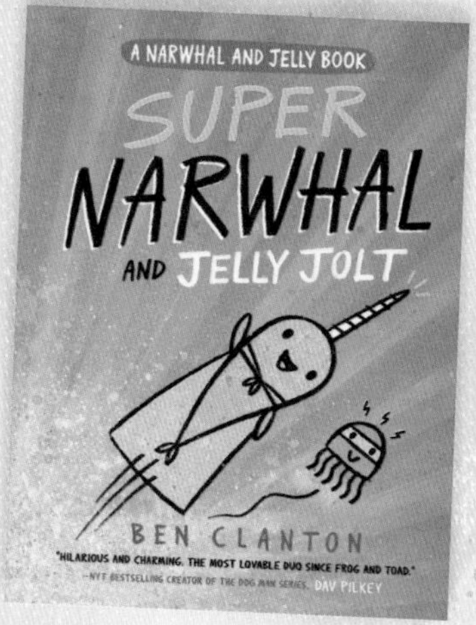
A NARWHAL AND JELLY BOOK
SUPER
NARWHAL
AND JELLY JOLT
BEN CLANTON
"HILARIOUS AND CHARMING. THE MOST LOVABLE DUO SINCE FROG AND TOAD."
—NYT BESTSELLING CREATOR OF THE DOG MAN SERIES, DAV PILKEY

1. NARWHAL: UNICORN OF THE SEA!
2. SUPER NARWHAL AND JELLY JOLT

BEN CLANTON

tundra

Tundra Books, an imprint of Tundra Book Group,
a division of Penguin Random House of Canada Limited

Library and Archives Canada Cataloguing in Publication

Title: Narwhal and Jelly : super pod party pack! / Ben Clanton.
Other titles: Graphic novels. Selections
Names: Clanton, Ben, 1988- author, artist. |
Container of (work): Clanton, Ben, 1988- Narwhal. |
Container of (work): Clanton, Ben, 1988- Super Narwhal and Jelly Jolt.
Identifiers: Canadiana 20220465339 | ISBN 9781774883730 (softcover)
Subjects: LCGFT: Graphic novels. | LCGFT: Animal fiction.
Classification: LCC PZ7.7.C53 Na 2023 | DDC j741.5/973–dc23

Published simultaneously in the United States of America by
Tundra Books of Northern New York, an imprint of Tundra Book Group,
a division of Penguin Random House of Canada Limited

Library of Congress Control Number: 2022951320

Edited by Tara Walker and Peter Phillips
Designed by Ben Clanton
The artwork in this book was rendered using mainly Procreate and Adobe Photoshop.
The text was set in a typeface based on hand-lettering by Ben Clanton.

Photos: (waffle) © Tiger Images/Shutterstock; (strawberry) © Valentina Razumova/ Shutterstock; (pickle) © dominitsky/Shutterstock; (tuba) Internet Archive Book Images

Printed in China

www.penguinrandomhouse.ca

1 2 3 4 5 27 26 25 24 23

tundra | Penguin Random House
TUNDRA BOOKS

NARWHAL

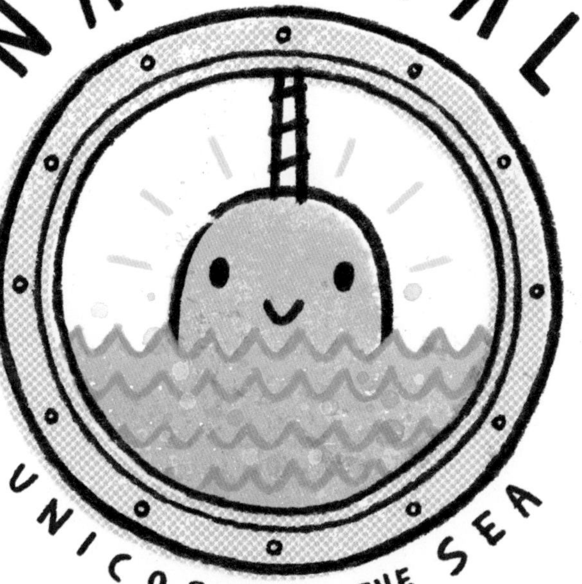

UNICORN OF THE SEA

NARWHAL
UNICORN OF THE SEA

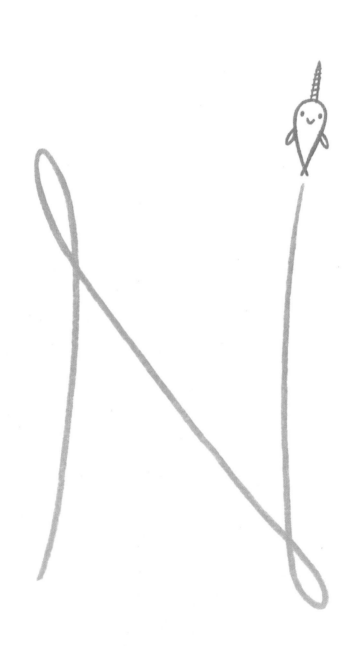

NARWHAL IS REALLY AWESOME

ONE DAY WHEN OUT FOR A SWIM, NARWHAL FOUND THEMSELF IN NEW WATERS . . .

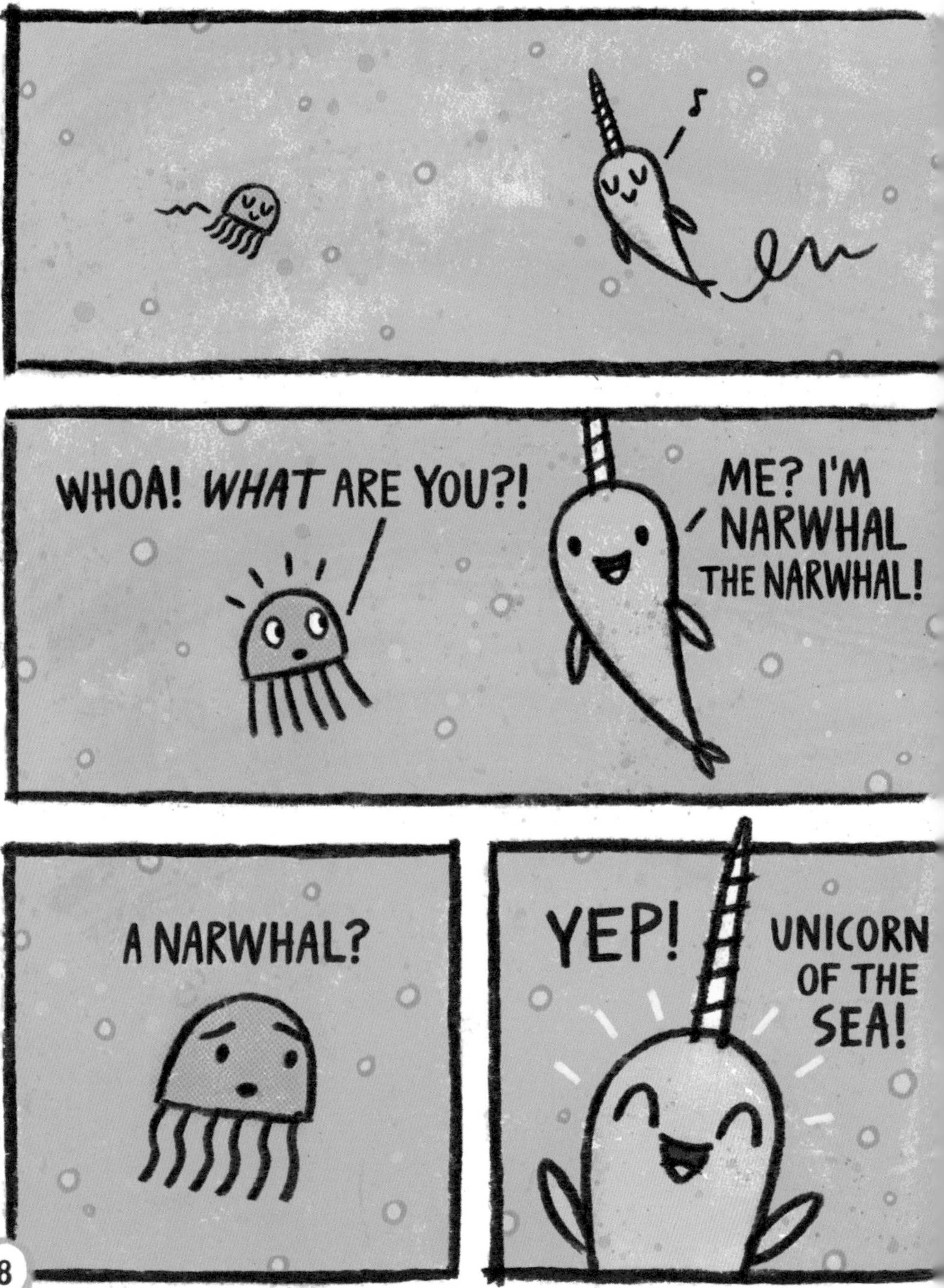
WHOA! *WHAT* ARE YOU?!
ME? I'M NARWHAL THE NARWHAL!
A NARWHAL?
YEP!
UNICORN OF THE SEA!

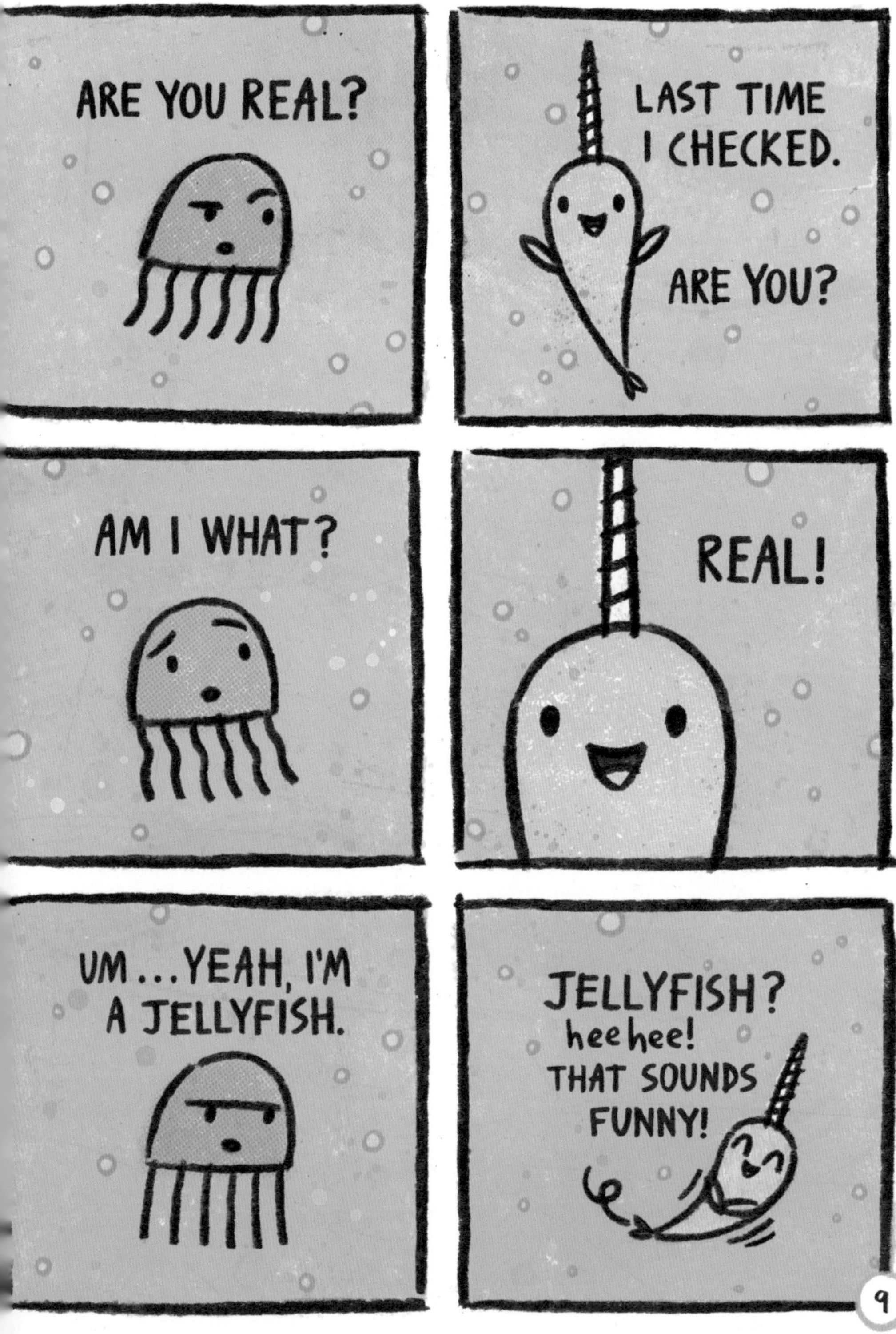
ARE YOU REAL?
LAST TIME I CHECKED.
ARE YOU?
AM I WHAT?
REAL!
UM...YEAH, I'M A JELLYFISH.
JELLYFISH?
heehee!
THAT SOUNDS FUNNY!

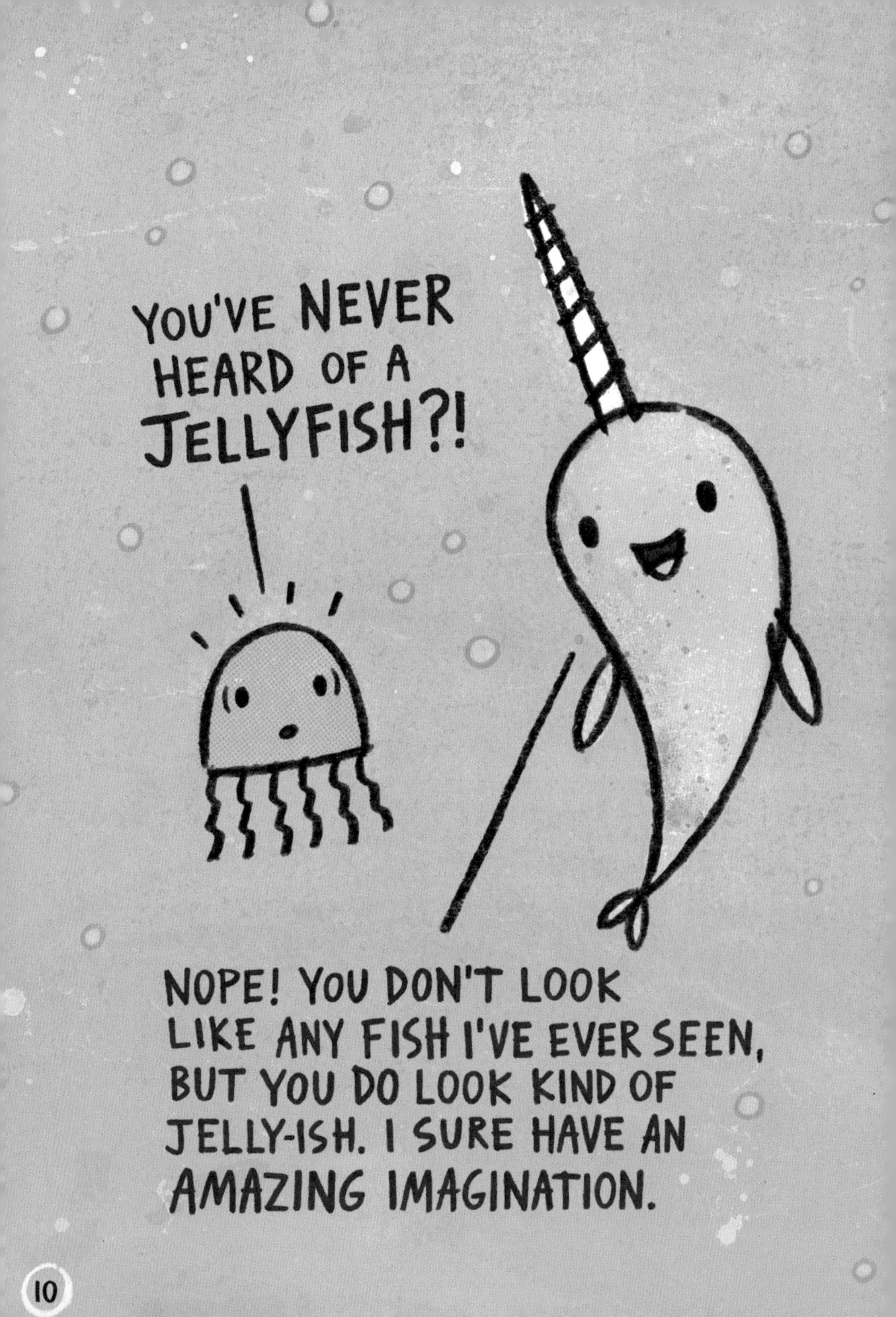
YOU'VE NEVER HEARD OF A JELLYFISH?!
NOPE! YOU DON'T LOOK LIKE ANY FISH I'VE EVER SEEN, BUT YOU DO LOOK KIND OF JELLY-ISH. I SURE HAVE AN AMAZING IMAGINATION.

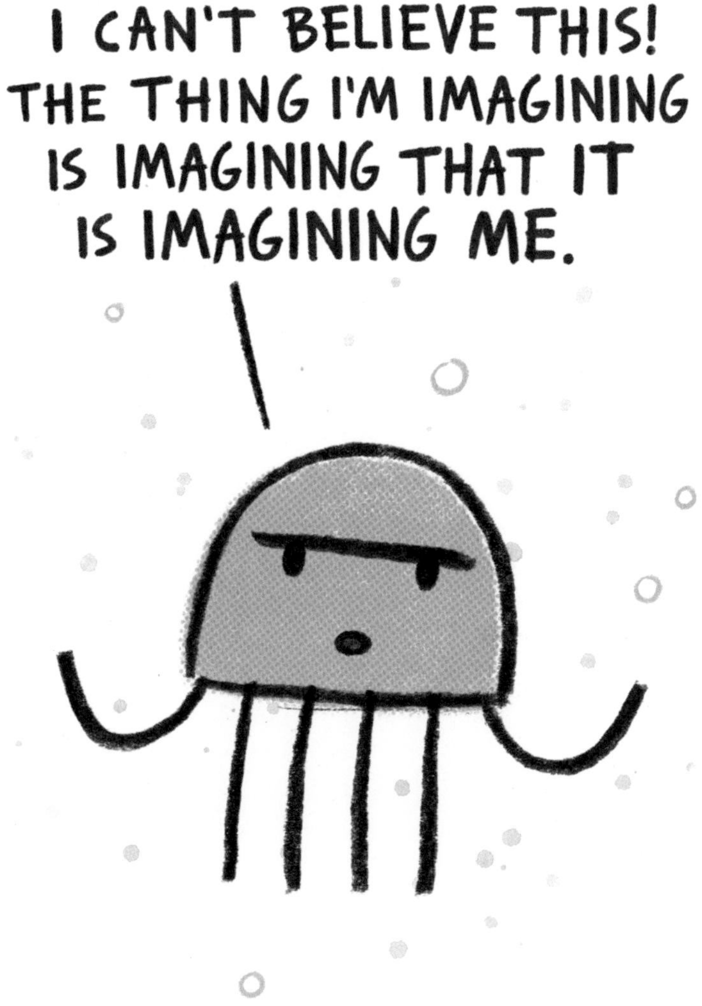
I CAN'T BELIEVE THIS! THE THING I'M IMAGINING IS IMAGINING THAT IT IS IMAGINING ME.

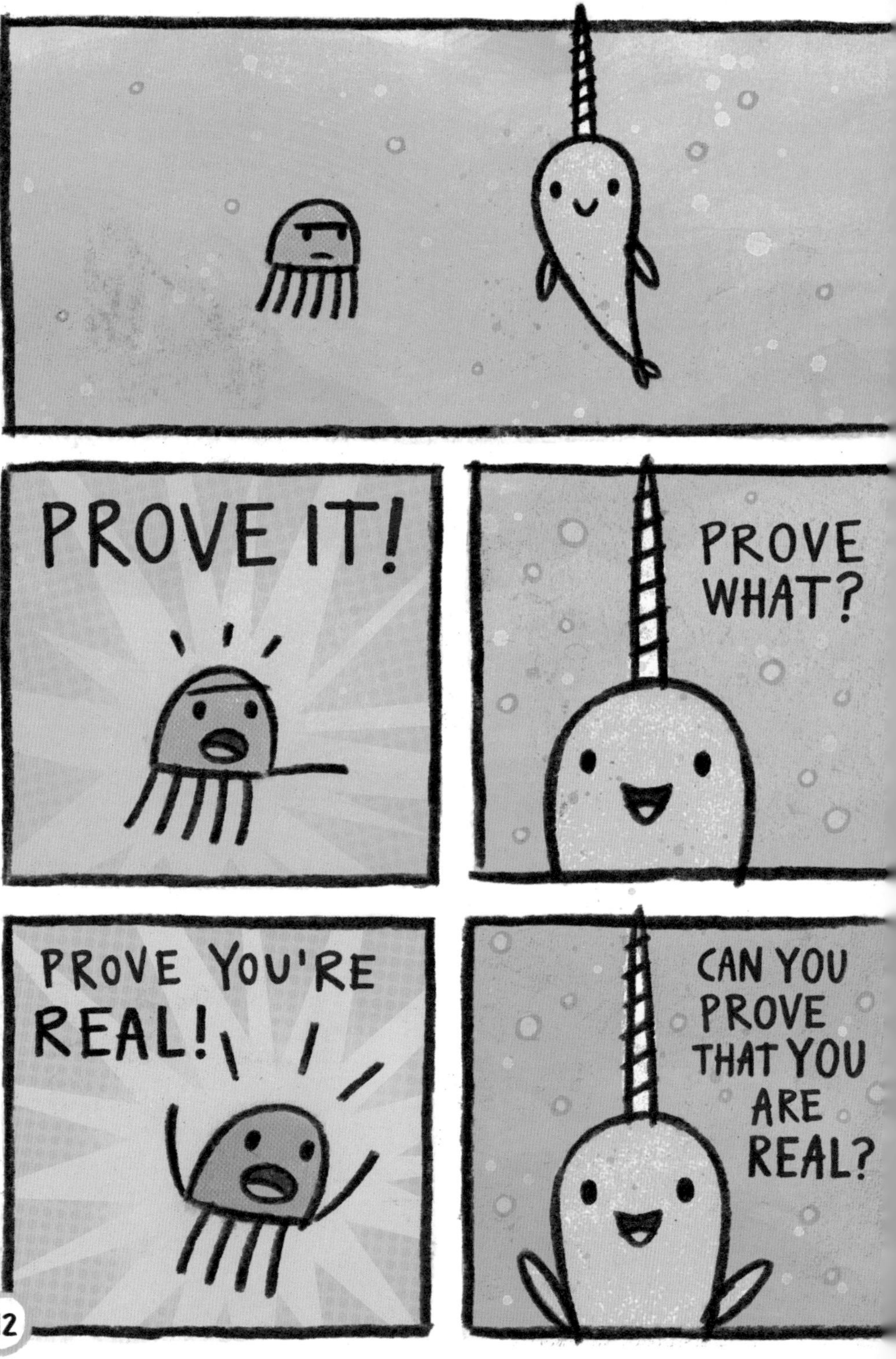
PROVE IT!
PROVE WHAT?
PROVE YOU'RE REAL!
CAN YOU PROVE THAT YOU ARE REAL?

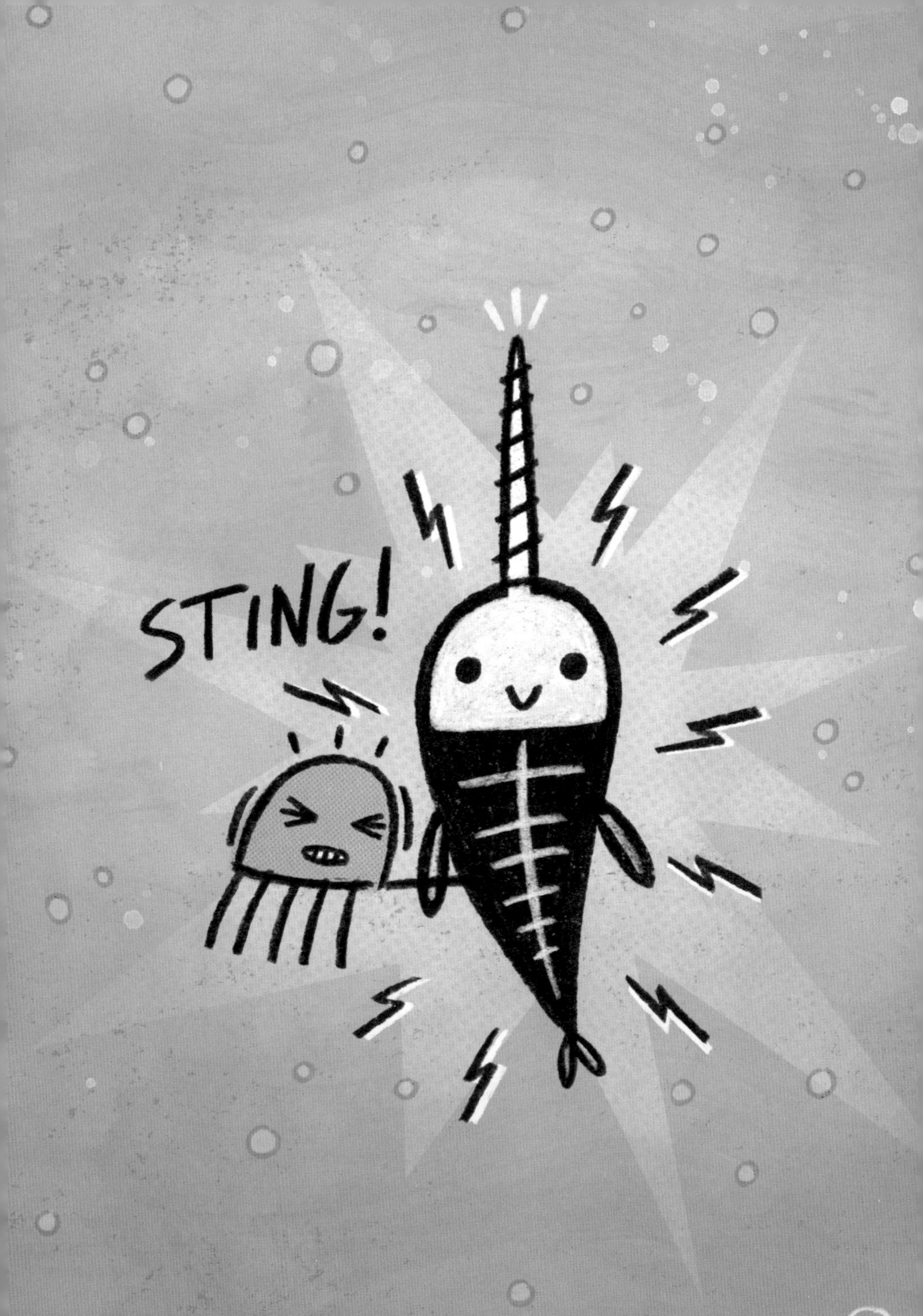
STING!

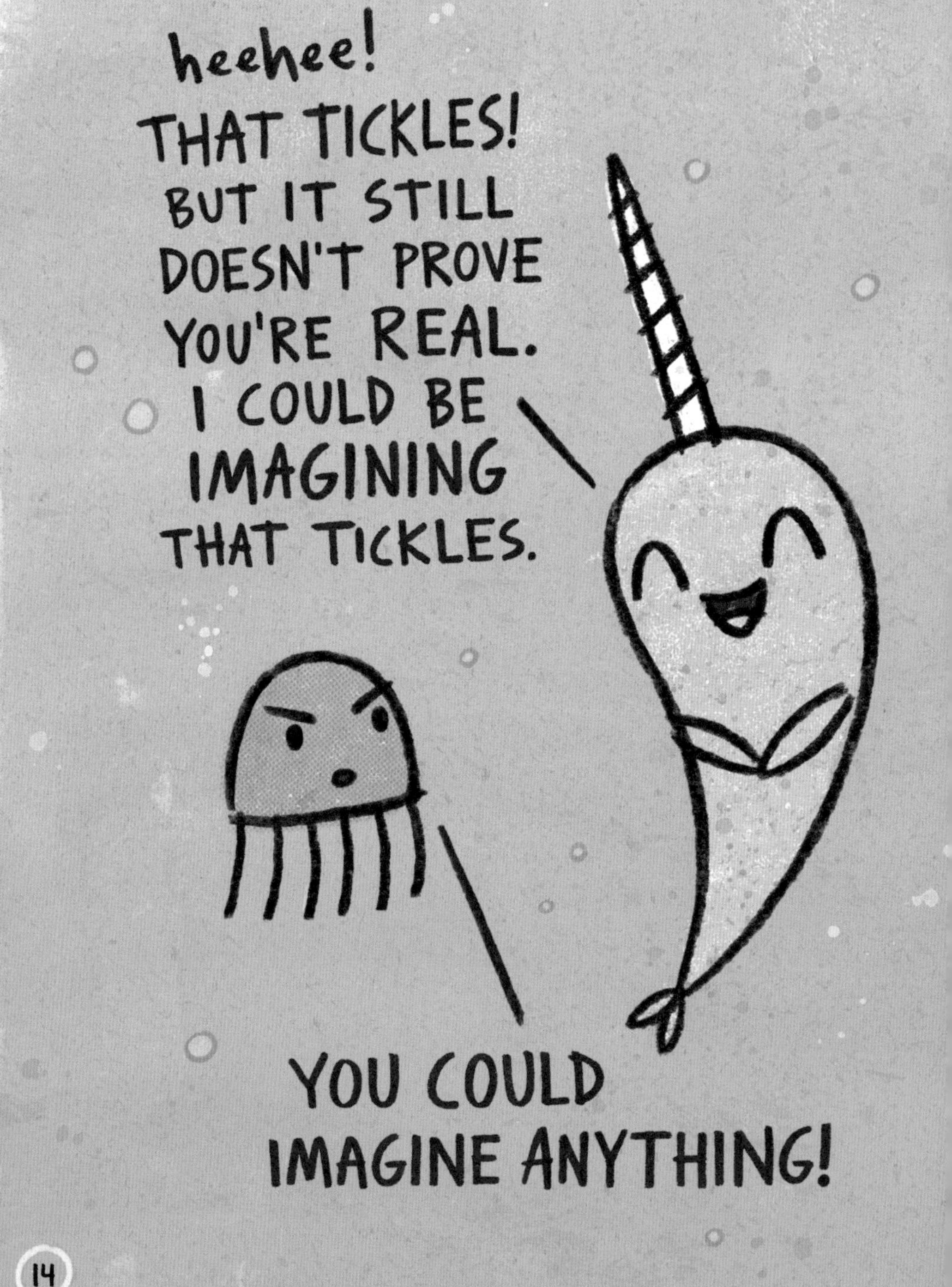
heehee!
THAT TICKLES! BUT IT STILL DOESN'T PROVE YOU'RE REAL. I COULD BE IMAGINING THAT TICKLES.
YOU COULD IMAGINE ANYTHING!

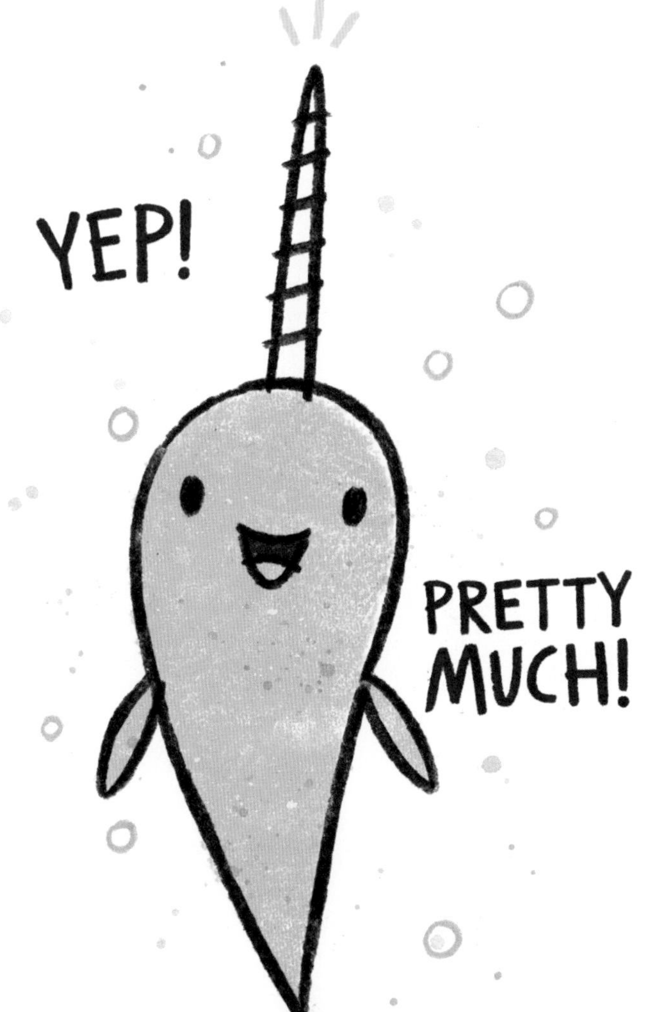
YEP!
PRETTY MUCH!

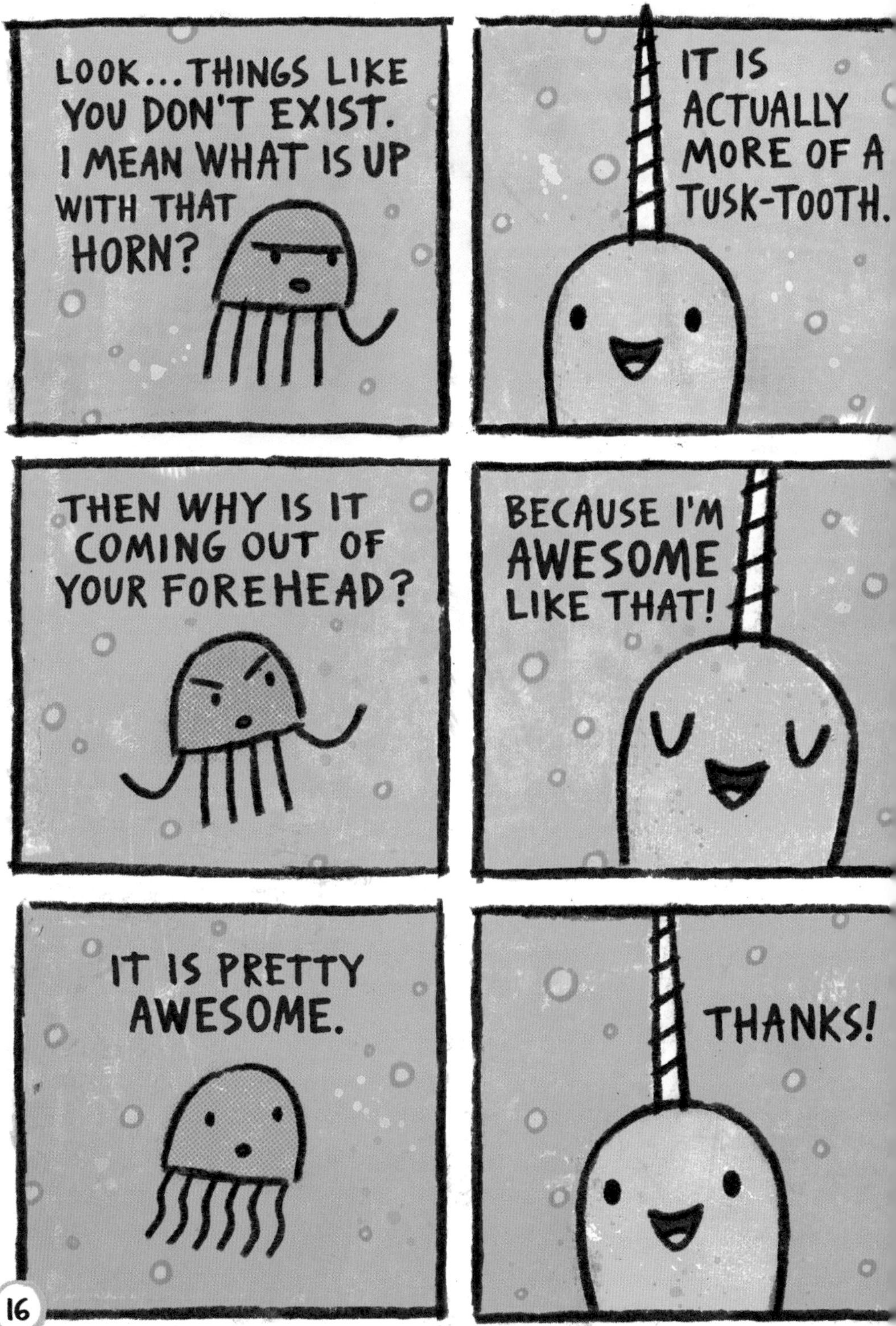
LOOK... THINGS LIKE YOU DON'T EXIST. I MEAN WHAT IS UP WITH THAT HORN?
IT IS ACTUALLY MORE OF A TUSK-TOOTH.
THEN WHY IS IT COMING OUT OF YOUR FOREHEAD?
BECAUSE I'M AWESOME LIKE THAT!
IT IS PRETTY AWESOME.
THANKS!

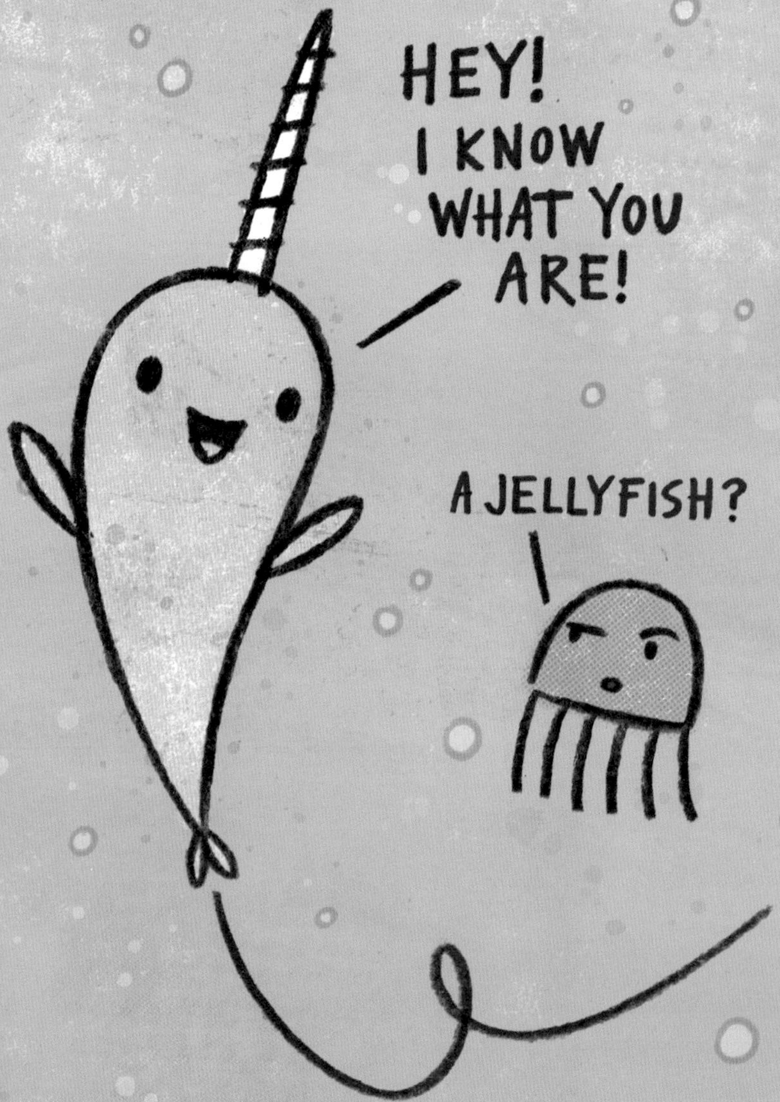
HEY! I KNOW WHAT YOU ARE!
A JELLYFISH?

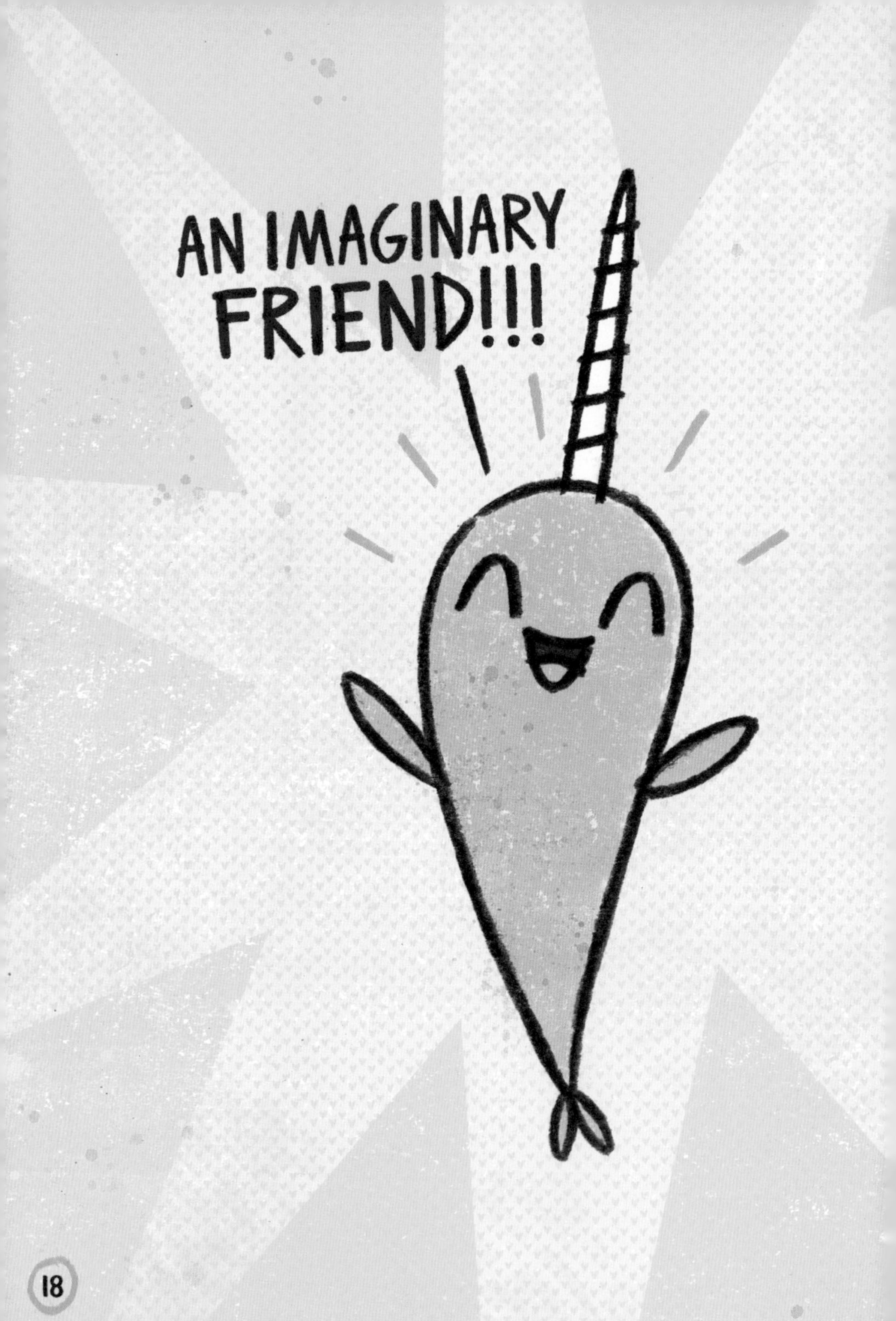
AN IMAGINARY
FRIEND!!!

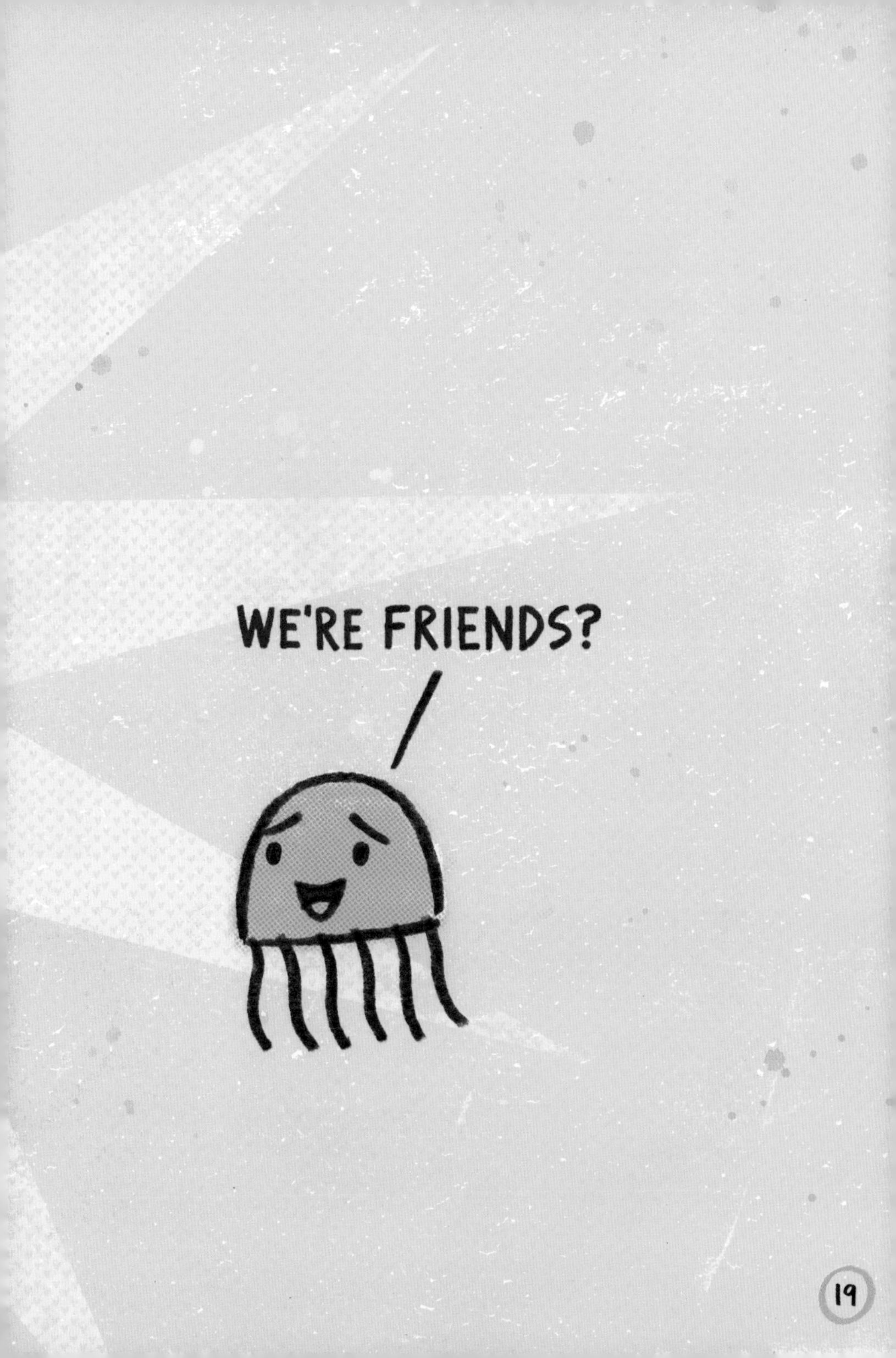
WE'RE FRIENDS?

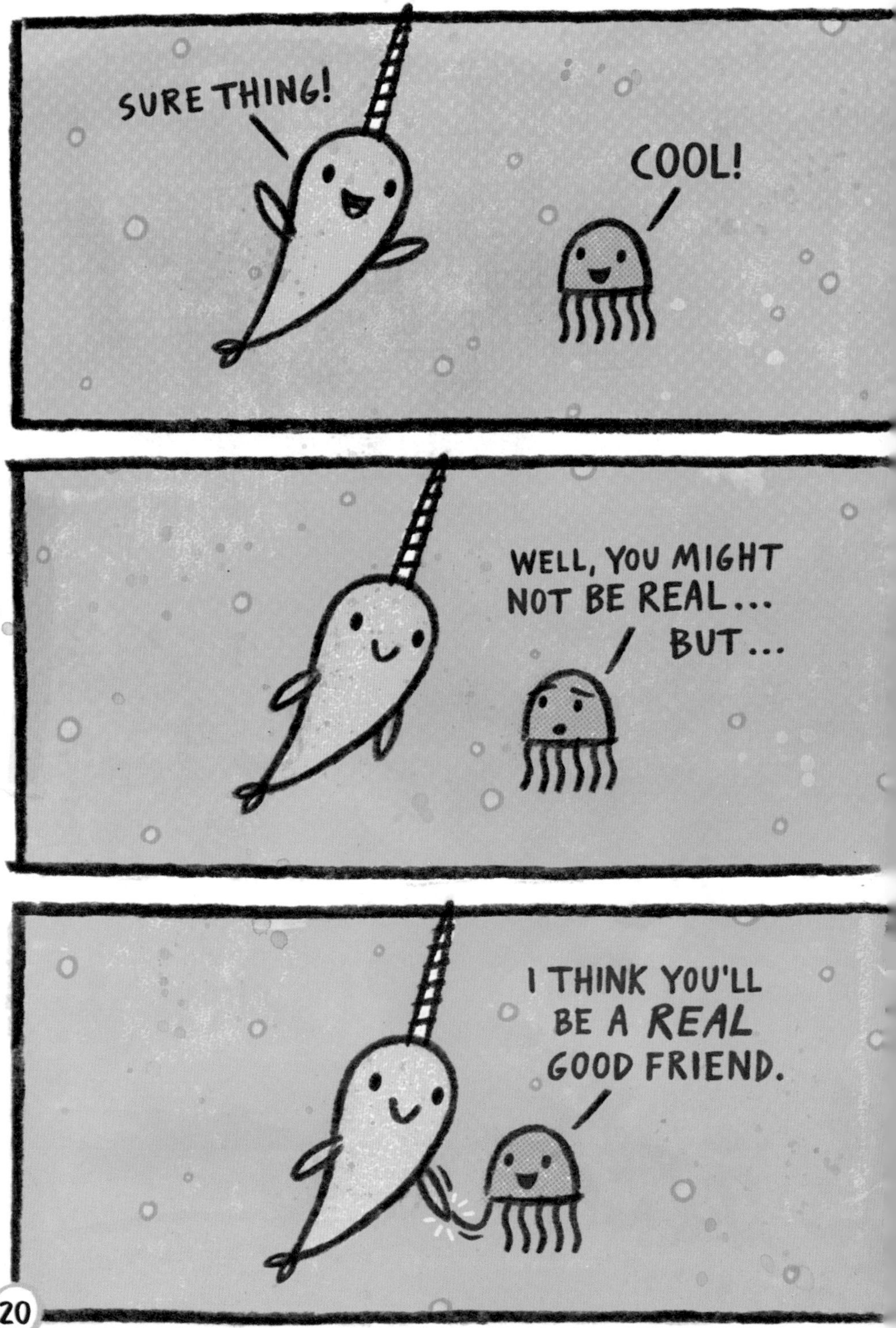
SURE THING!
COOL!
WELL, YOU MIGHT NOT BE REAL... BUT...
I THINK YOU'LL BE A REAL GOOD FRIEND.

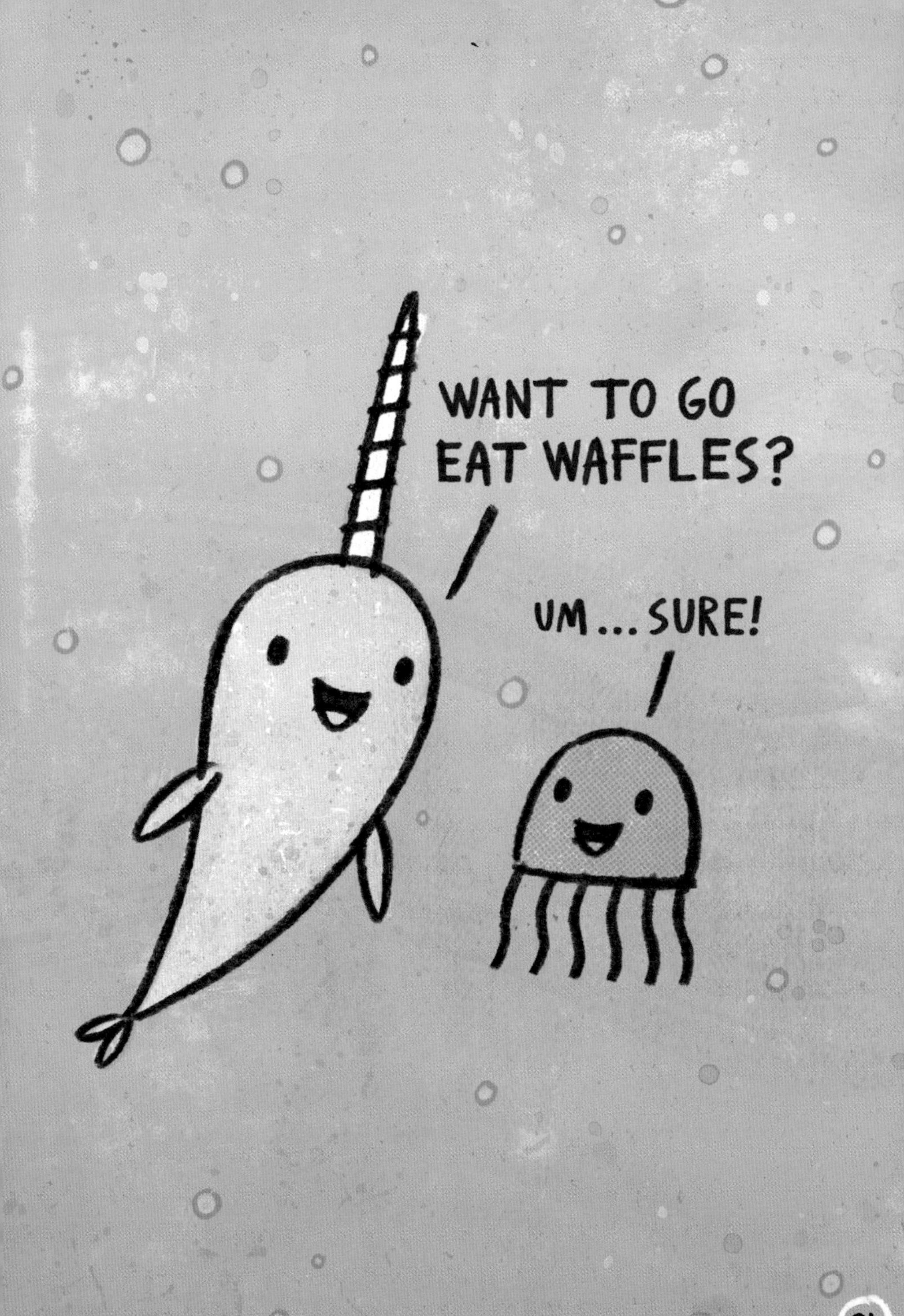
WANT TO GO EAT WAFFLES?
UM... SURE!

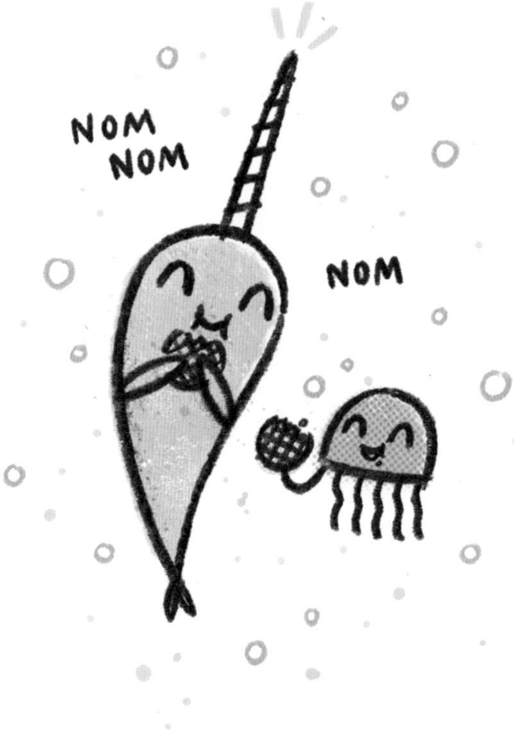
NOM
NOM
NOM

REALLY FUN FACTS

A NARWHAL'S LONG, HORN-LIKE TOOTH CAN REACH UP TO 3 m (10 ft.) LONG!

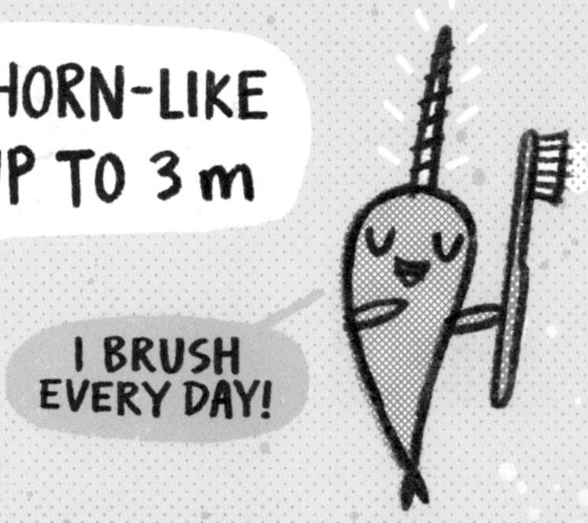
I BRUSH EVERY DAY!

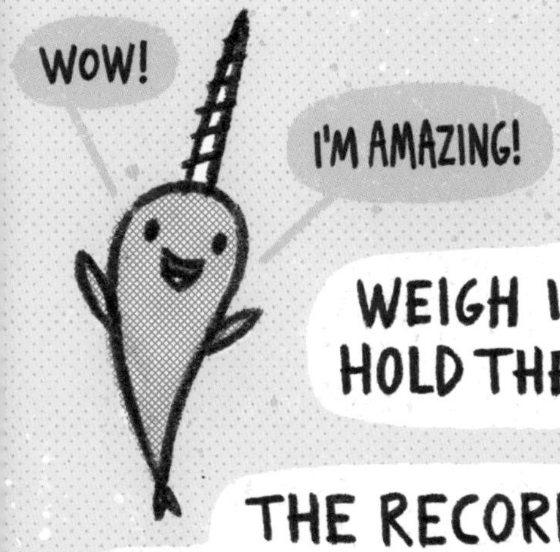
WOW!
I'M AMAZING!

NARWHALS CAN WEIGH 1,600 kg (3,500 lb.) AND HOLD THEIR BREATH FOR 25 min.

THE RECORD DIVE DEPTH FOR A NARWHAL IS 1,800 m (5,905 ft., OVER ONE MILE).

RECENT RESEARCH SUGGESTS NARWHALS CAN LIVE UP TO 90 YEARS.

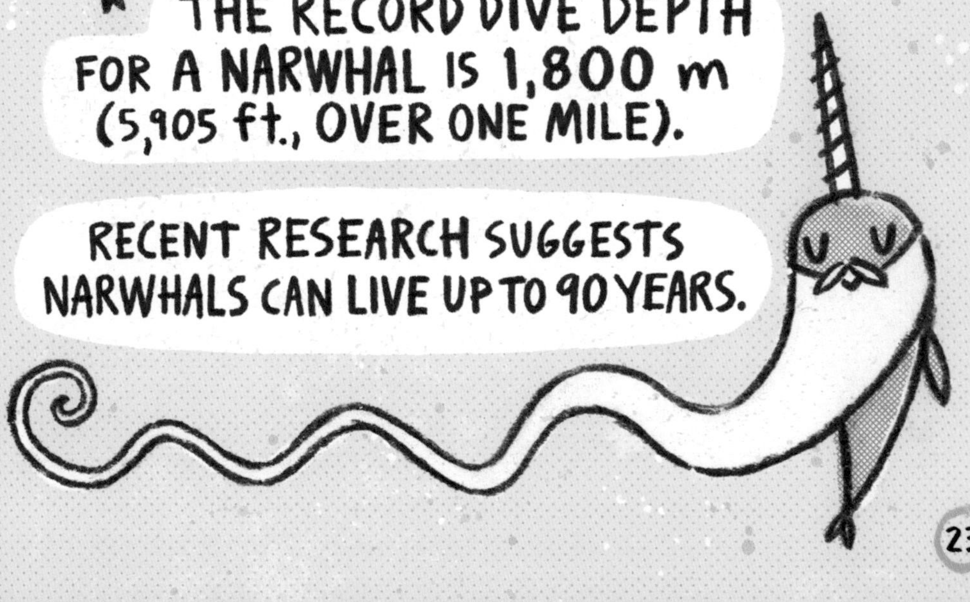

MORE REALLY FUN FACTS

THERE ARE NEARLY 4,000 TYPES OF JELLYFISH IN THE WORLD.

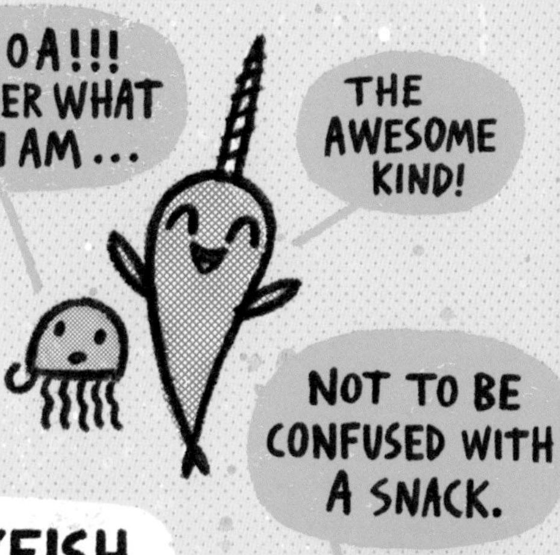
WHOA!!! I WONDER WHAT KIND I AM...
THE AWESOME KIND!
NOT TO BE CONFUSED WITH A SNACK.

A GROUP OF JELLYFISH IS CALLED A SMACK.

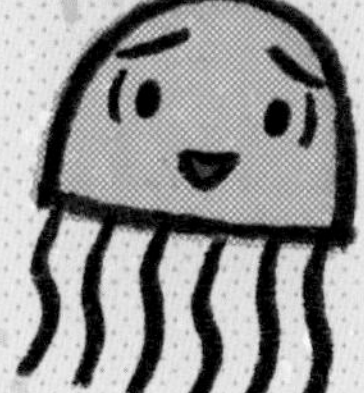

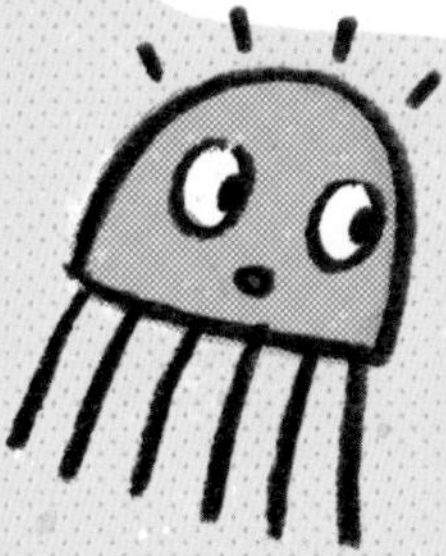

JELLYFISH HAVE BEEN AROUND FOR MILLIONS OF YEARS. WELL BEFORE DINOSAURS!

THE STING FROM SOME JELLYFISH CAN BE DEADLY FOR HUMANS.

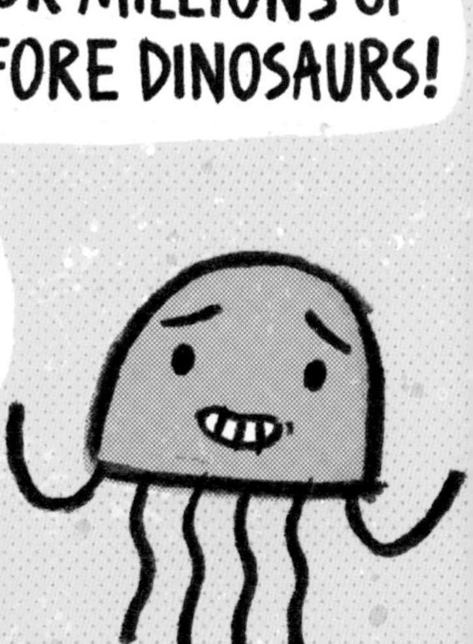

NARWHAL'S POD OF AWESOMENESS

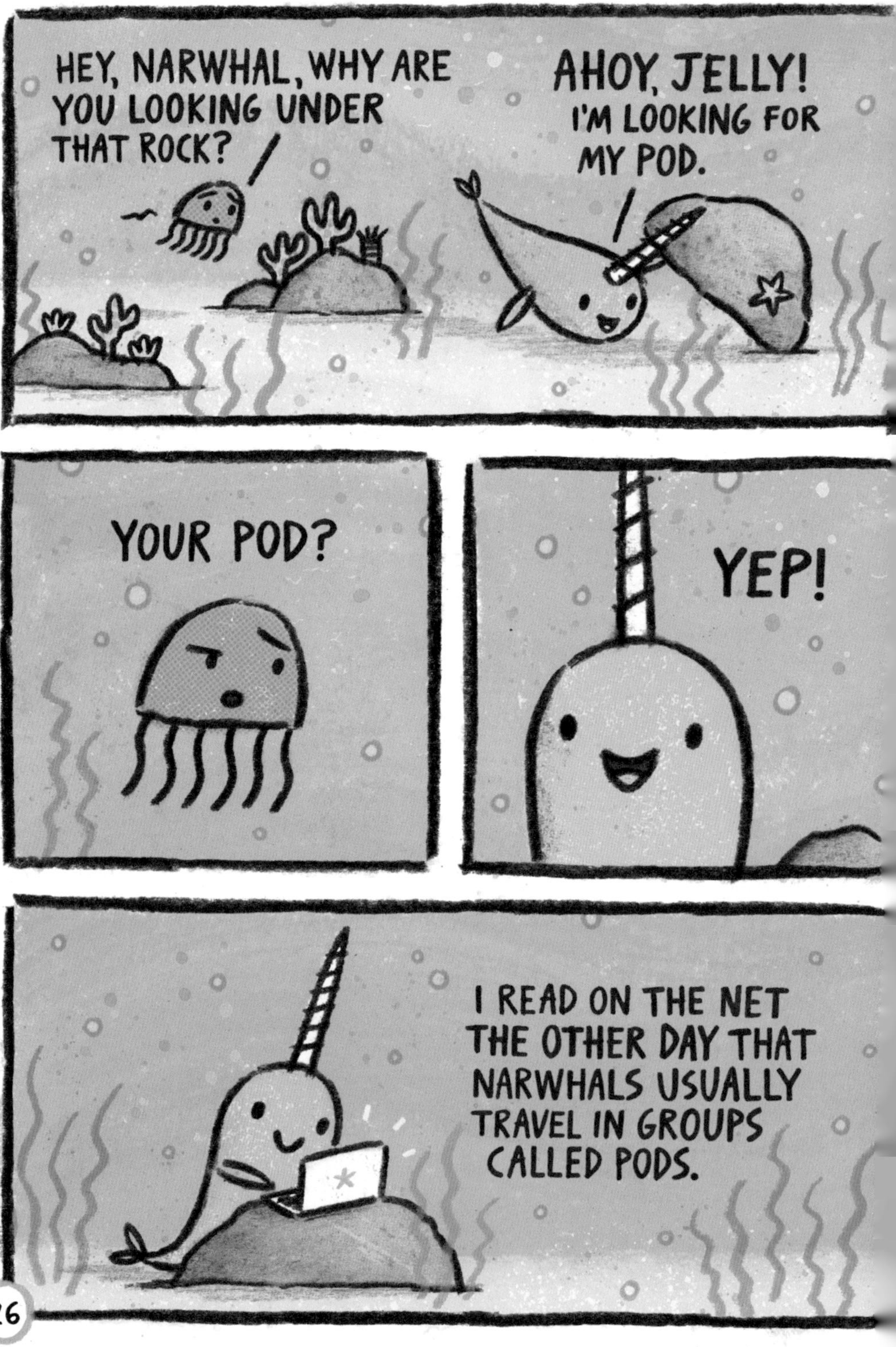
HEY, NARWHAL, WHY ARE YOU LOOKING UNDER THAT ROCK?
AHOY, JELLY! I'M LOOKING FOR MY POD.
YOUR POD?
YEP!
I READ ON THE NET THE OTHER DAY THAT NARWHALS USUALLY TRAVEL IN GROUPS CALLED PODS.

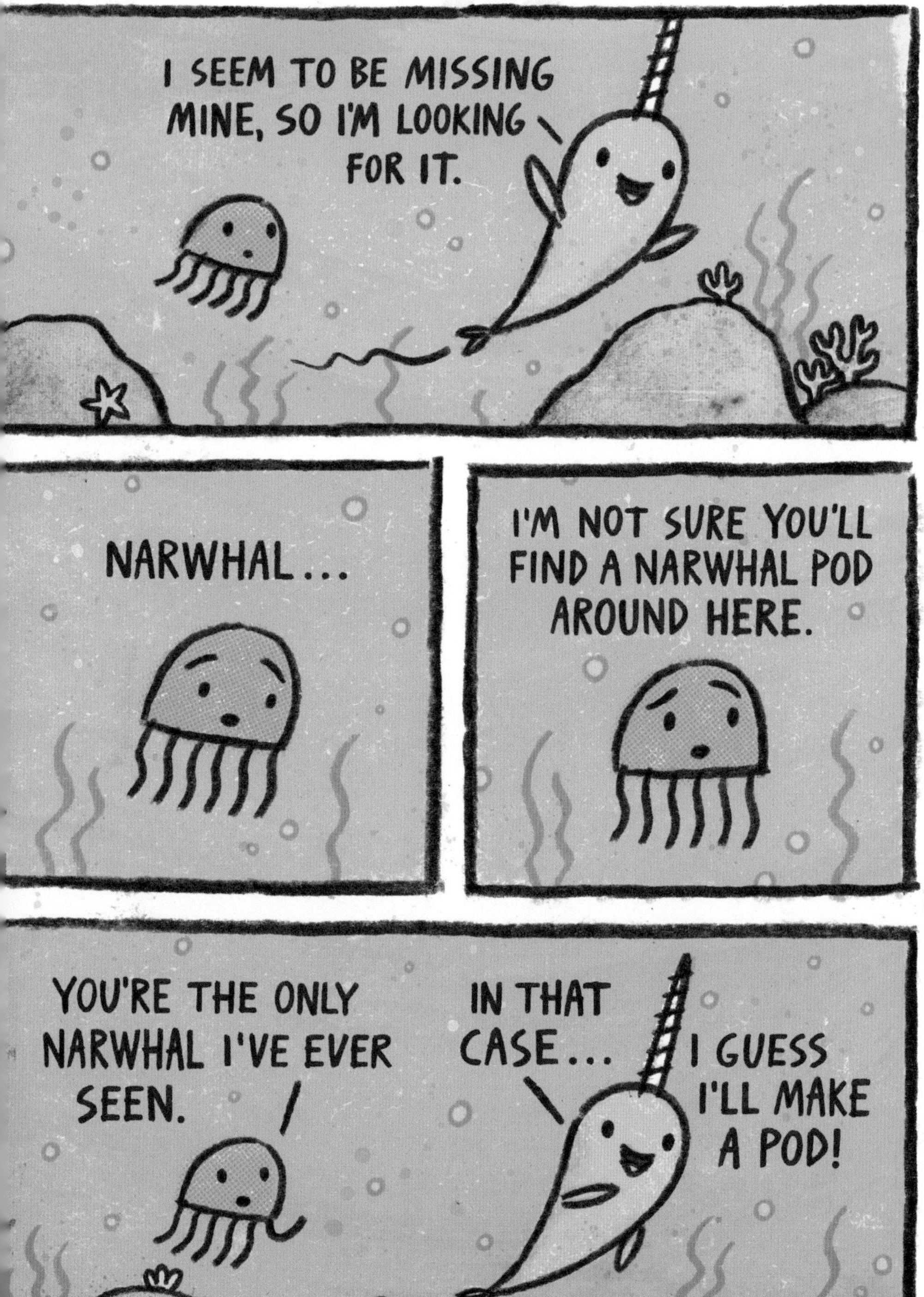
I SEEM TO BE MISSING MINE, SO I'M LOOKING FOR IT.
NARWHAL...
I'M NOT SURE YOU'LL FIND A NARWHAL POD AROUND HERE.
YOU'RE THE ONLY NARWHAL I'VE EVER SEEN.
IN THAT CASE...
I GUESS I'LL MAKE A POD!

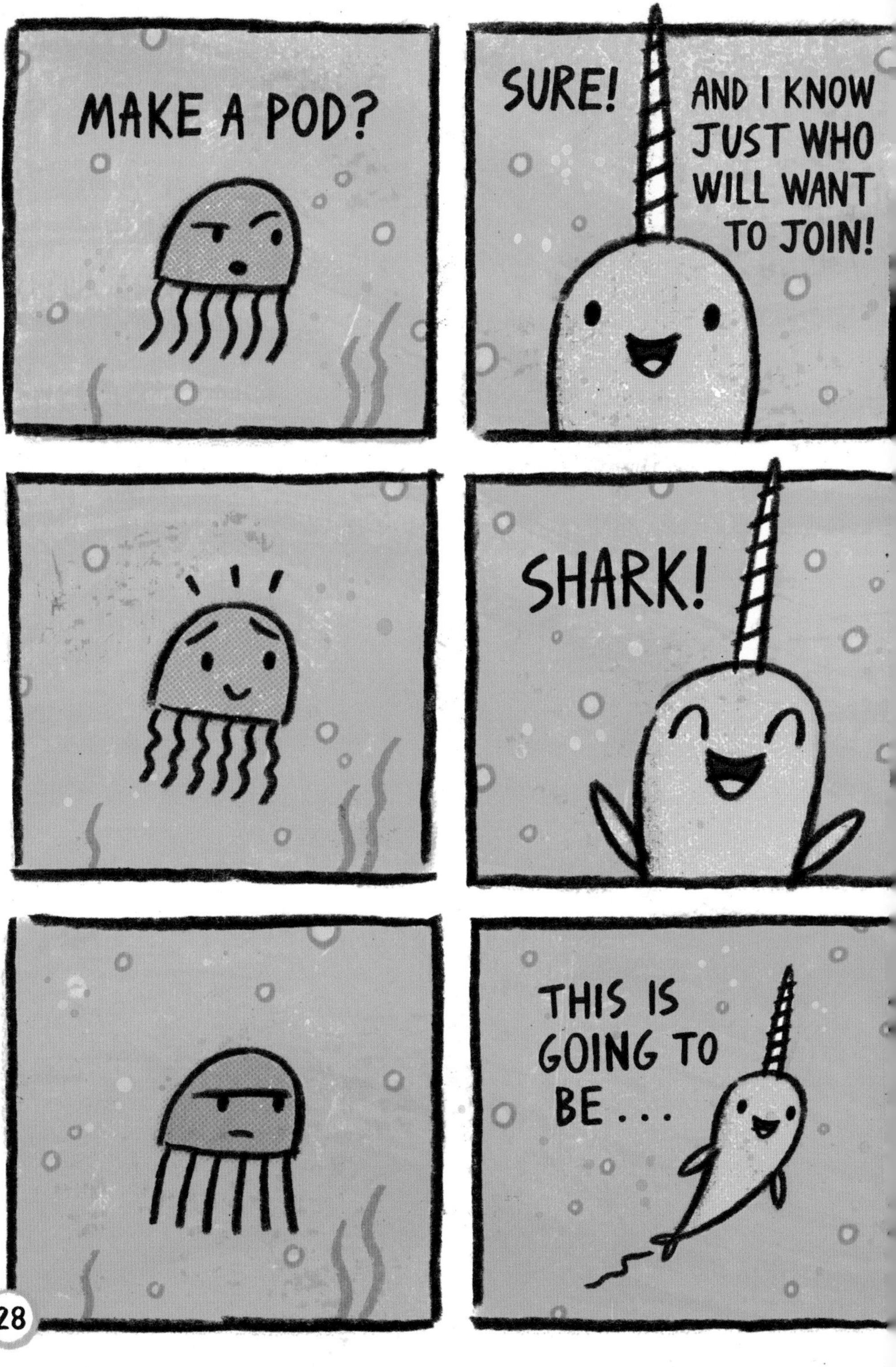
MAKE A POD?
SURE!
AND I KNOW JUST WHO WILL WANT TO JOIN!
SHARK!
THIS IS GOING TO BE . . .

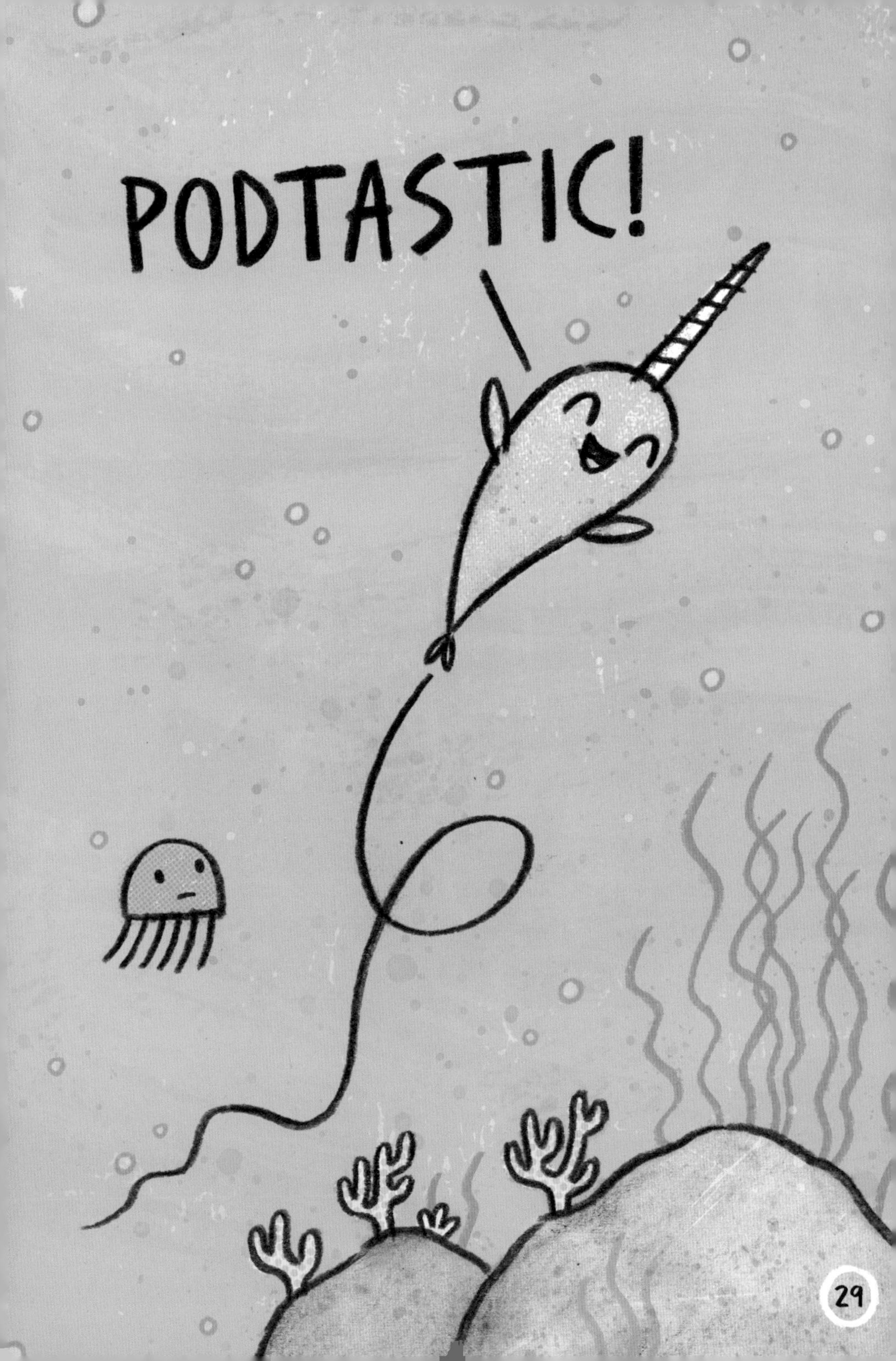
PODTASTIC!

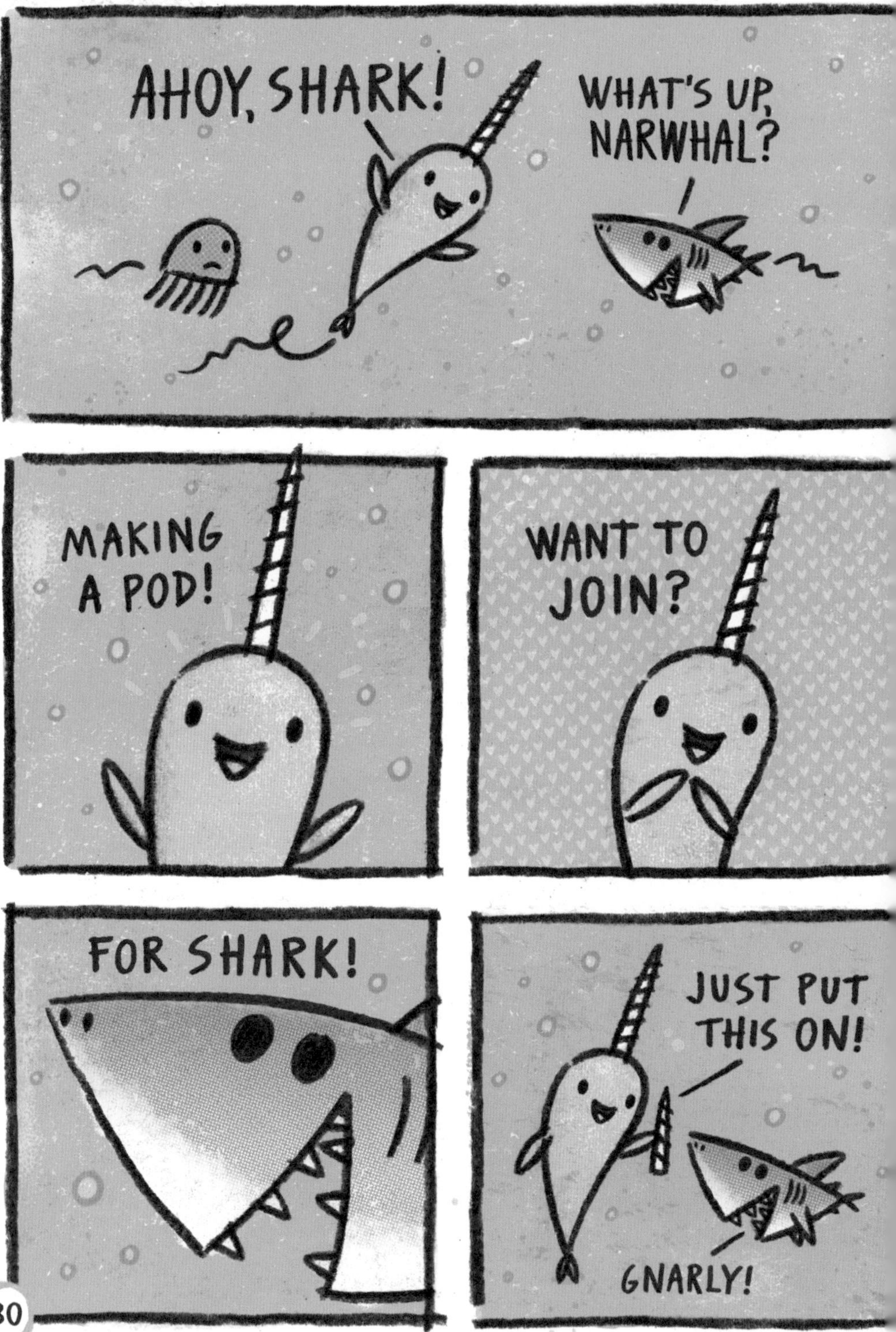
AHOY, SHARK!
WHAT'S UP, NARWHAL?
MAKING A POD!
WANT TO JOIN?
FOR SHARK!
JUST PUT THIS ON!
GNARLY!

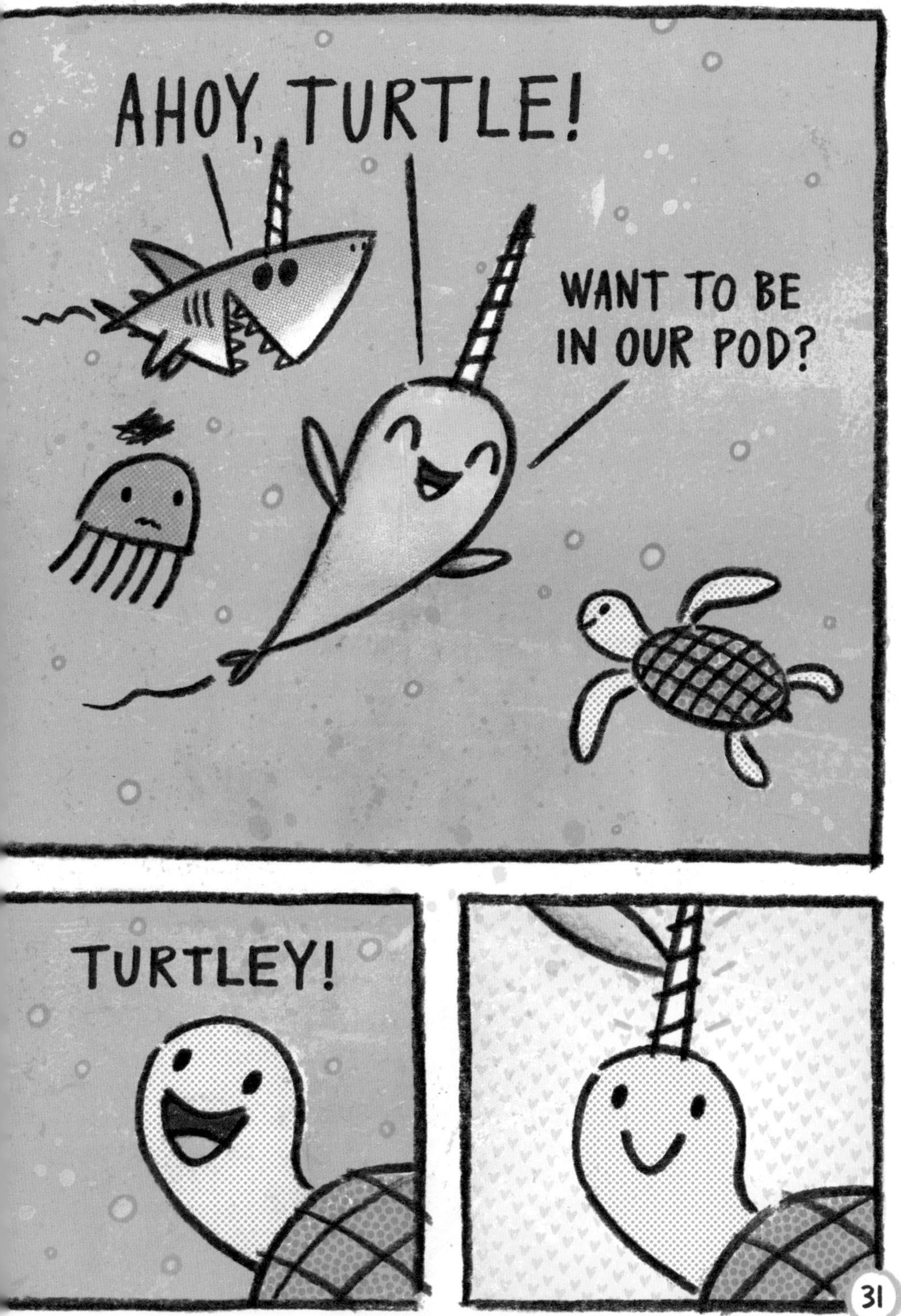
AHOY, TURTLE!
WANT TO BE IN OUR POD?
TURTLEY!

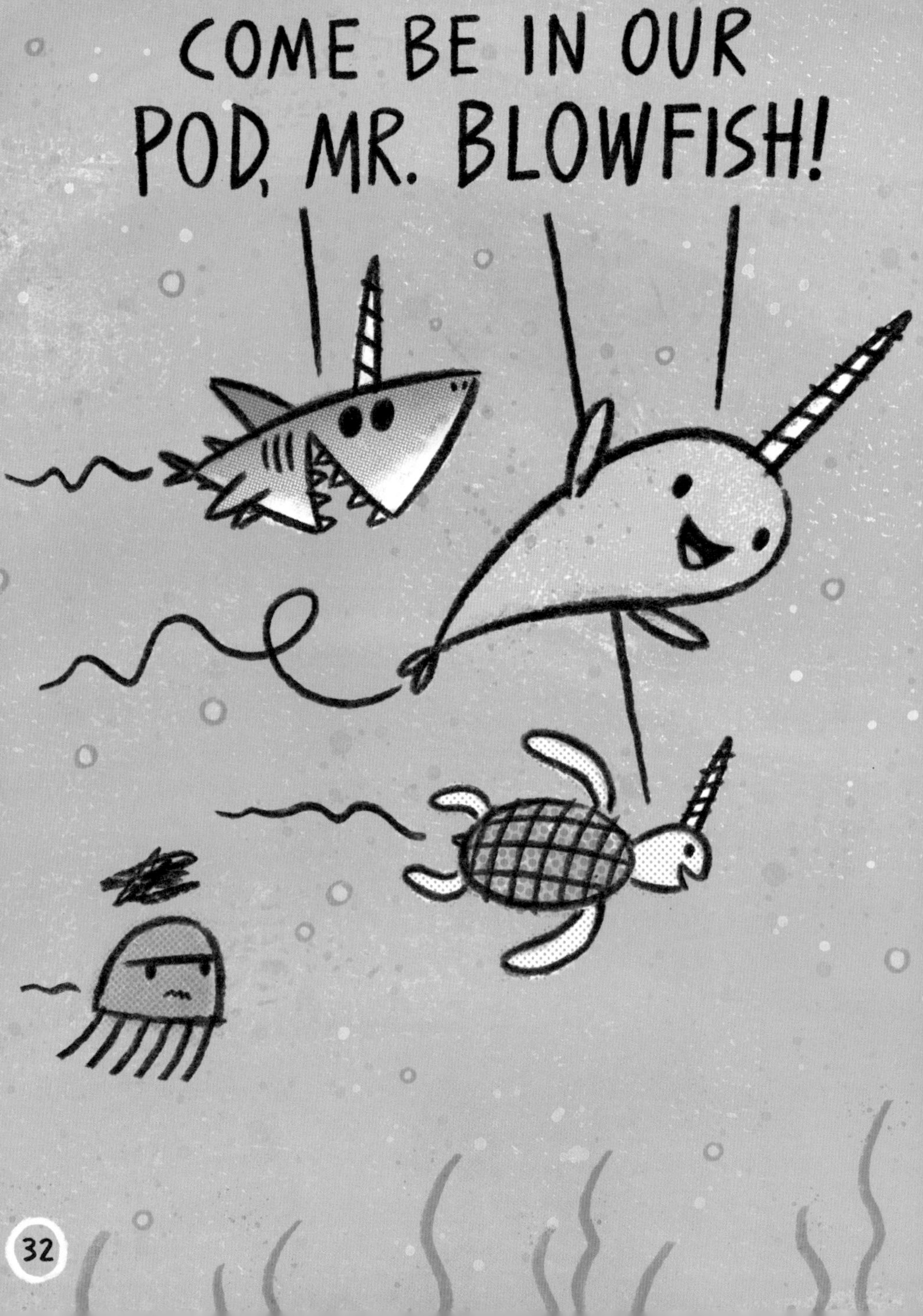
COME BE IN OUR POD, MR. BLOWFISH!

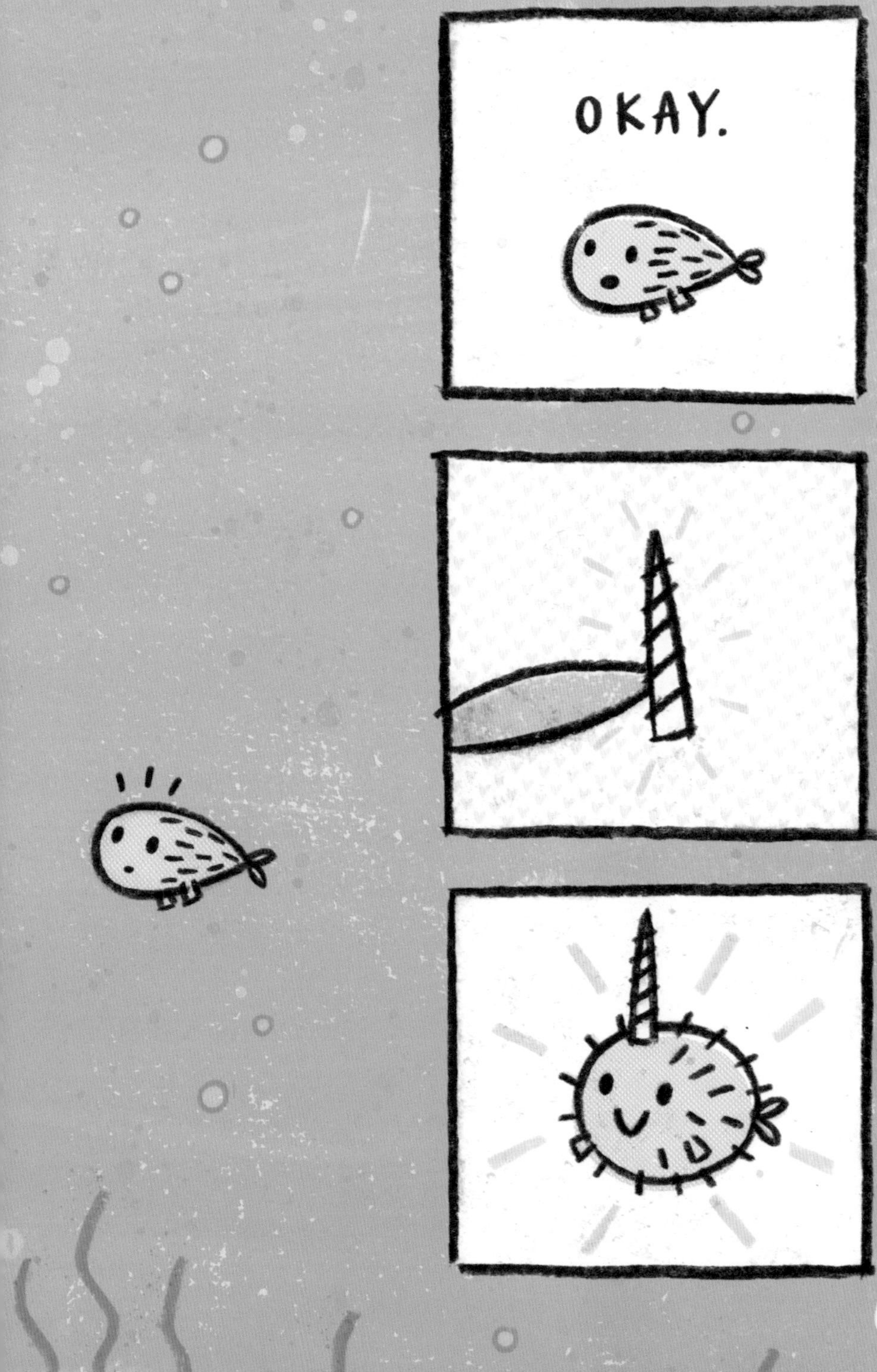
OKAY.

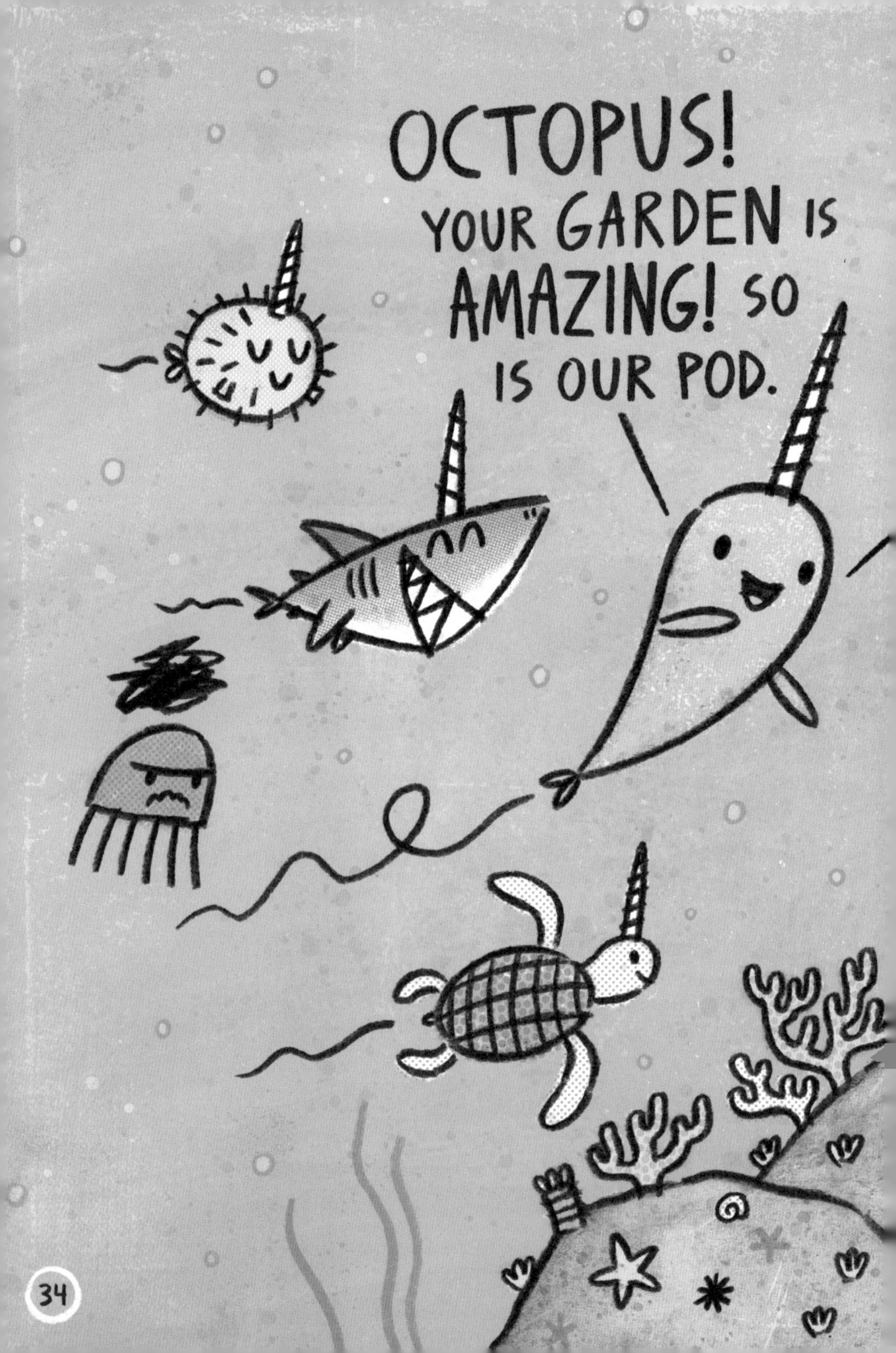
OCTOPUS! YOUR GARDEN IS AMAZING! SO IS OUR POD.

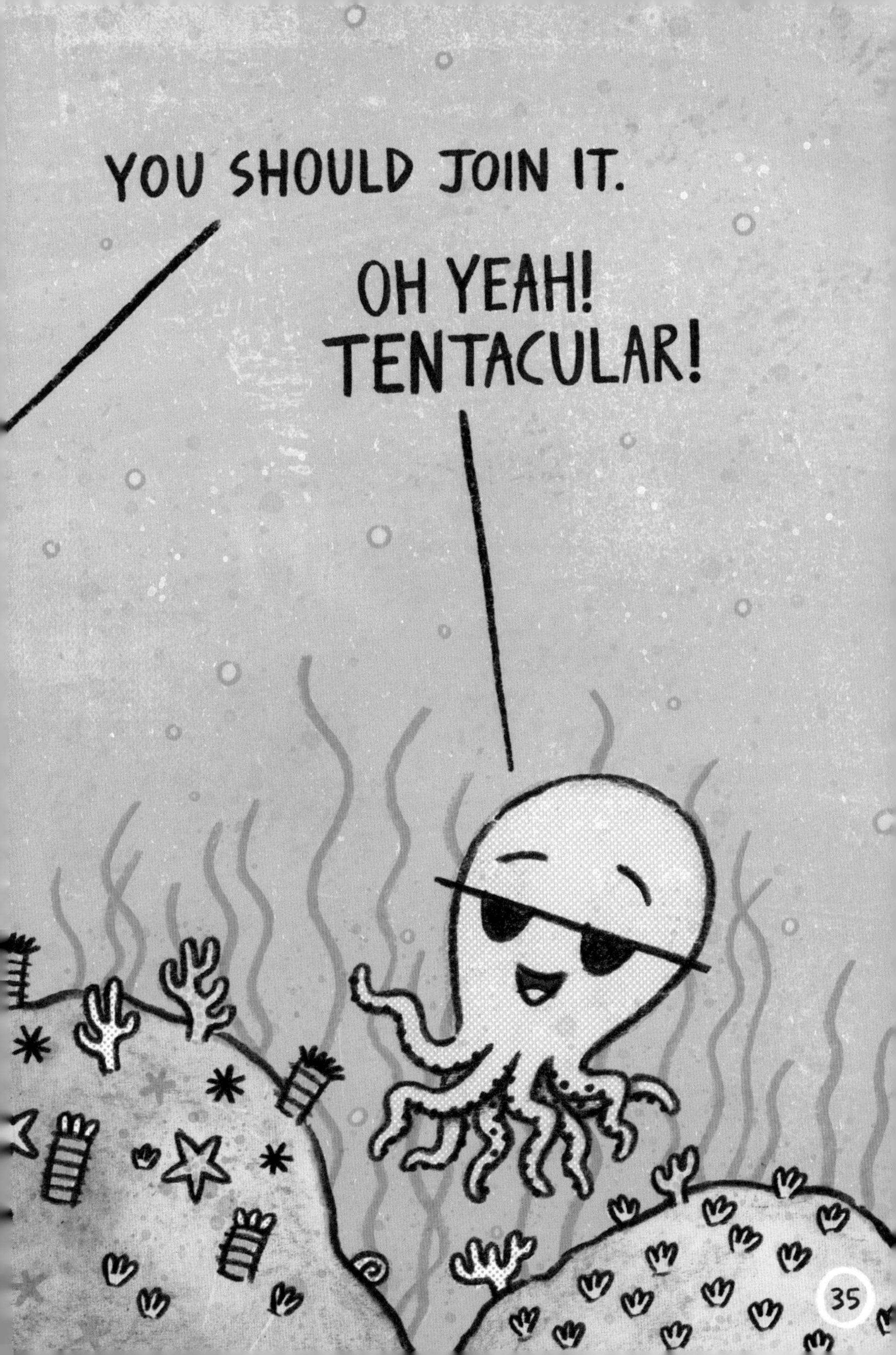
YOU SHOULD JOIN IT.
OH YEAH! TENTACULAR!

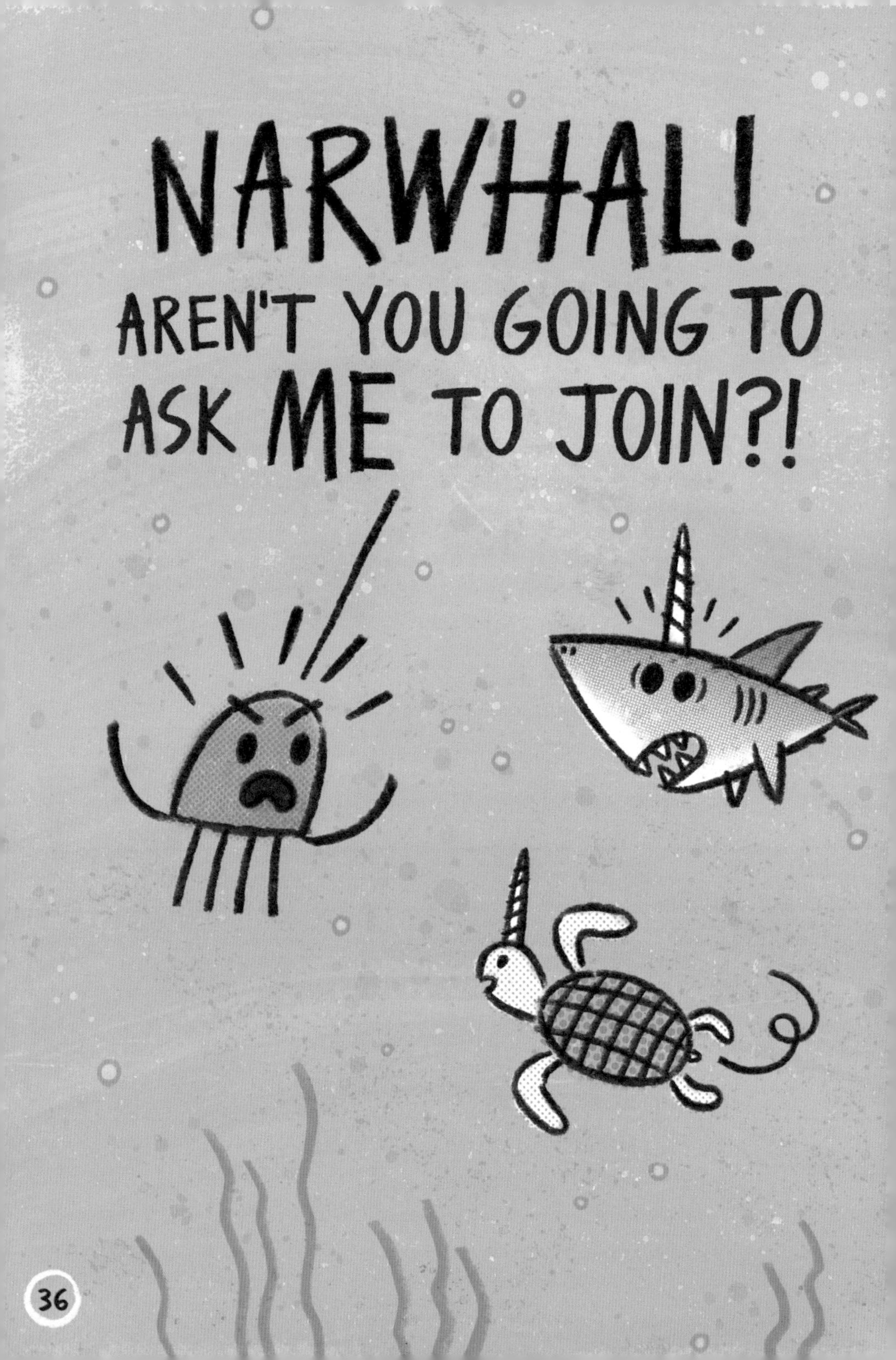
NARWHAL! AREN'T YOU GOING TO ASK ME TO JOIN?!

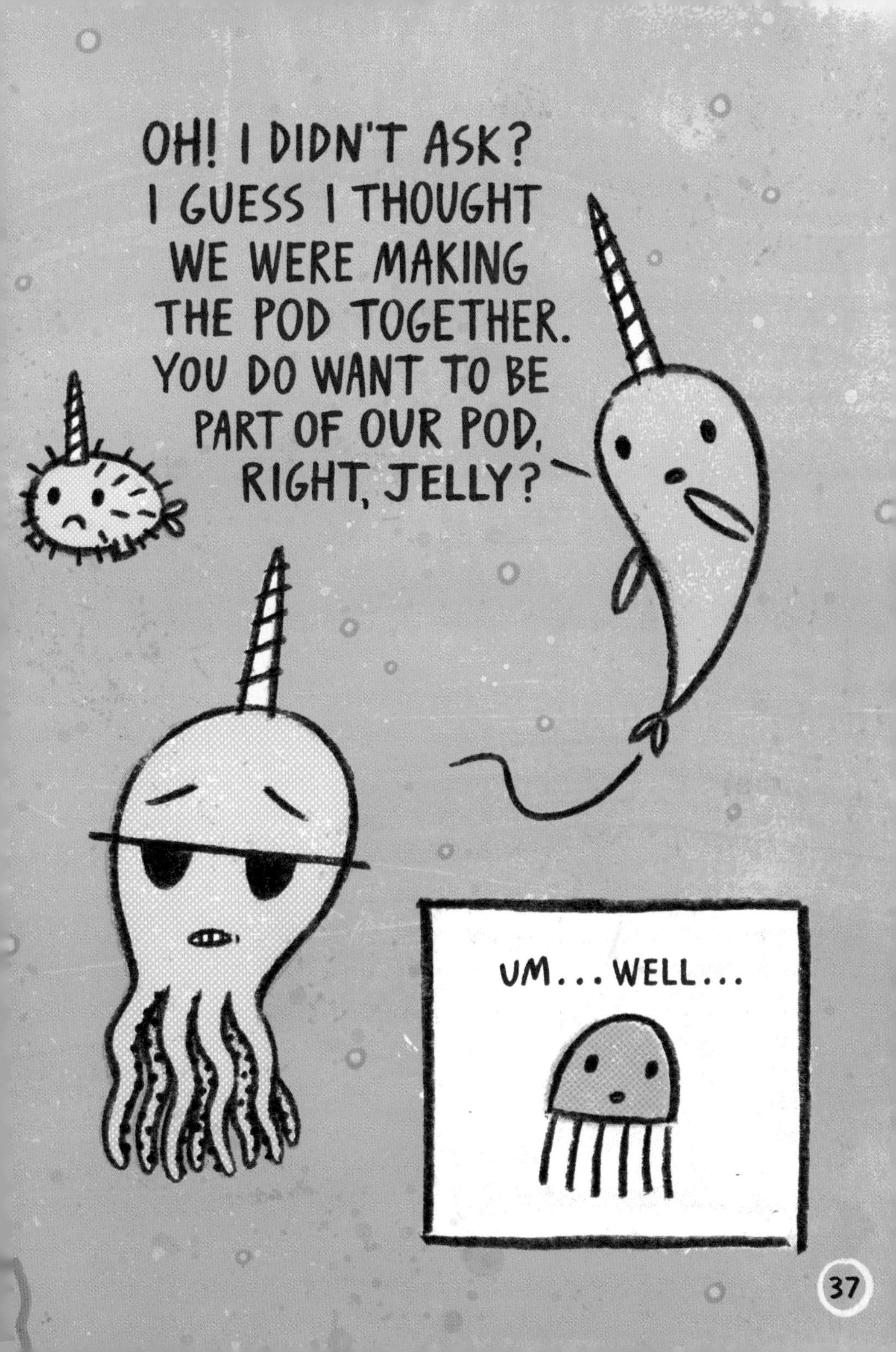
OH! I DIDN'T ASK? I GUESS I THOUGHT WE WERE MAKING THE POD TOGETHER. YOU DO WANT TO BE PART OF OUR POD, RIGHT, JELLY?
UM... WELL...

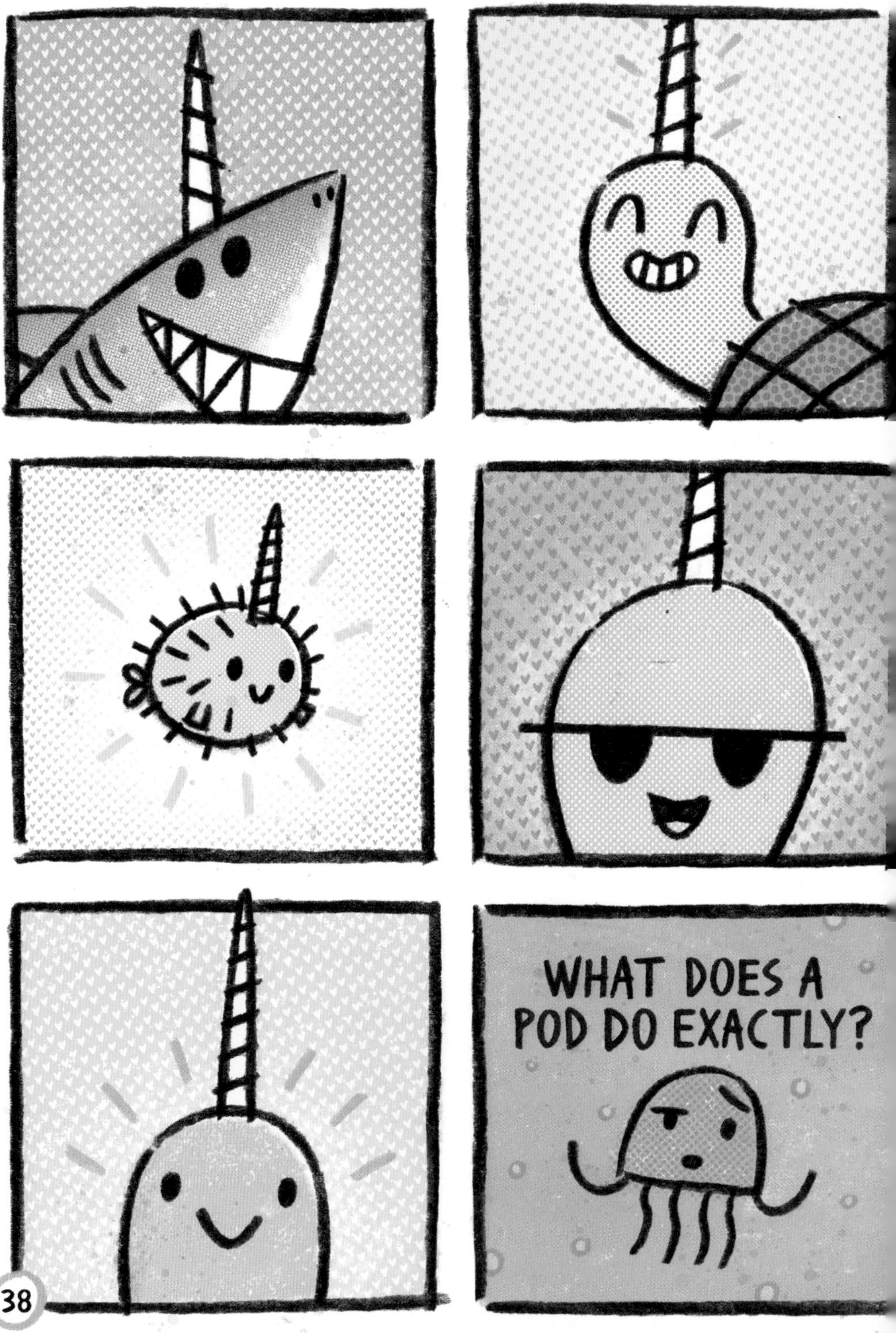
WHAT DOES A
POD DO EXACTLY?

I'M NOT REALLY SURE!

BUT I IMAGINE A POD PLAYS
ULTIMATE CANNONBALL, EATS
WAFFLES, FIGHTS CRIME AND...

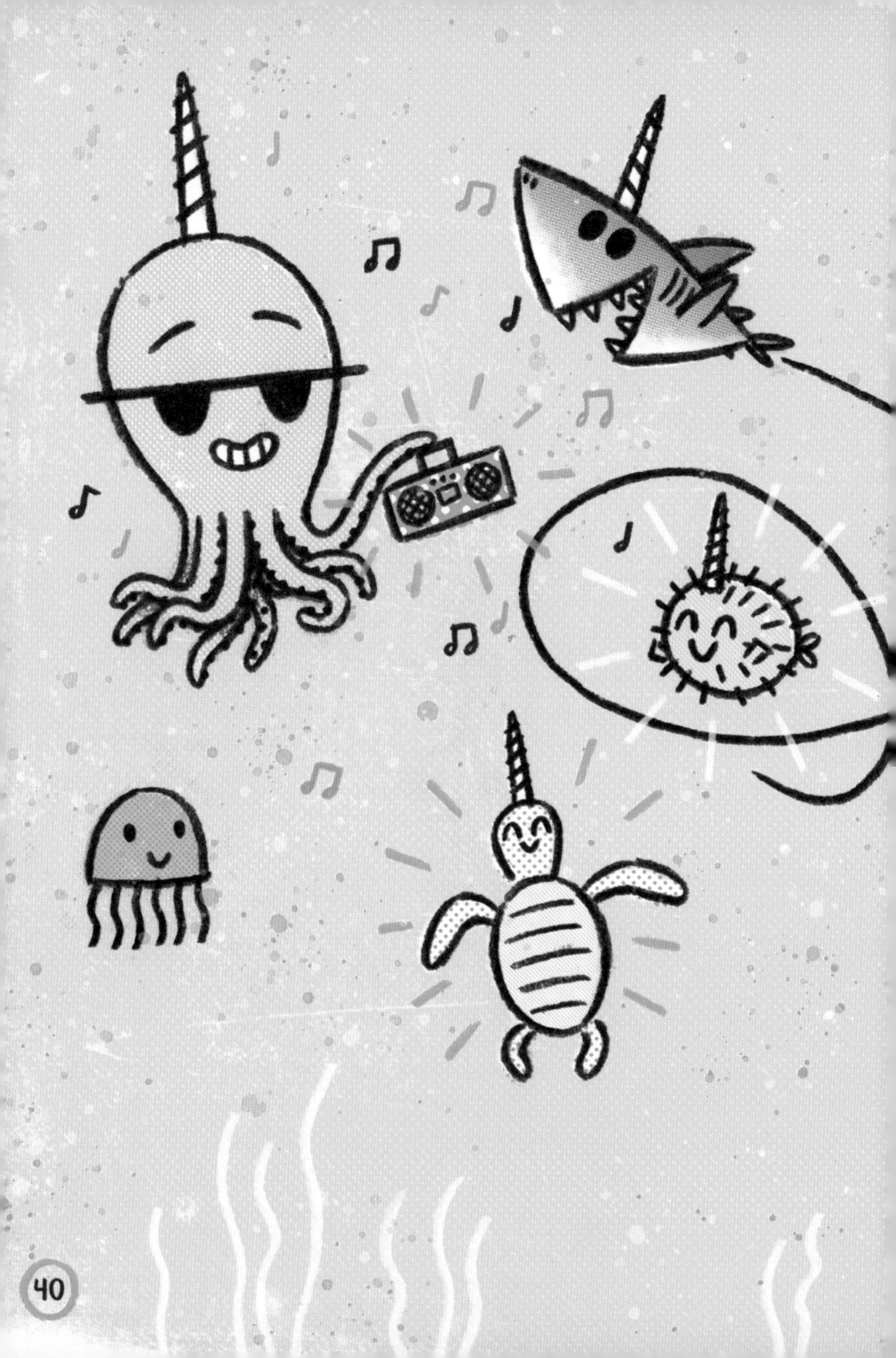

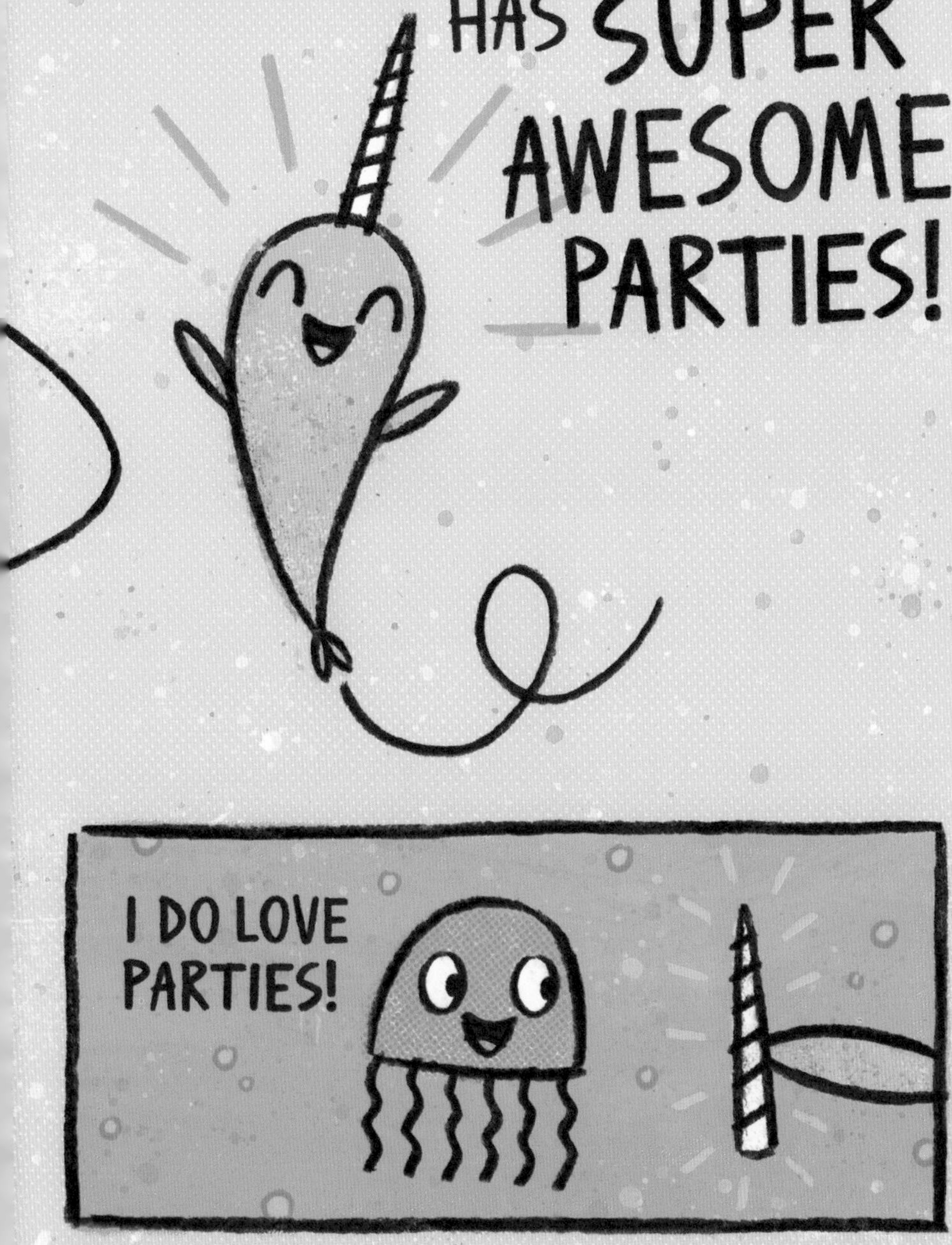
HAS SUPER AWESOME PARTIES!
I DO LOVE PARTIES!

PODTASTIC!

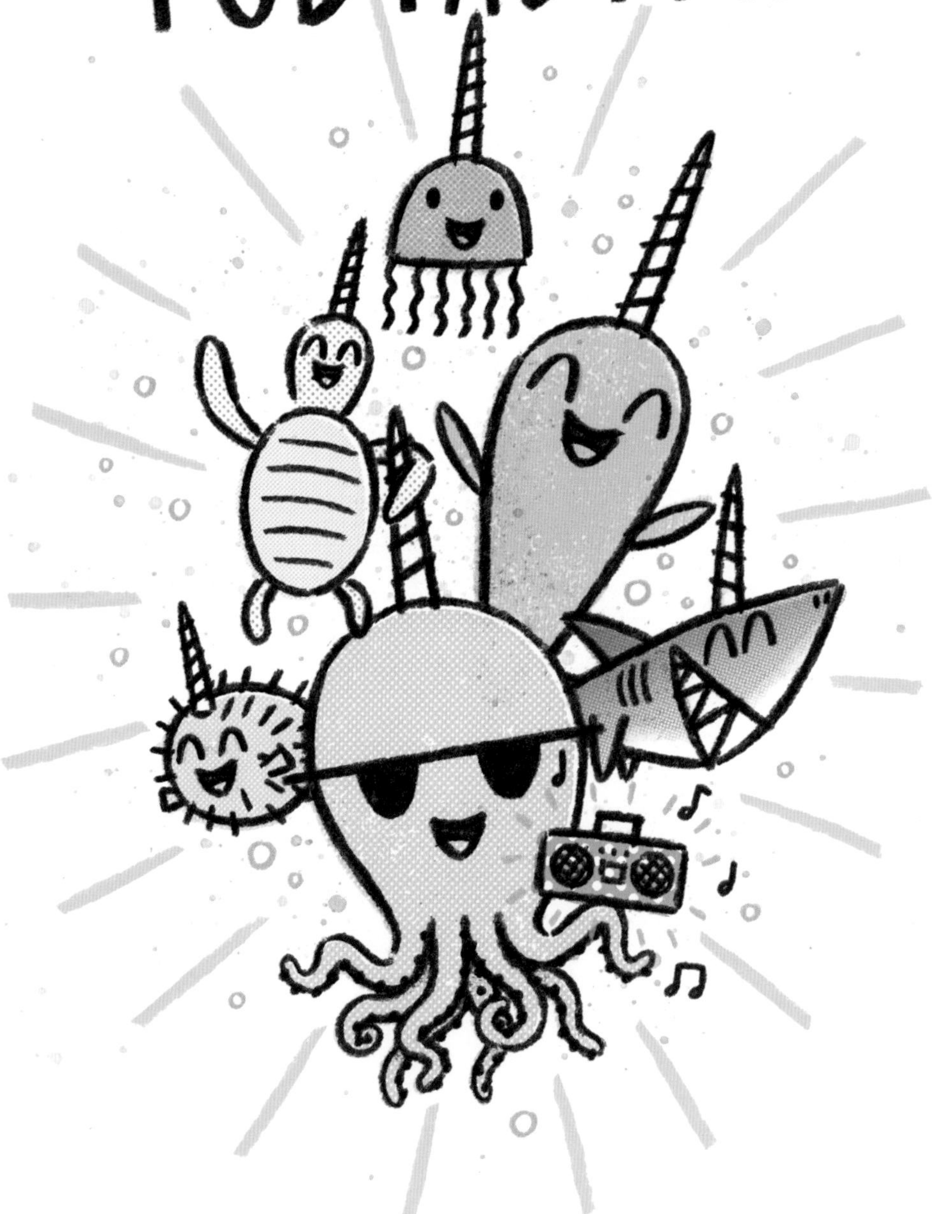

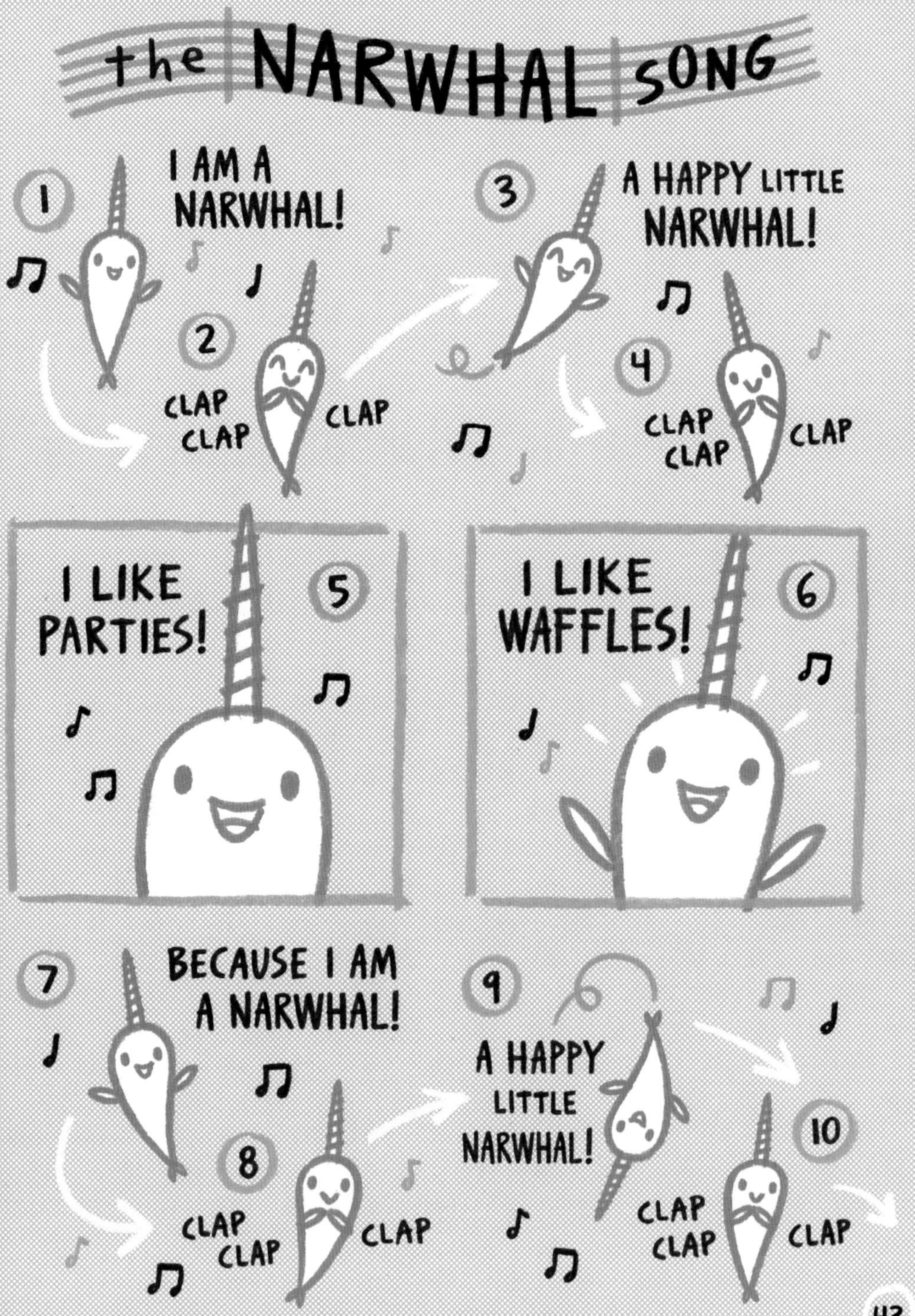
the NARWHAL SONG
1
I AM A NARWHAL!
2
CLAP CLAP
CLAP
3
A HAPPY LITTLE NARWHAL!
4
CLAP CLAP
CLAP
I LIKE PARTIES!
5
I LIKE WAFFLES!
6
7
BECAUSE I AM A NARWHAL!
8
CLAP CLAP
CLAP
9
A HAPPY LITTLE NARWHAL!
10
CLAP CLAP
CLAP

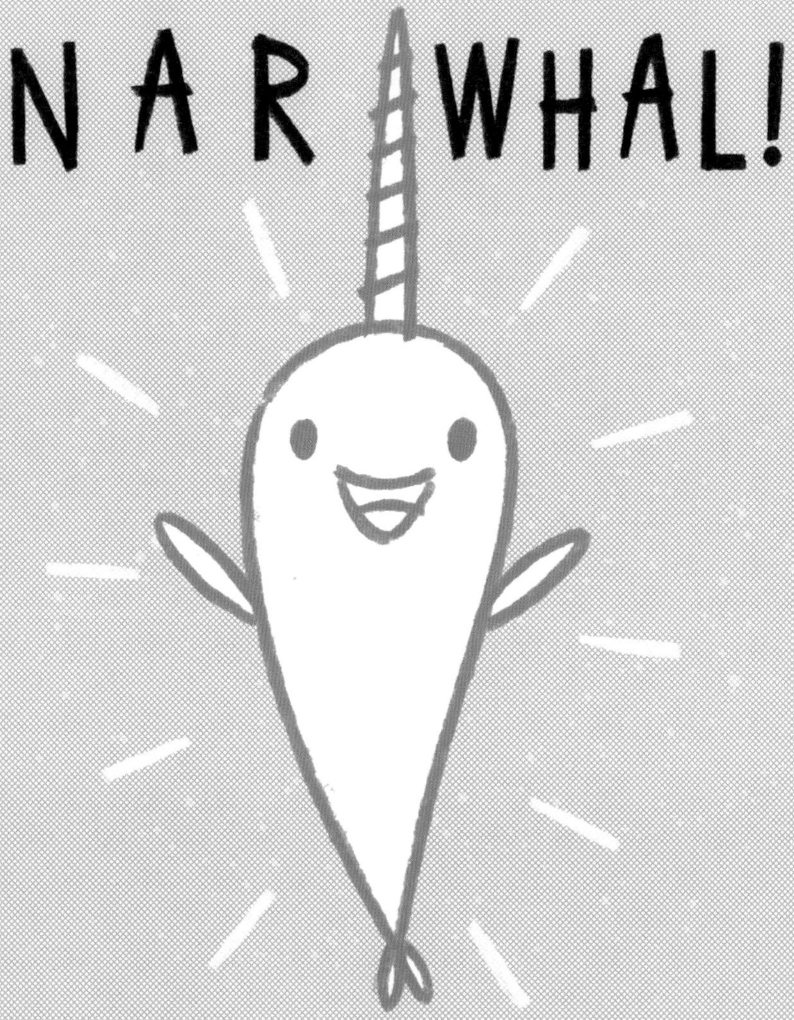
NARWHAL!

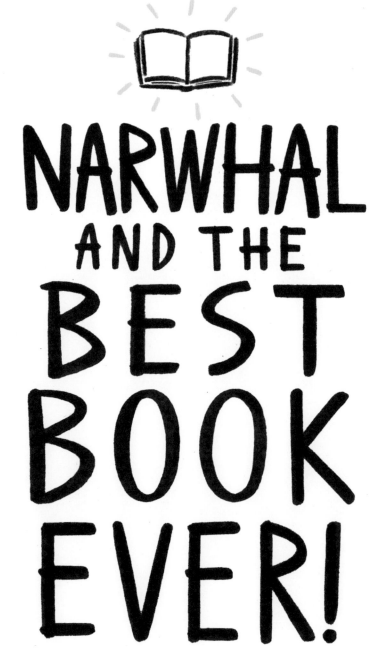

NARWHAL
AND THE
BEST
BOOK
EVER!

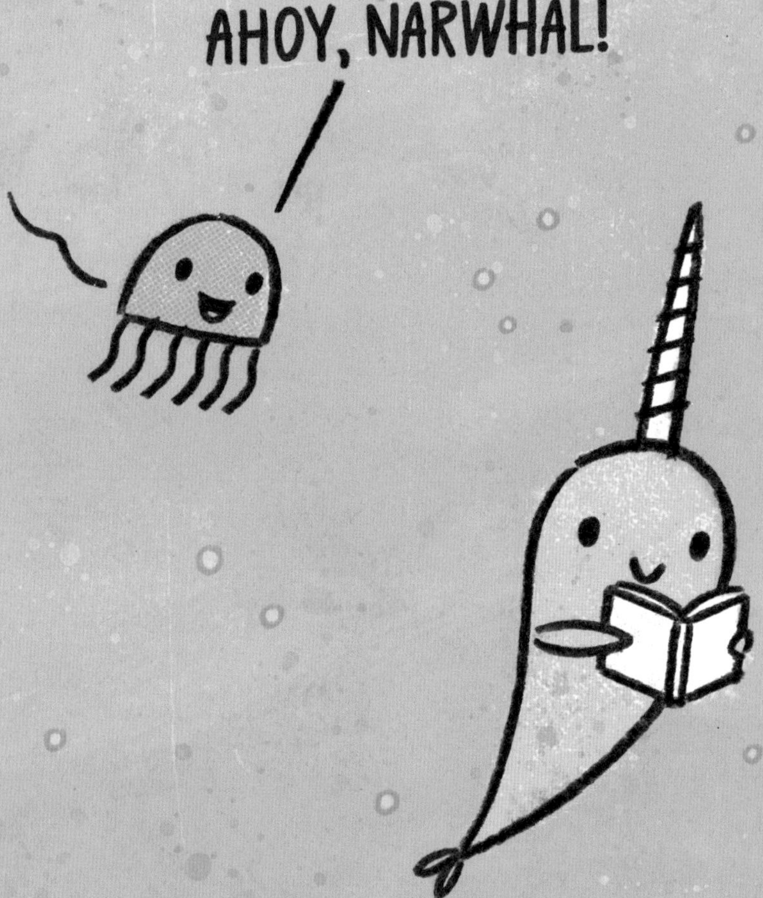
AHOY, NARWHAL!

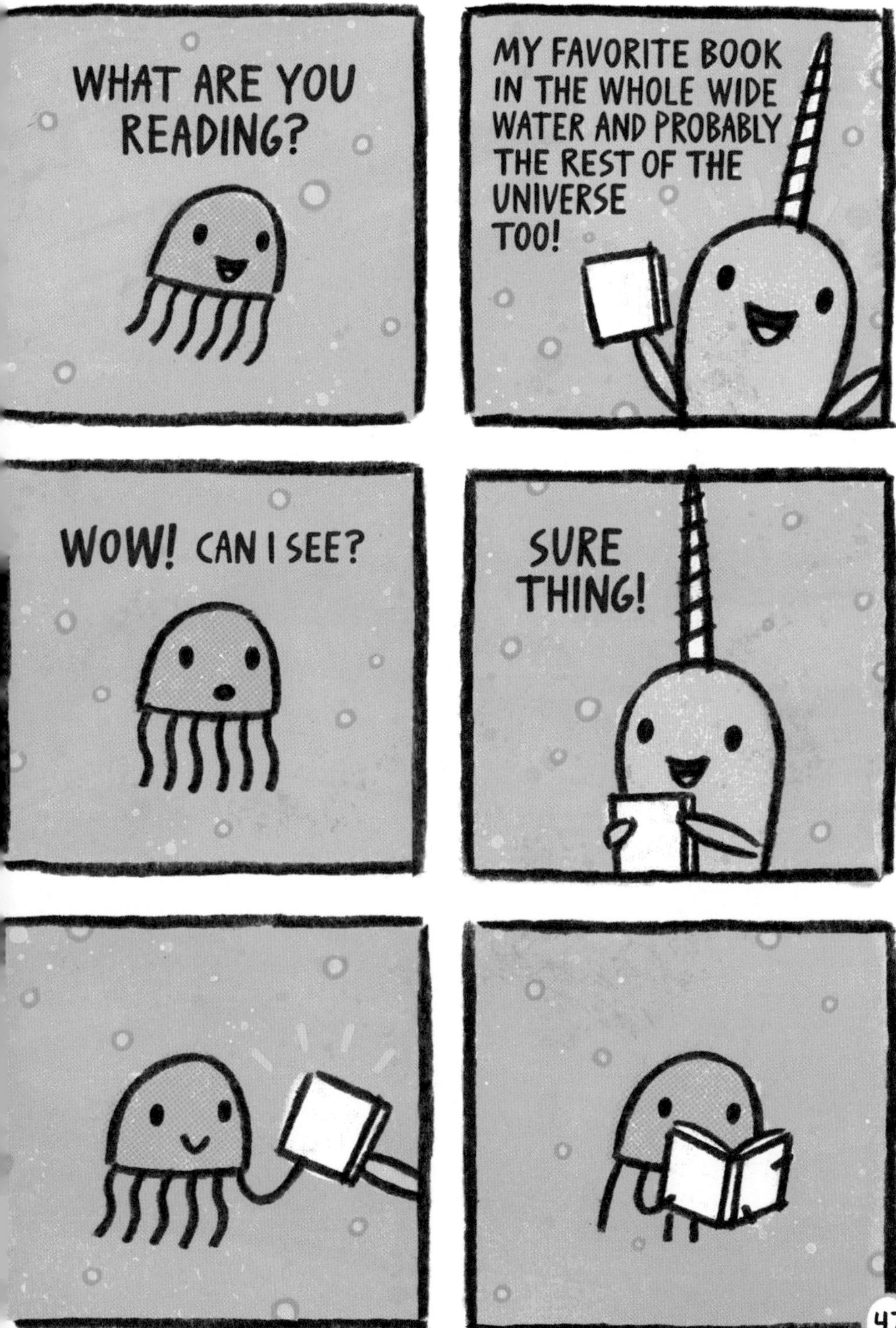
WHAT ARE YOU READING?
MY FAVORITE BOOK IN THE WHOLE WIDE WATER AND PROBABLY THE REST OF THE UNIVERSE TOO!
WOW! CAN I SEE?
SURE THING!

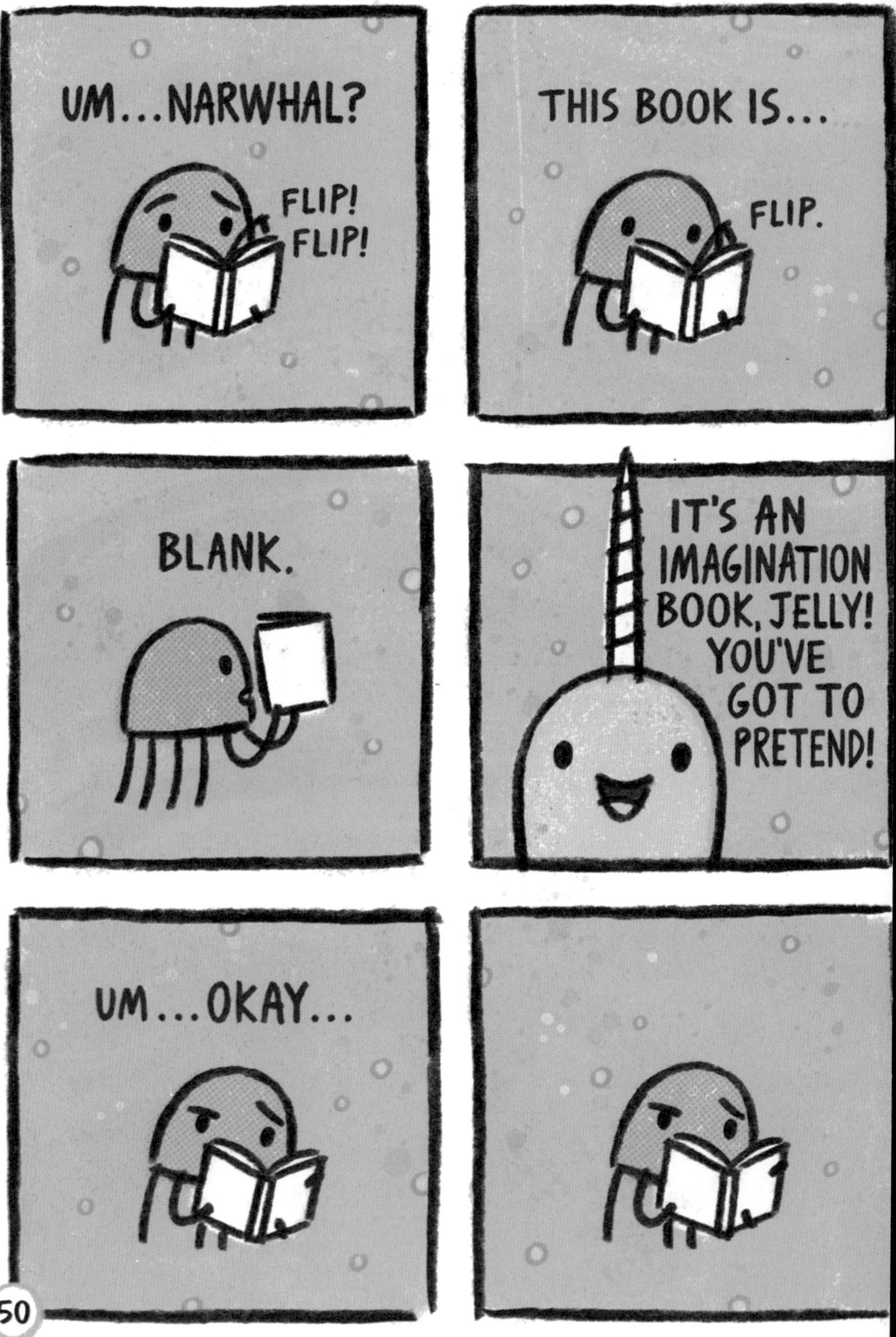
UM...NARWHAL?
FLIP! FLIP!
THIS BOOK IS...
FLIP.
BLANK.
IT'S AN IMAGINATION BOOK, JELLY! YOU'VE GOT TO PRETEND!
UM...OKAY...

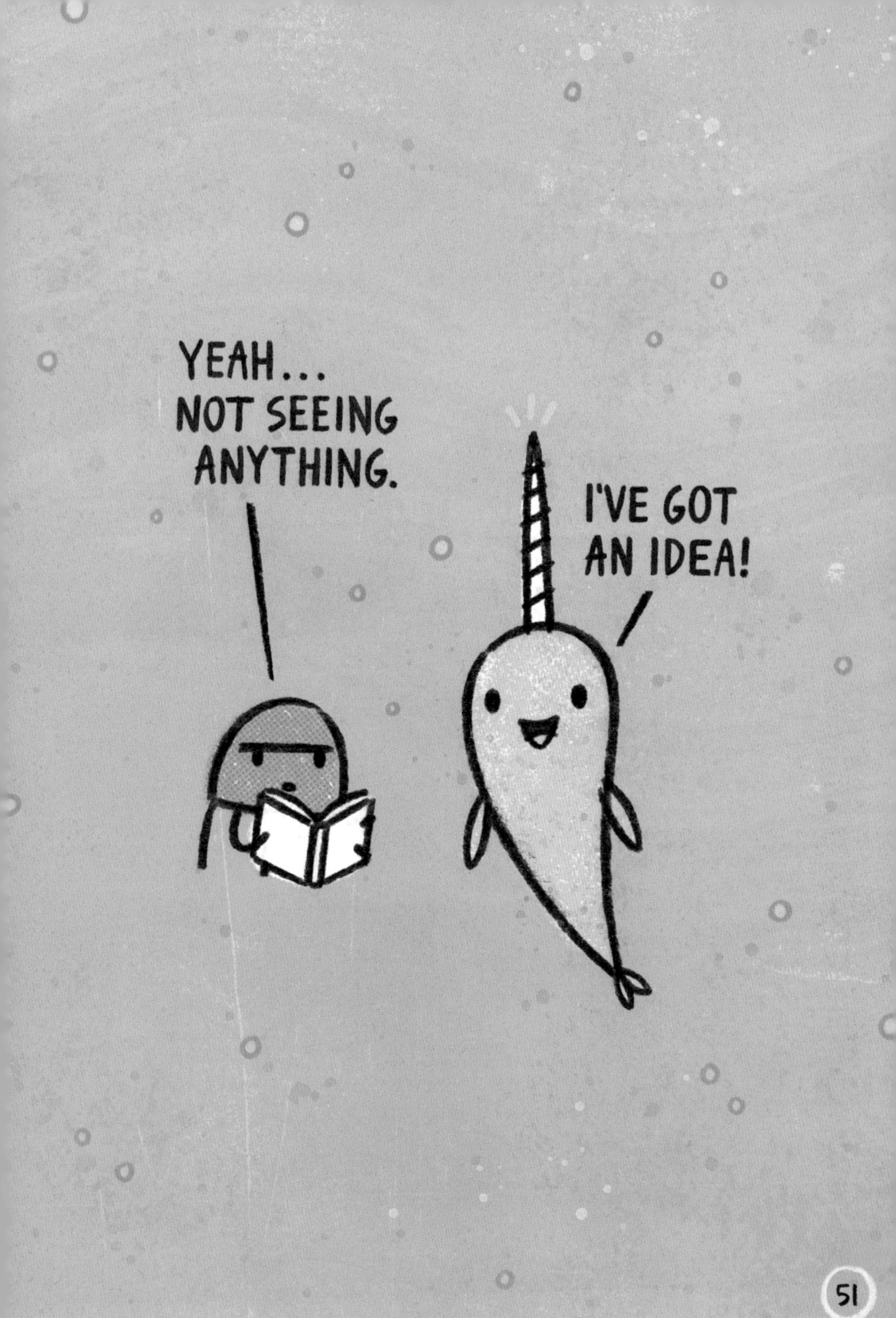
YEAH... NOT SEEING ANYTHING.
I'VE GOT AN IDEA!

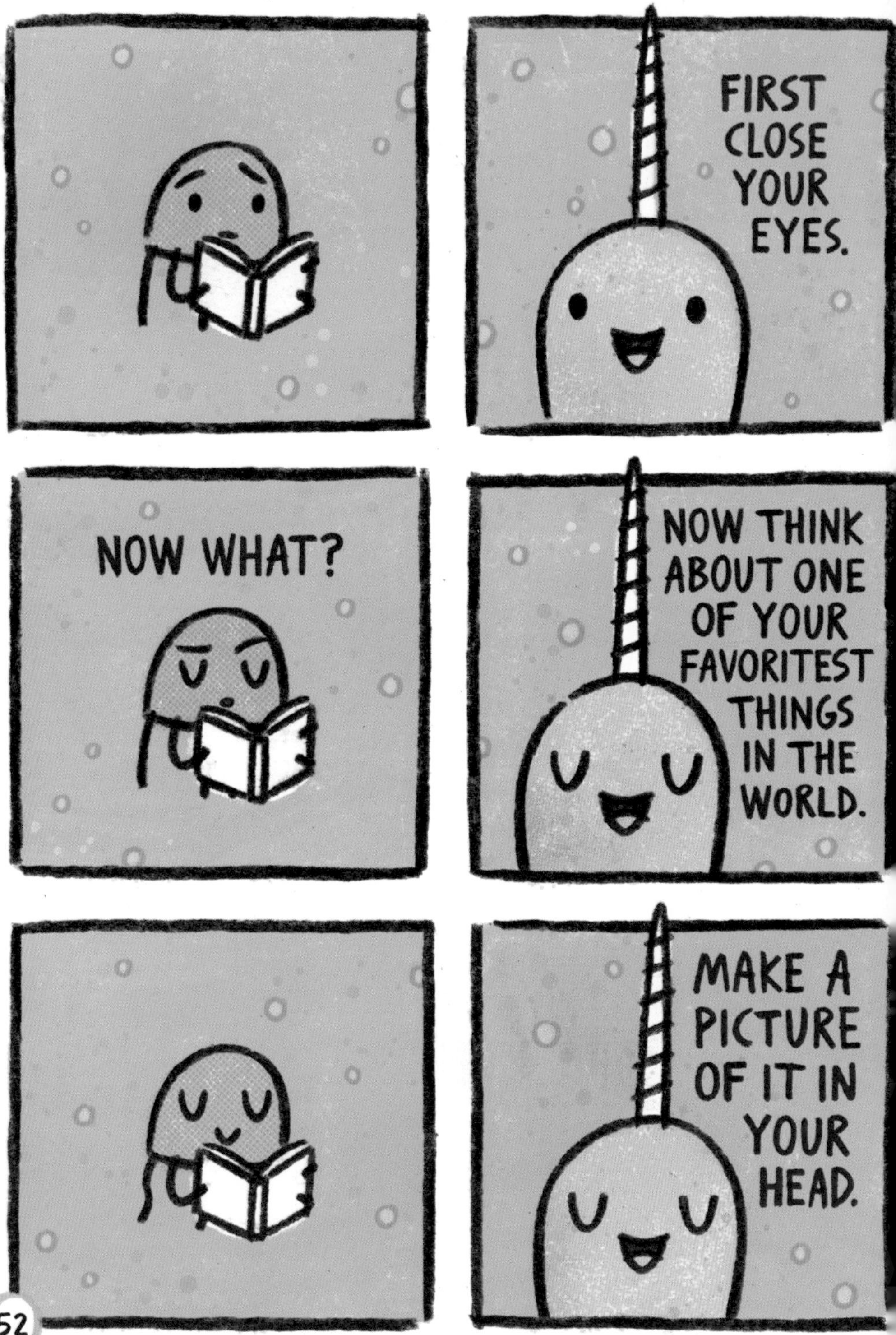
FIRST CLOSE YOUR EYES.
NOW WHAT?
NOW THINK ABOUT ONE OF YOUR FAVORITEST THINGS IN THE WORLD.
MAKE A PICTURE OF IT IN YOUR HEAD.

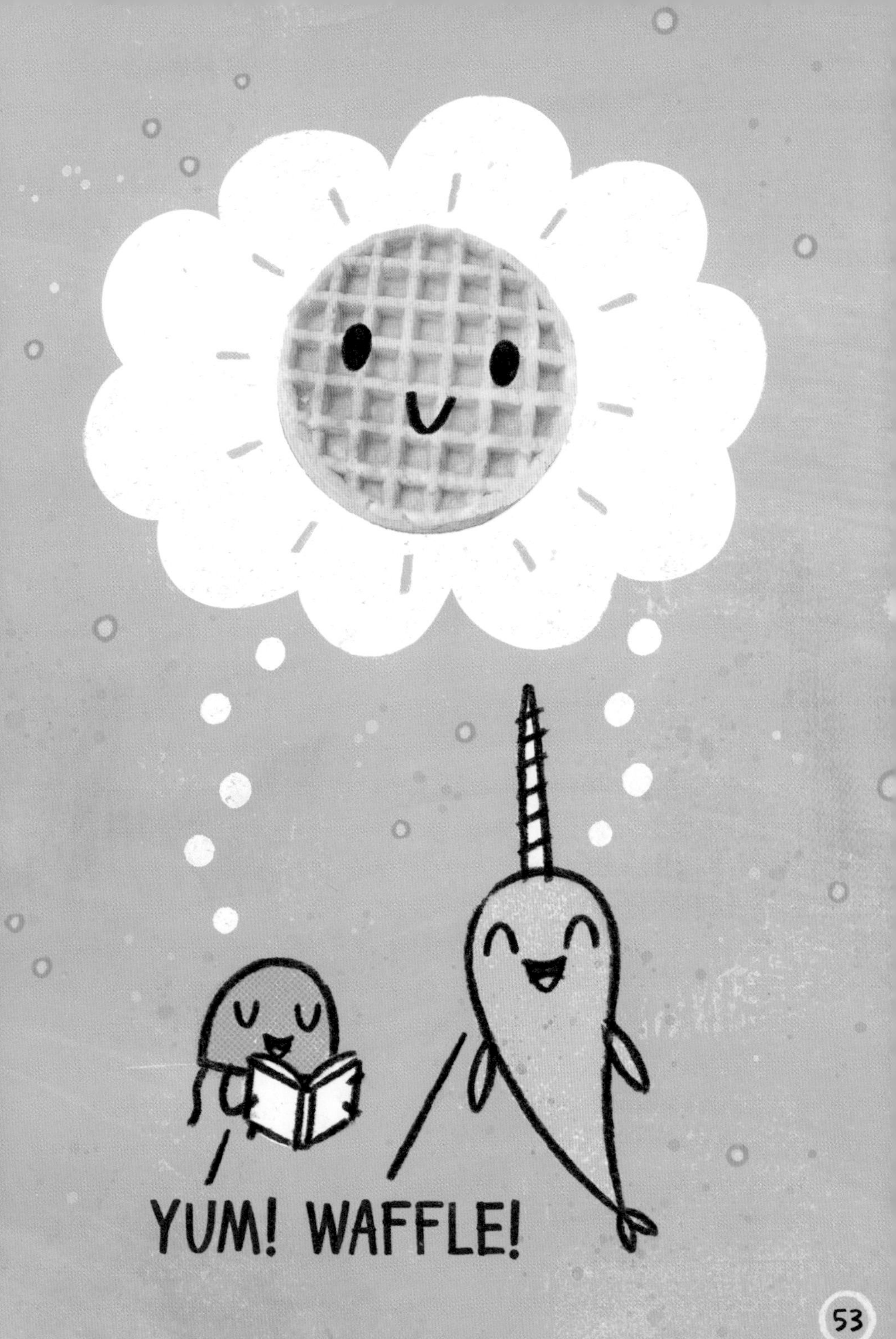
YUM! WAFFLE!

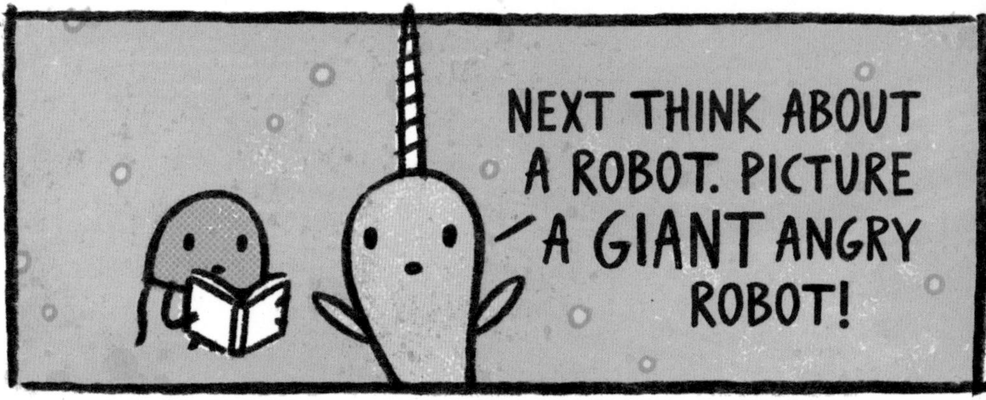
NEXT THINK ABOUT A ROBOT. PICTURE A GIANT ANGRY ROBOT!

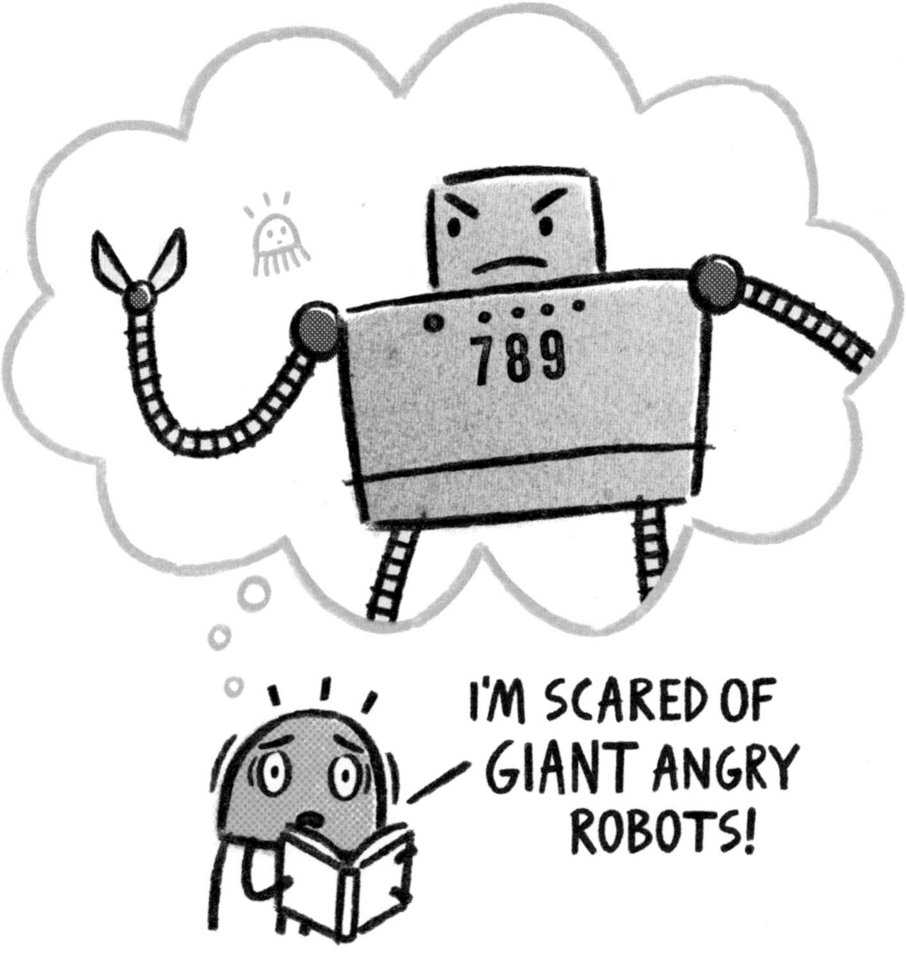
789
I'M SCARED OF GIANT ANGRY ROBOTS!

GOOD THING THAT WAFFLE
IS A KUNG FU MASTER!

LOOK AT THE BOOK AND SEE
A PICTURE OF IT BATTLING
THE ROBOT!

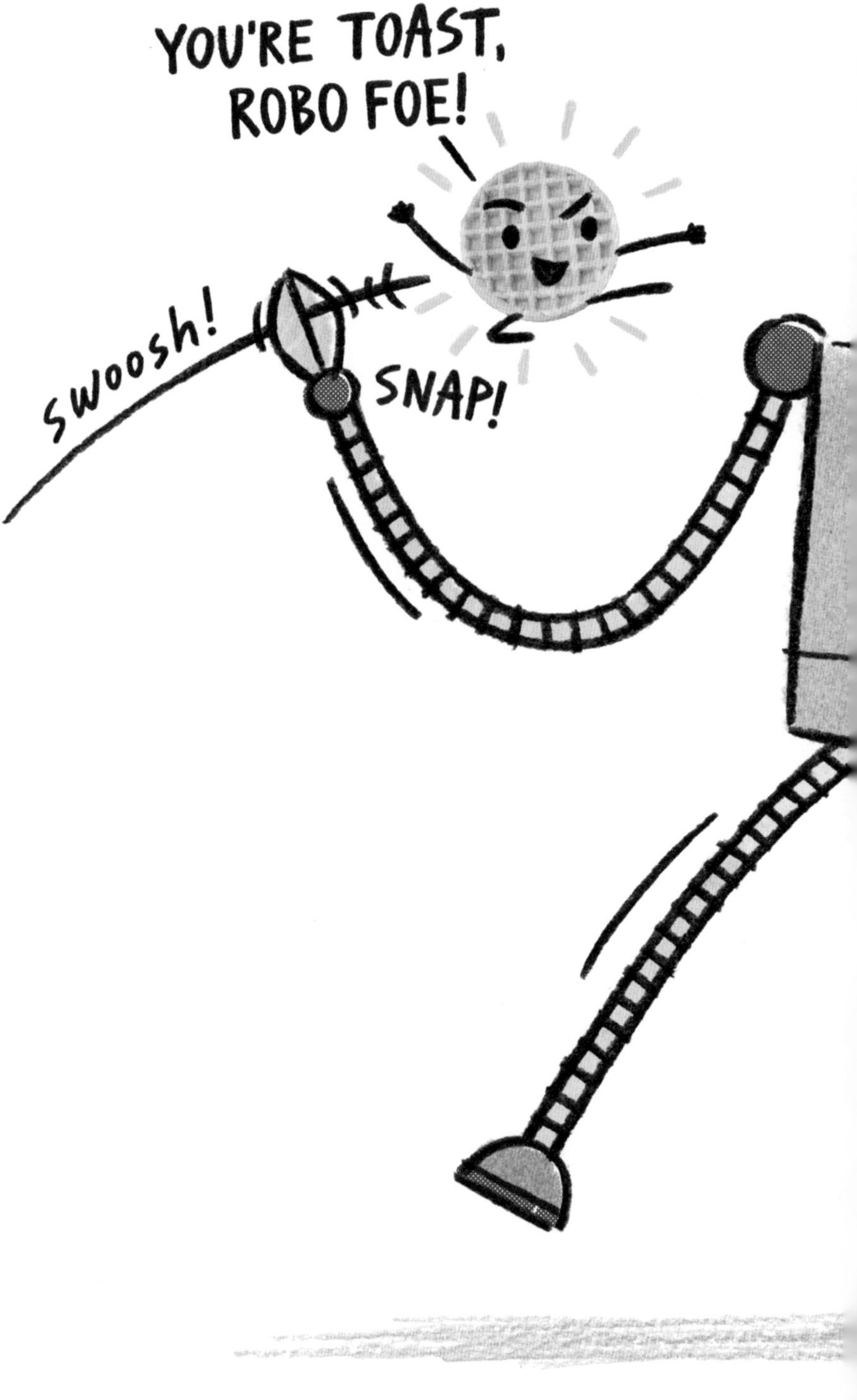
YOU'RE TOAST,
ROBO FOE!
SWOOSH!
SNAP!

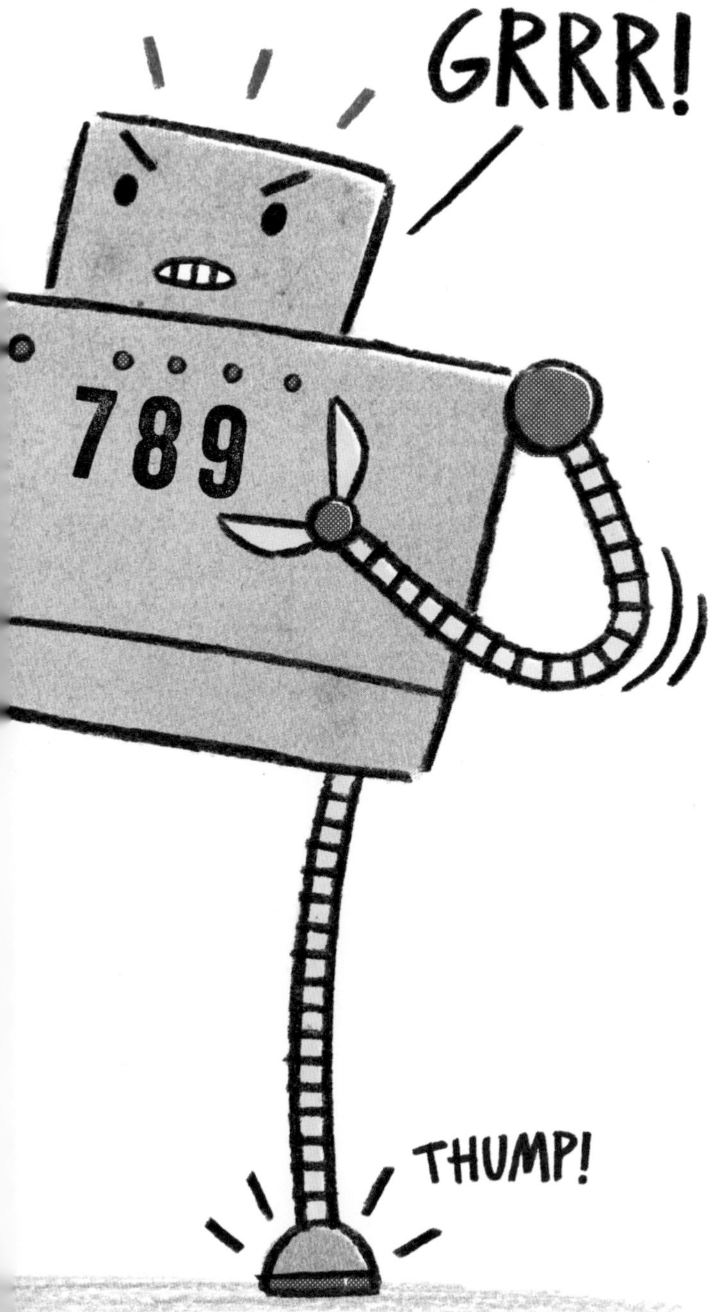
GRRR!
789
THUMP!

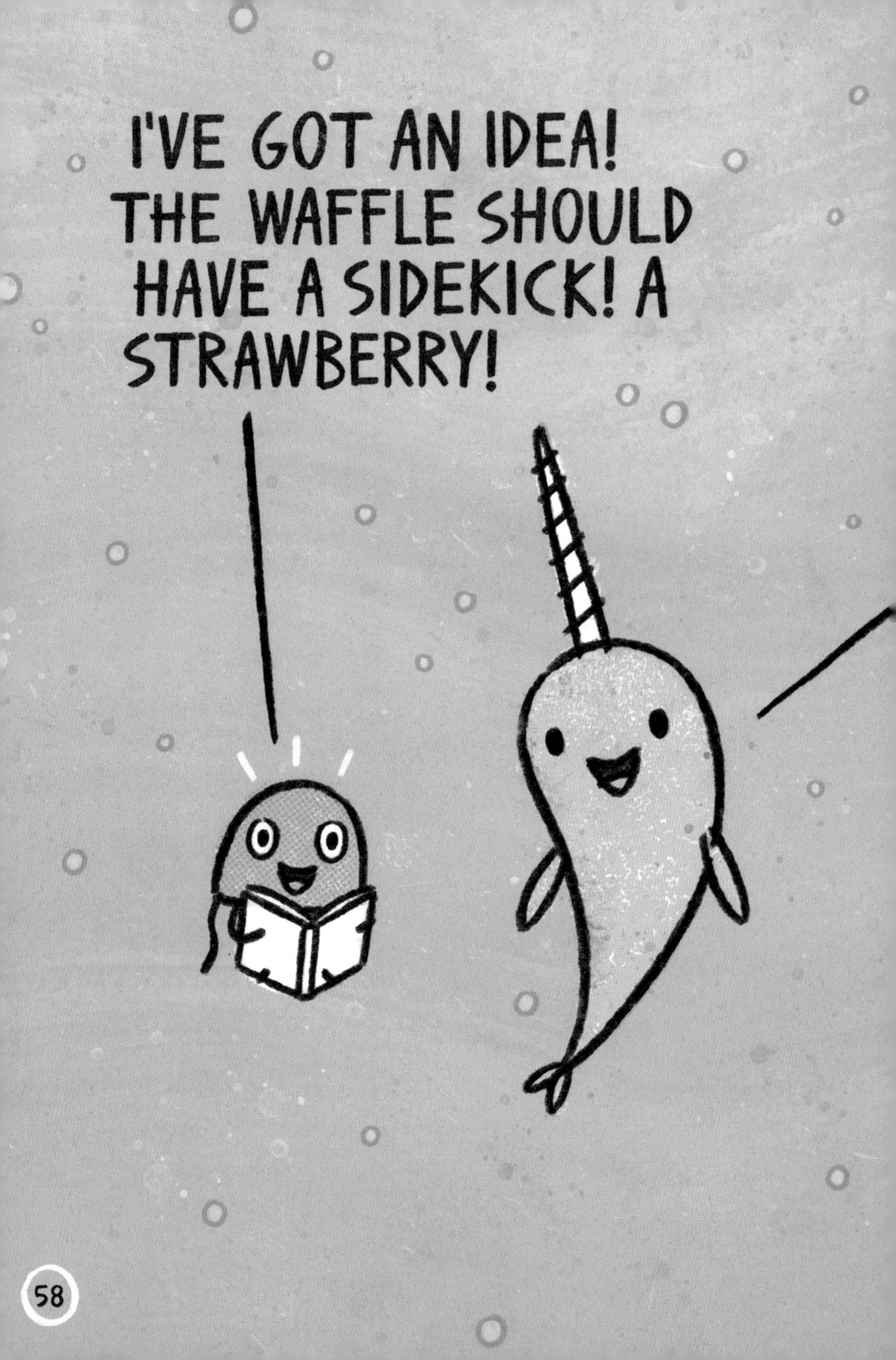
I'VE GOT AN IDEA! THE WAFFLE SHOULD HAVE A SIDEKICK! A STRAWBERRY!

NICE ONE, JELLY!

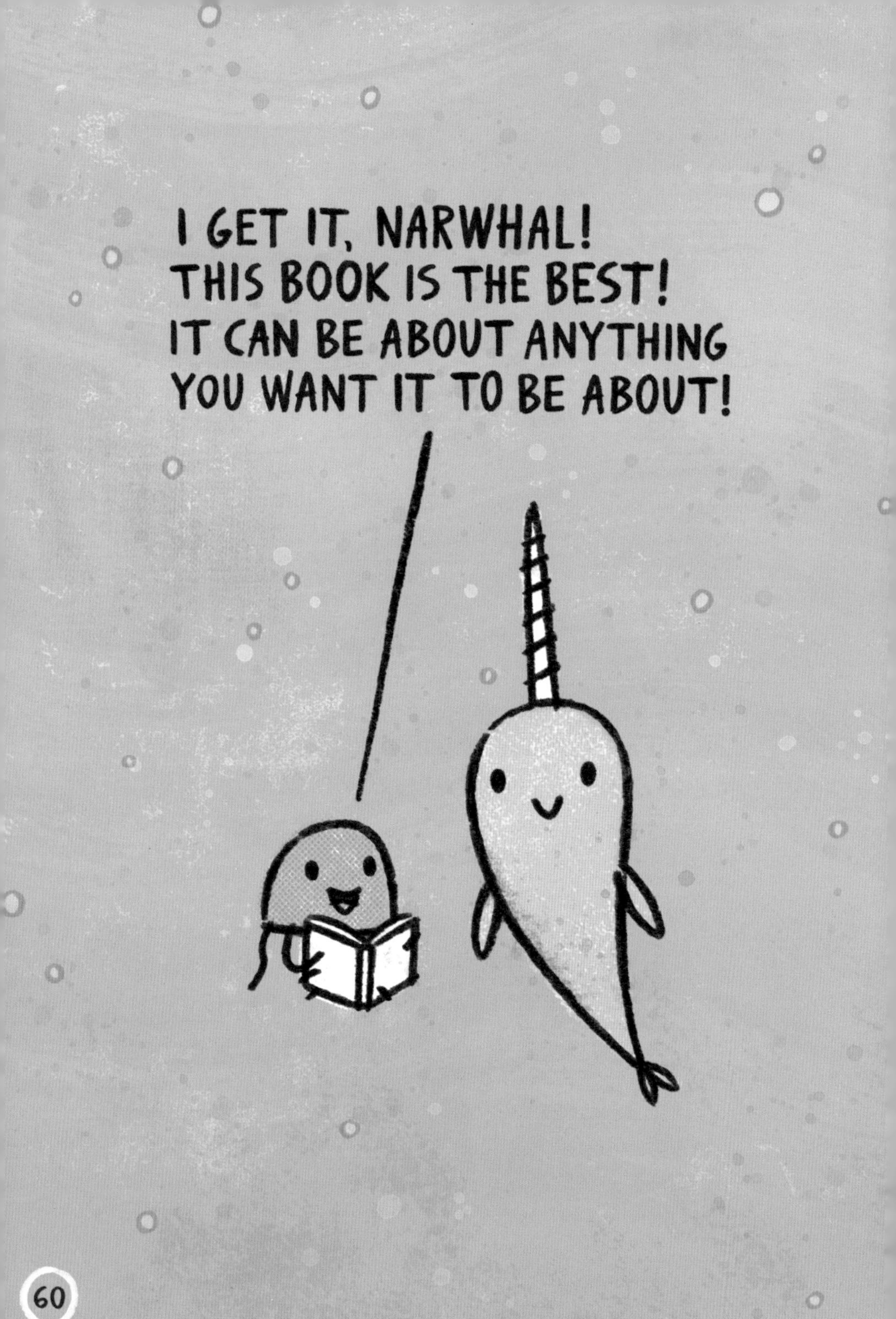
I GET IT, NARWHAL!
THIS BOOK IS THE BEST!
IT CAN BE ABOUT ANYTHING
YOU WANT IT TO BE ABOUT!

TURN THE PAGE!
I WANT TO SEE
WHAT HAPPENS NEXT.

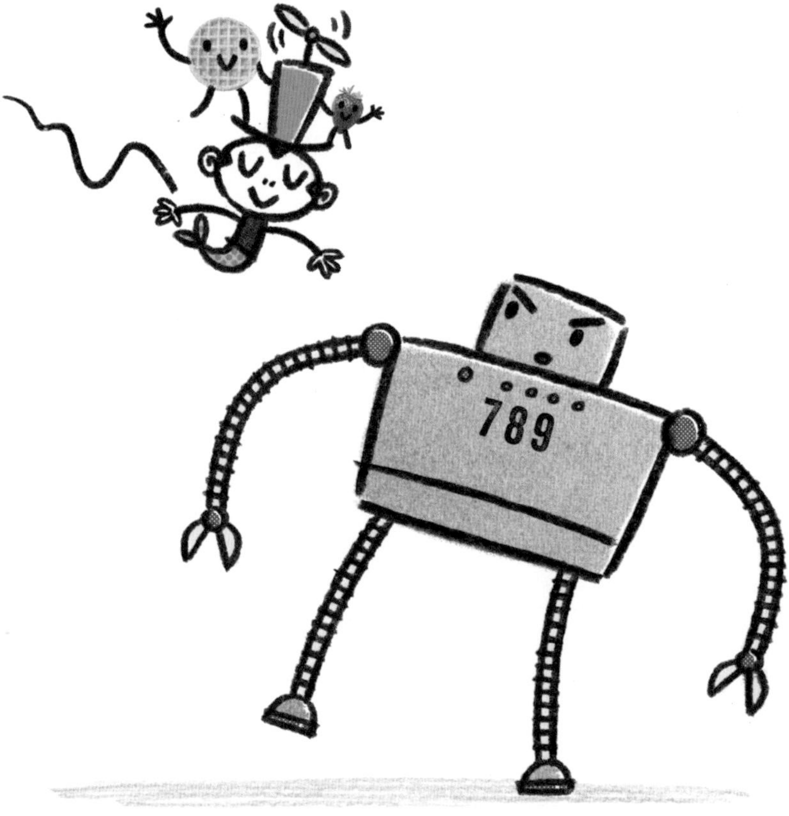
789

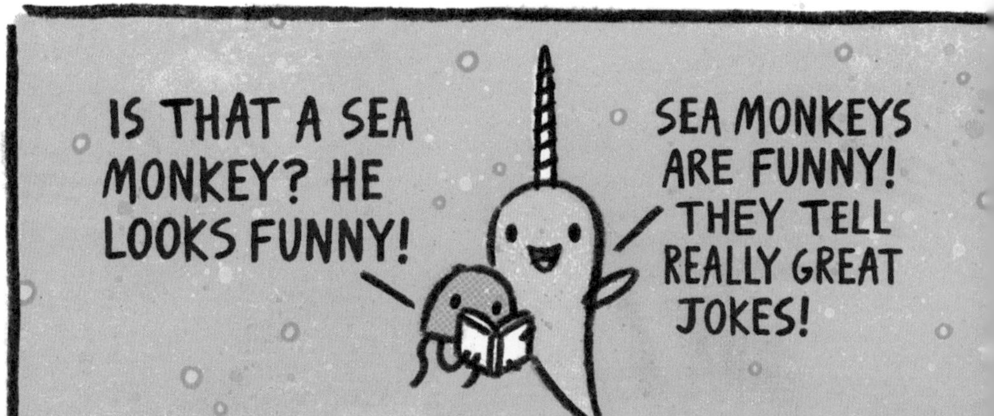
IS THAT A SEA MONKEY? HE LOOKS FUNNY!
SEA MONKEYS ARE FUNNY! THEY TELL REALLY GREAT JOKES!

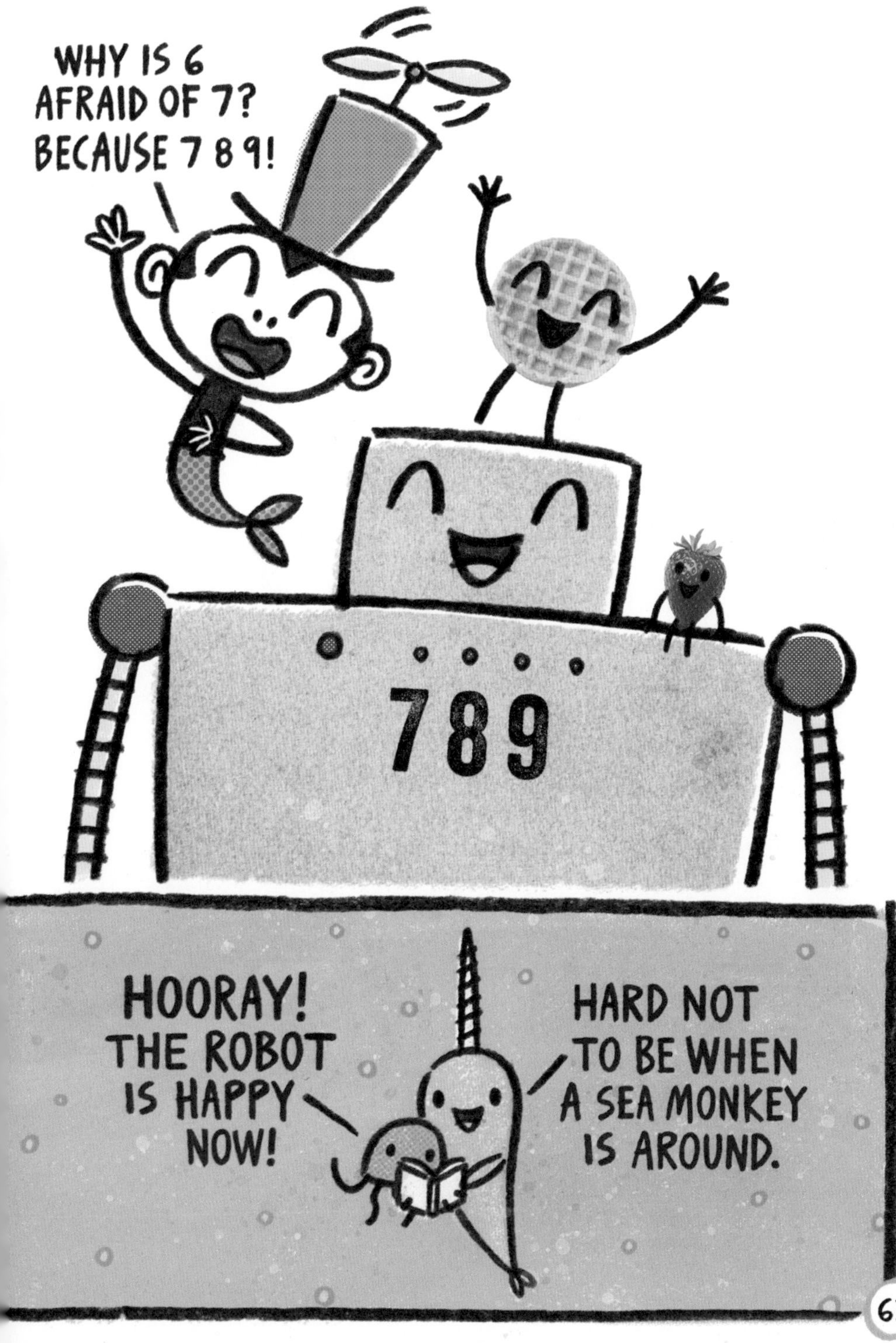
WHY IS 6 AFRAID OF 7? BECAUSE 7 8 9!
789
HOORAY! THE ROBOT IS HAPPY NOW!
HARD NOT TO BE WHEN A SEA MONKEY IS AROUND.

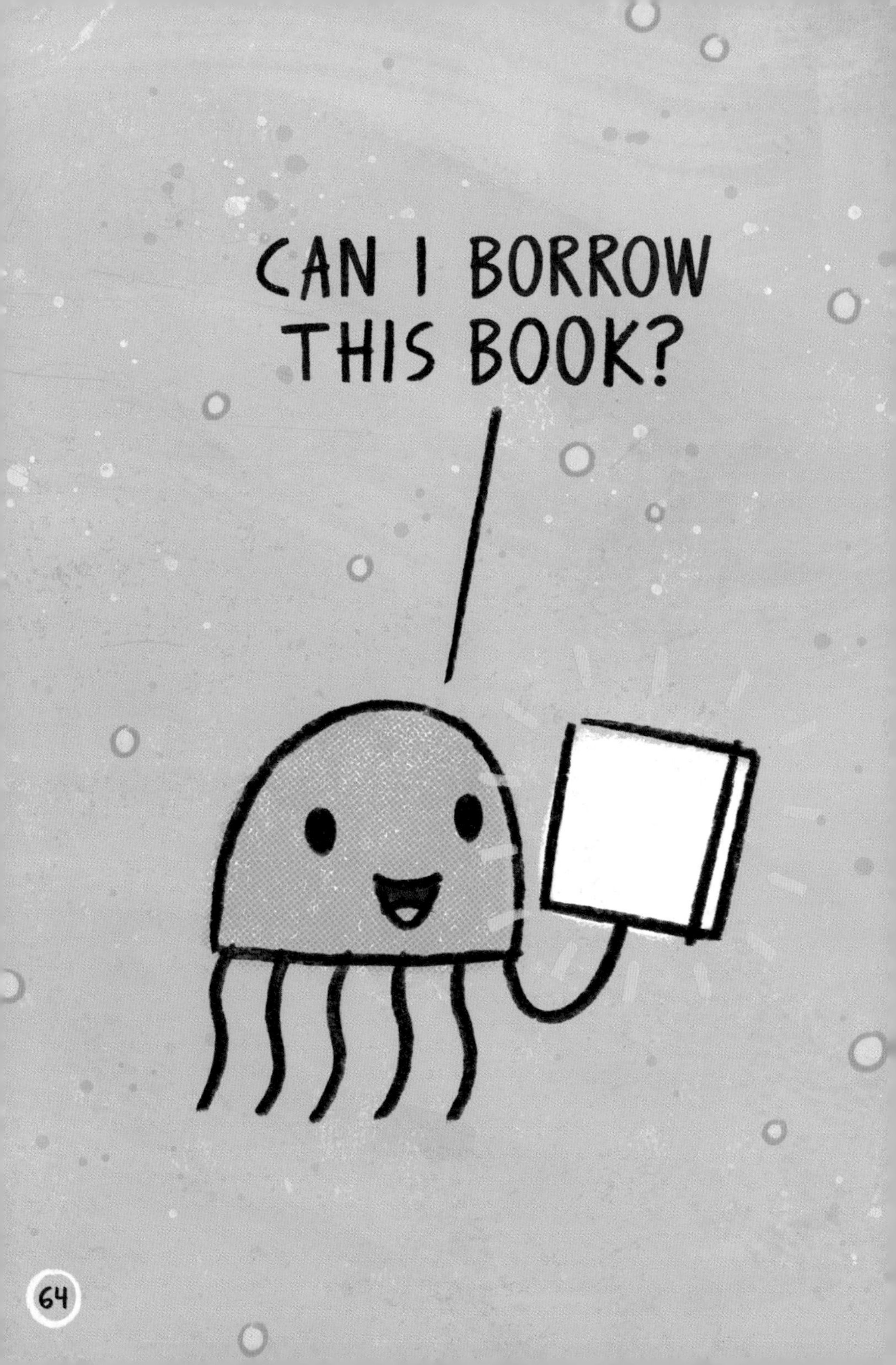
CAN I BORROW THIS BOOK?

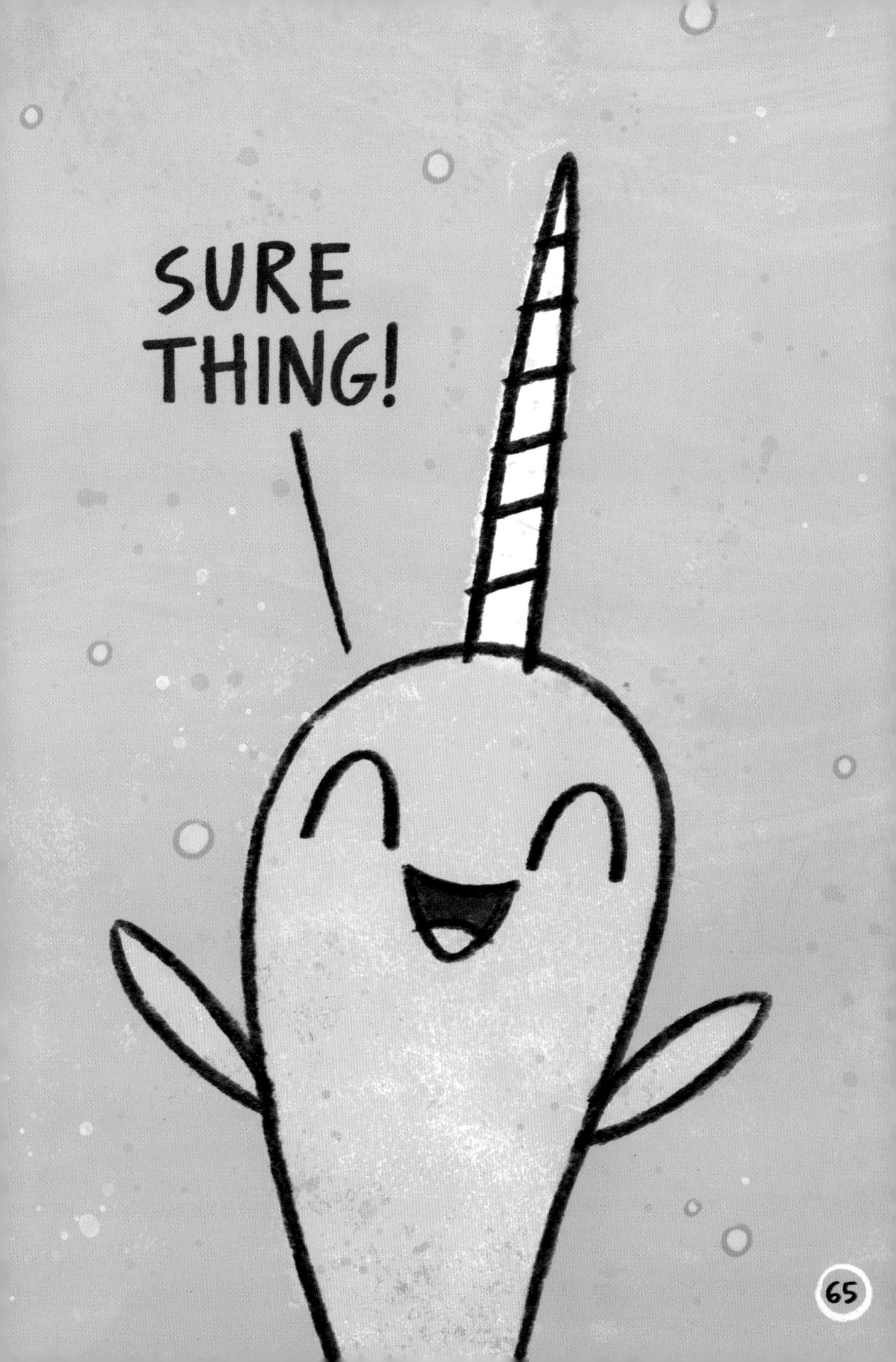
SURE THING!

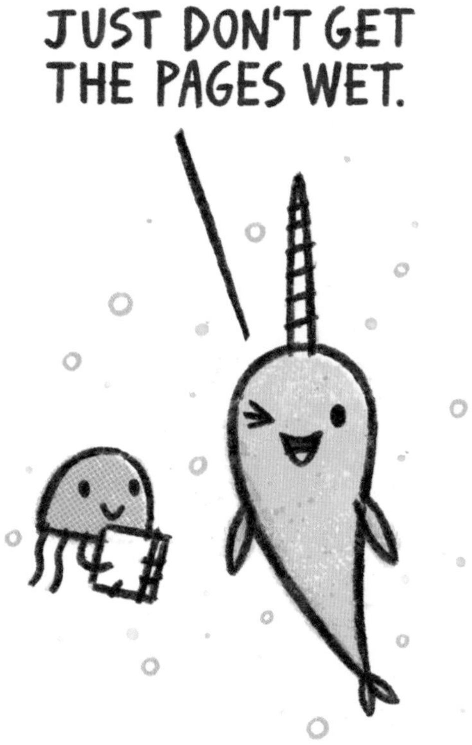
JUST DON'T GET THE PAGES WET.

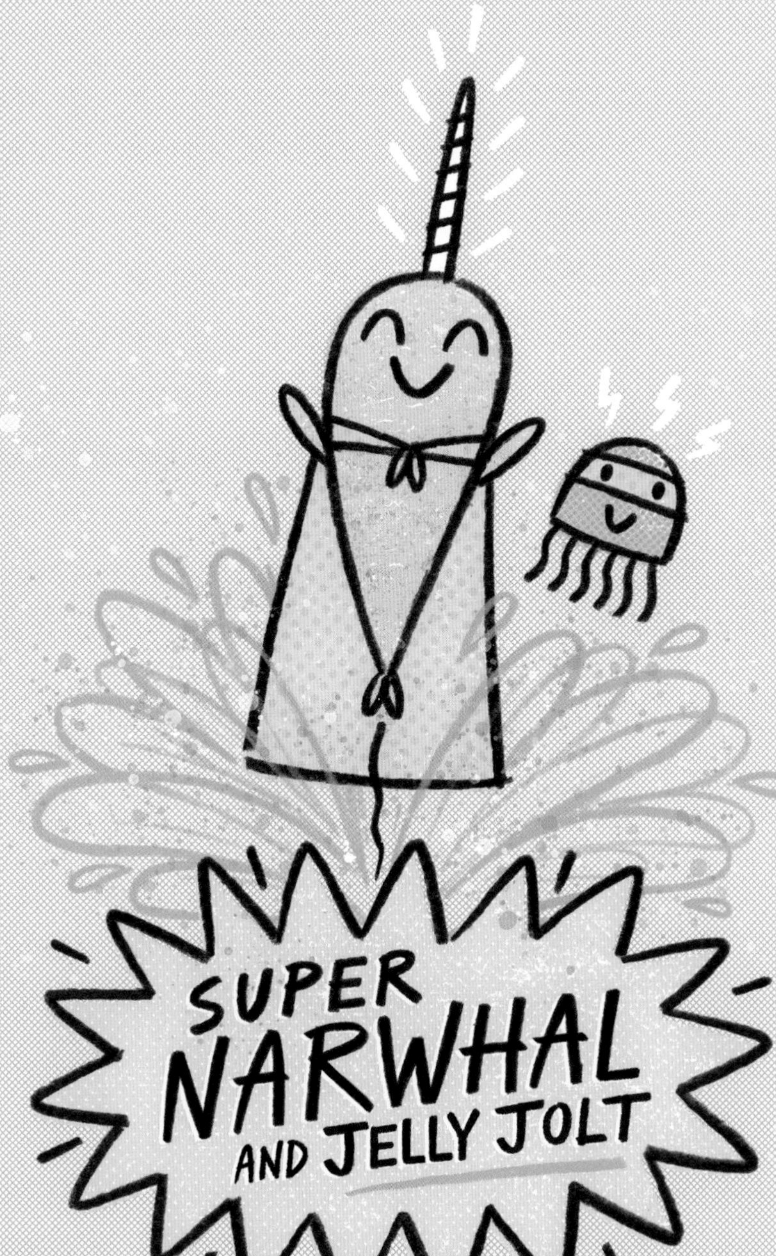
SUPER NARWHAL
AND JELLY JOLT

SUPER NARWHAL AND JELLY JOLT

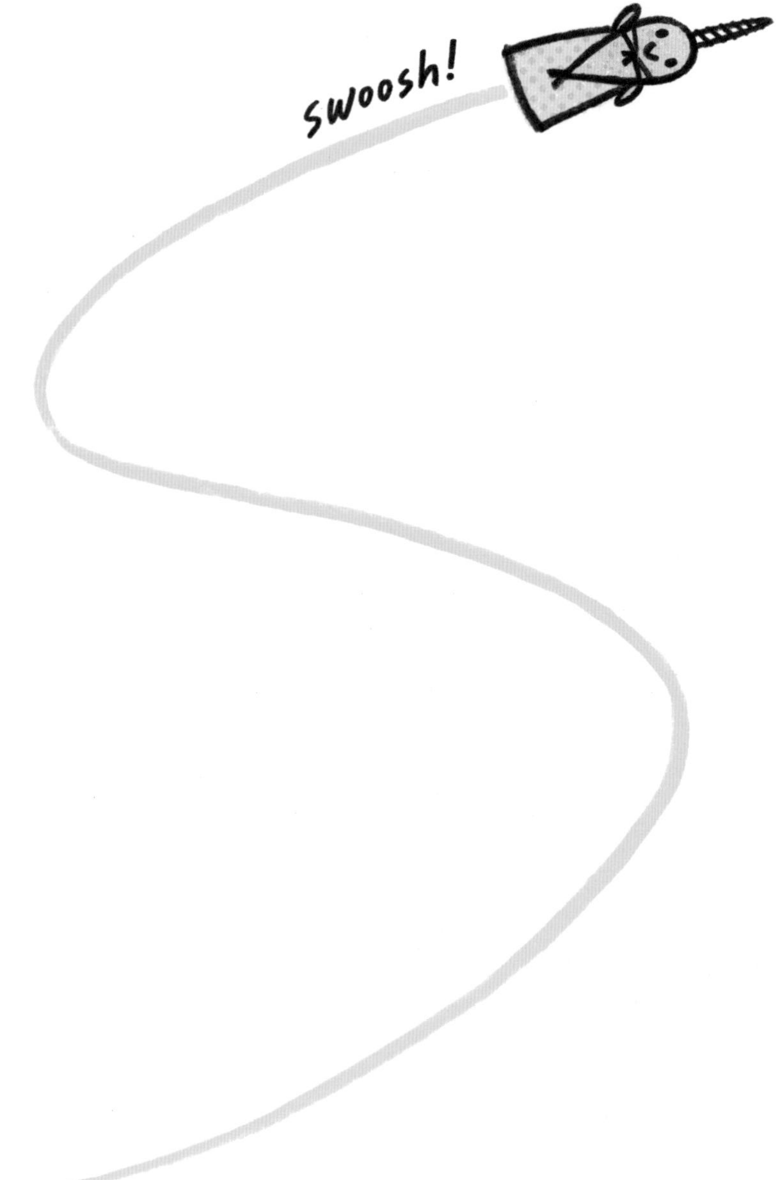
swoosh!

A SUPER START!

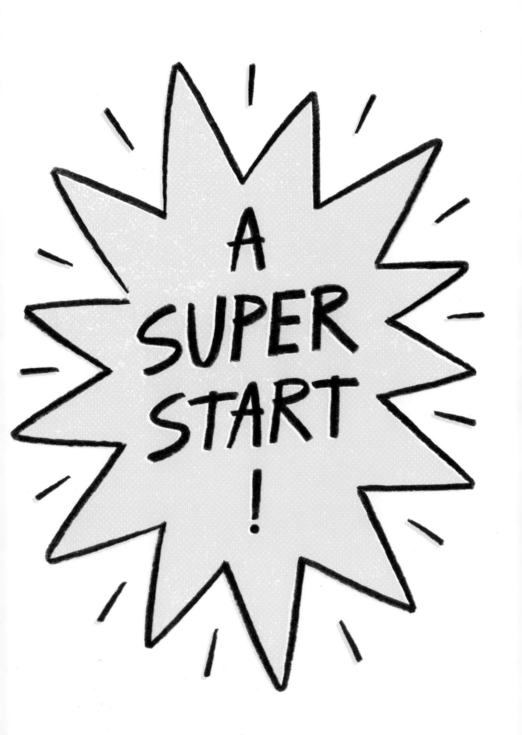

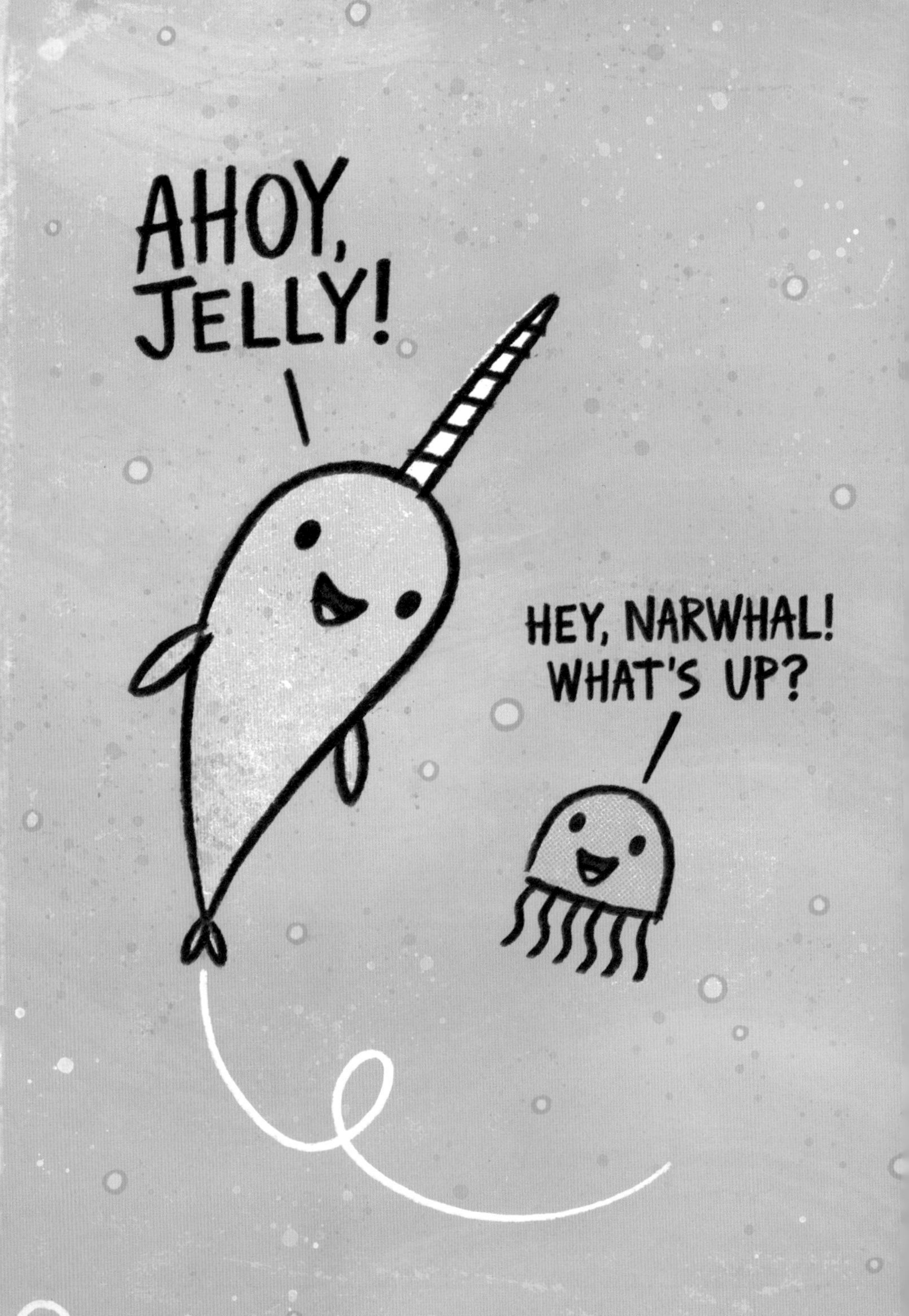
AHOY, JELLY!
HEY, NARWHAL! WHAT'S UP?

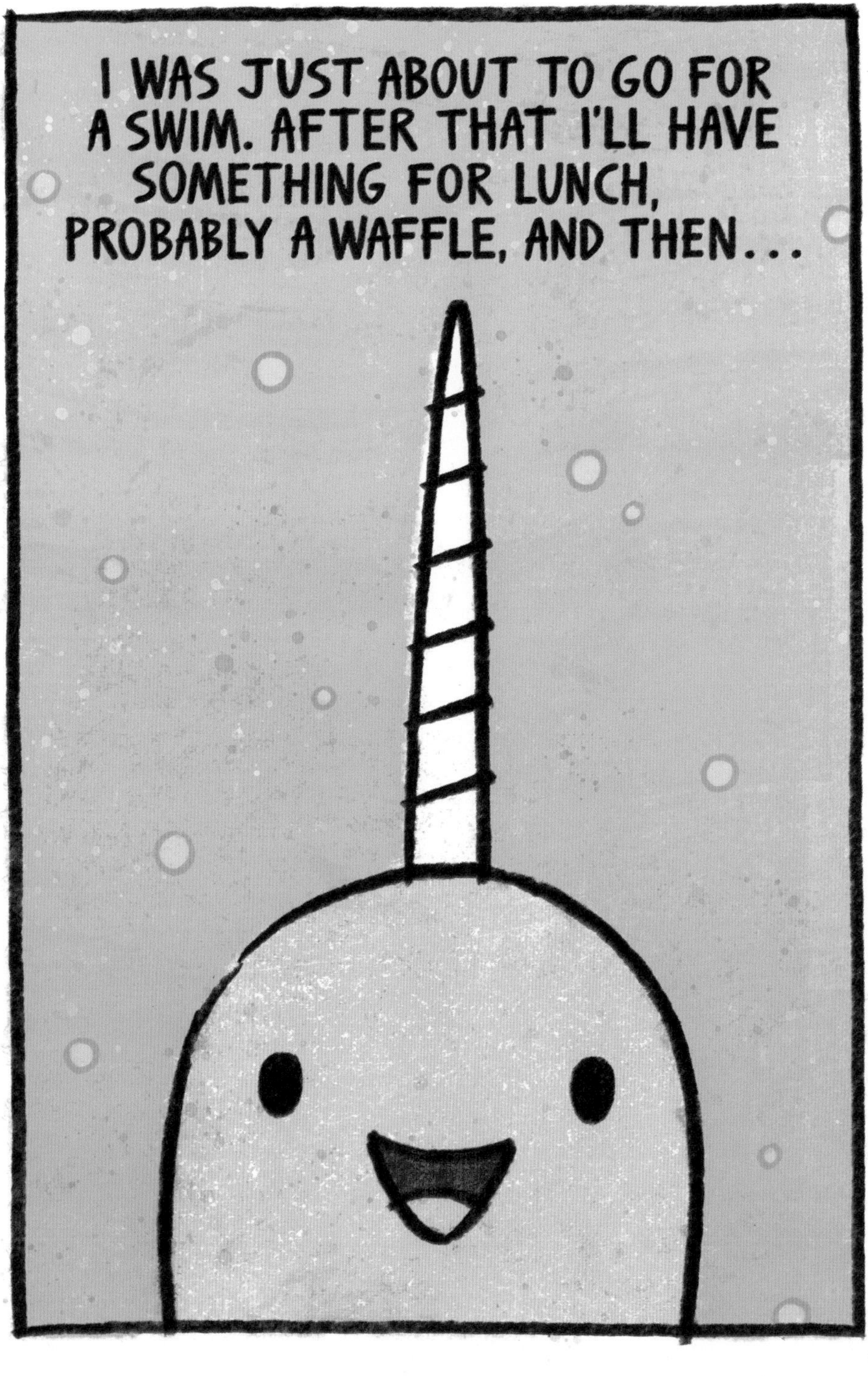
I WAS JUST ABOUT TO GO FOR A SWIM. AFTER THAT I'LL HAVE SOMETHING FOR LUNCH, PROBABLY A WAFFLE, AND THEN...

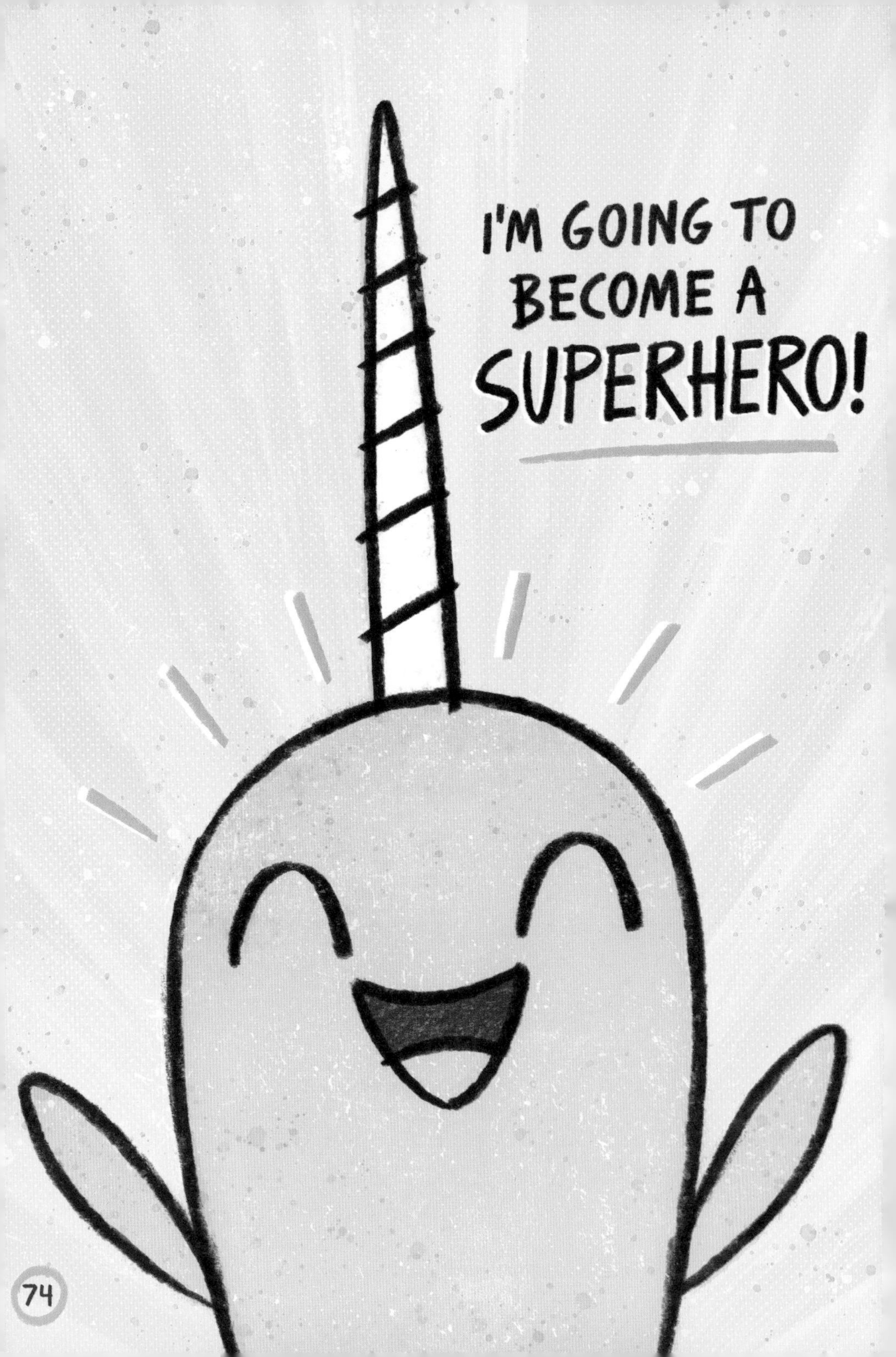
I'M GOING TO BECOME A SUPERHERO!

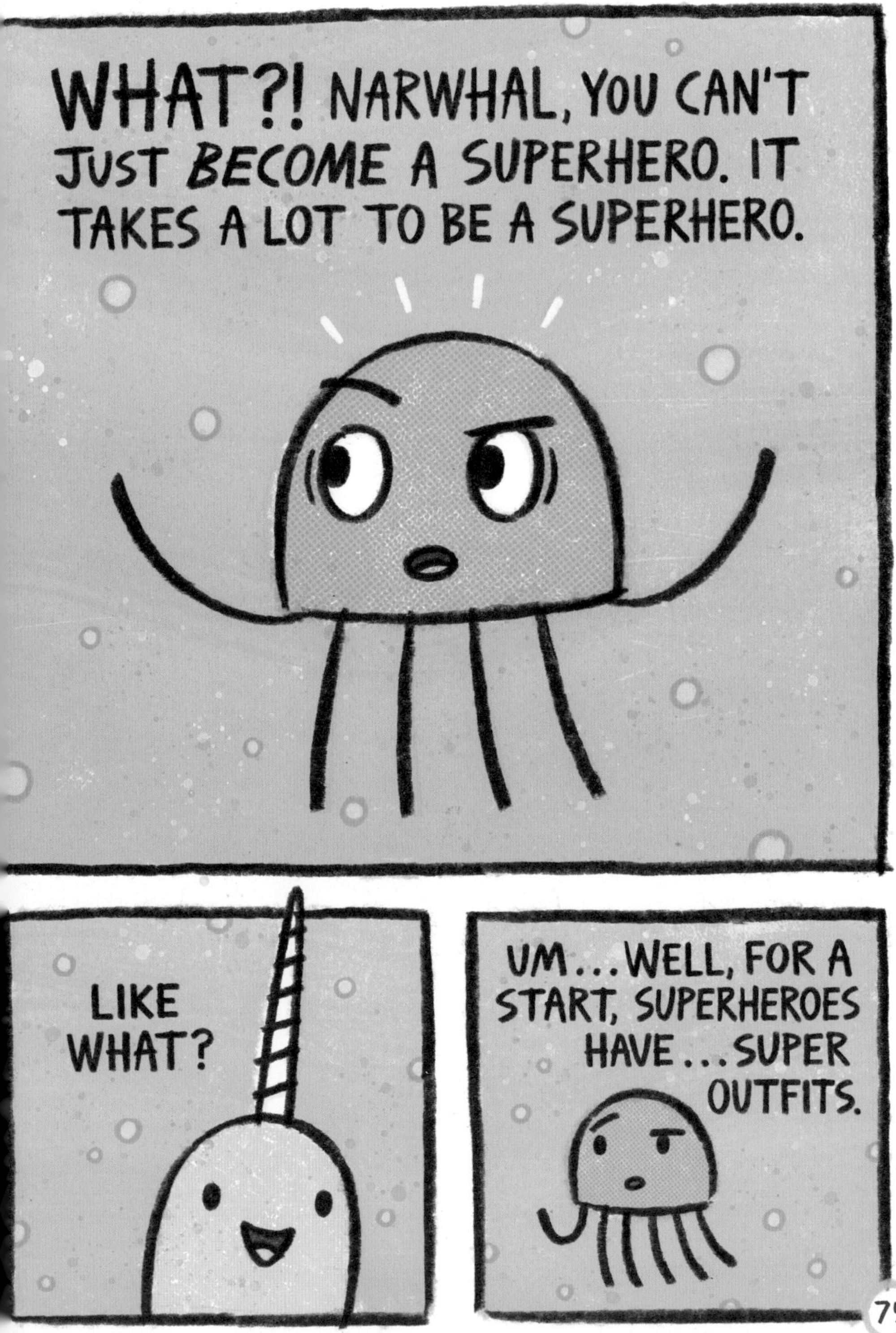
WHAT?! NARWHAL, YOU CAN'T JUST *BECOME* A SUPERHERO. IT TAKES A LOT TO BE A SUPERHERO.
LIKE WHAT?
UM... WELL, FOR A START, SUPERHEROES HAVE... SUPER OUTFITS.

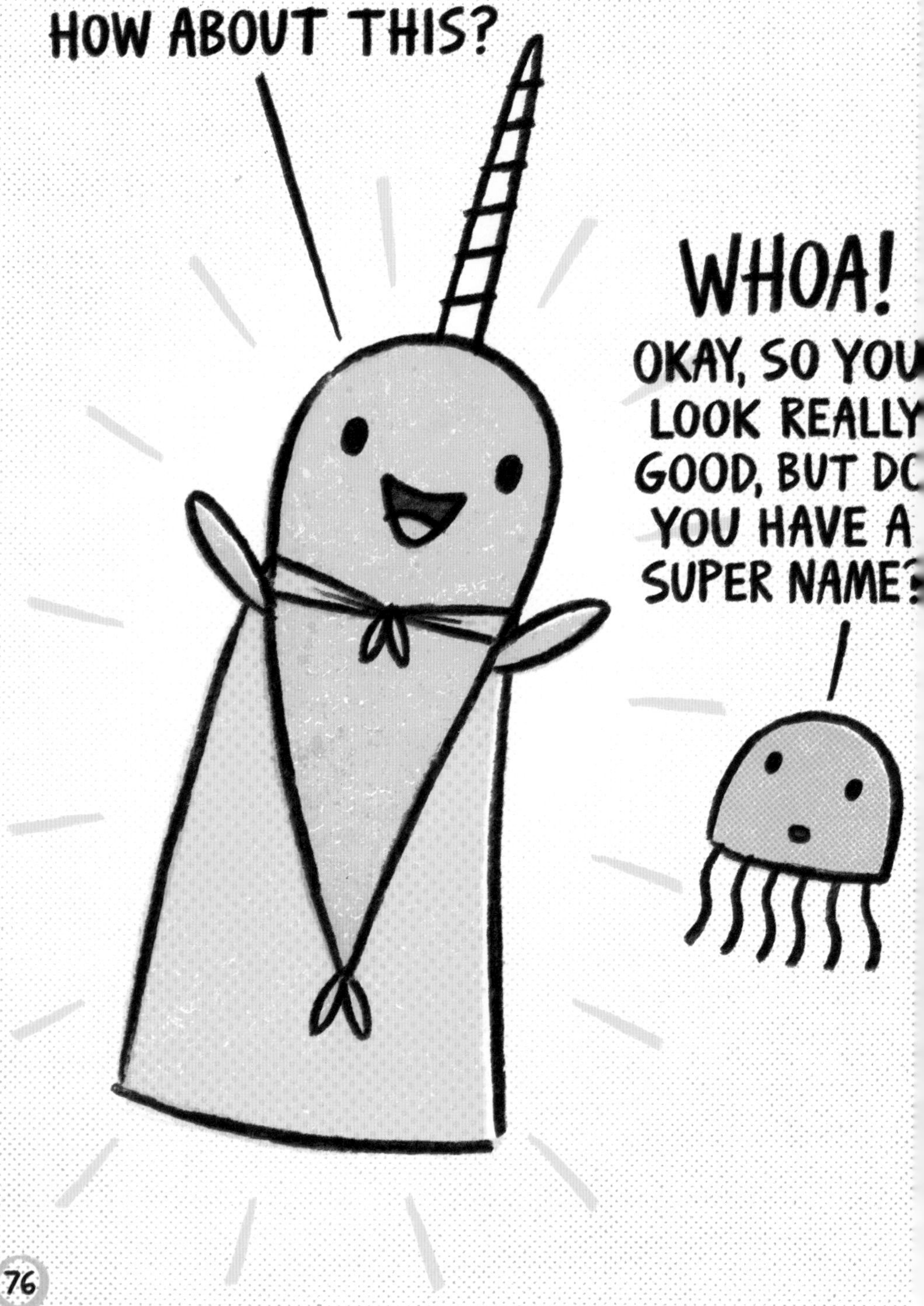
HOW ABOUT THIS?
WHOA!
OKAY, SO YOU LOOK REALLY GOOD, BUT DO YOU HAVE A SUPER NAME?

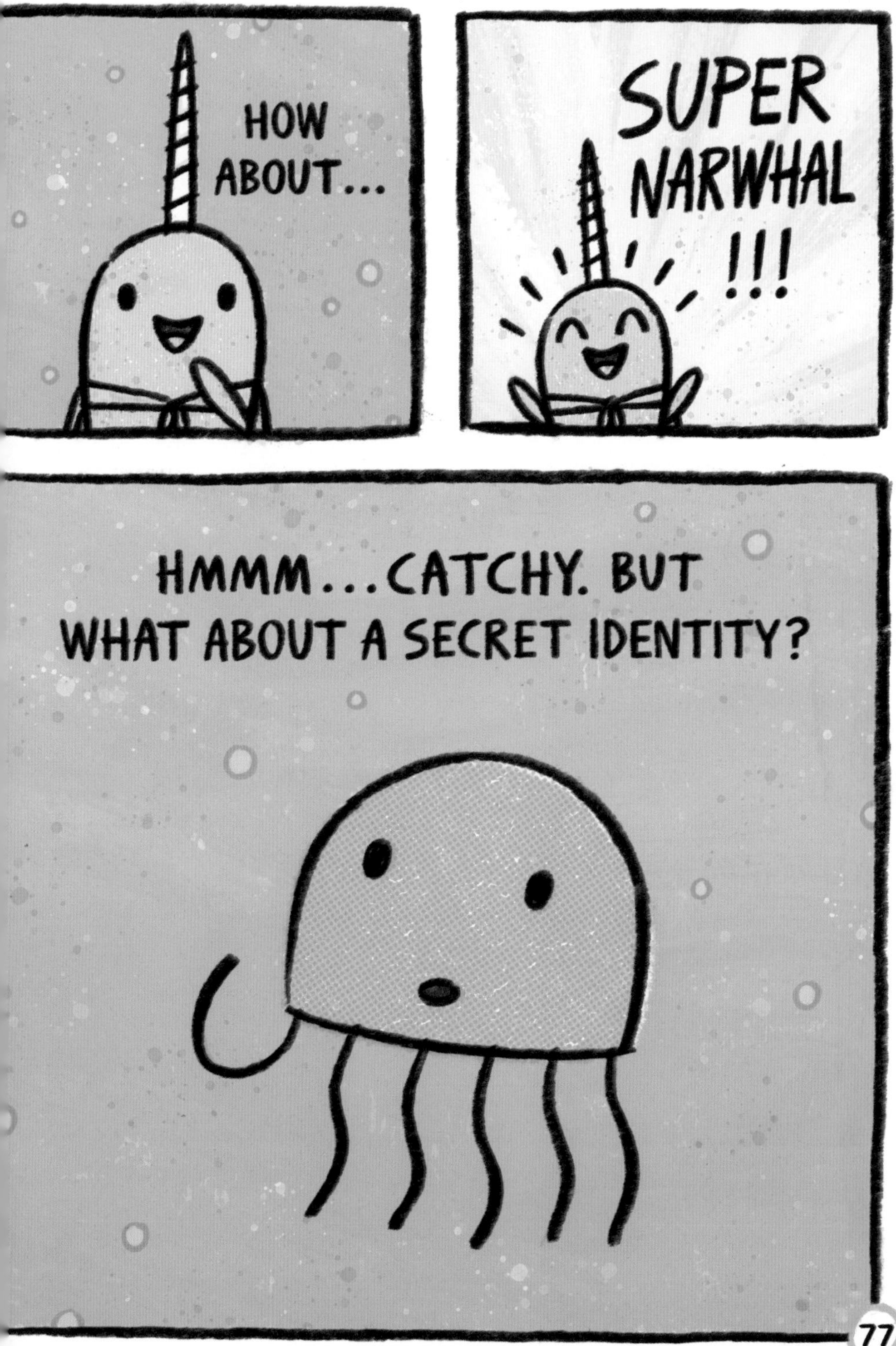
HOW ABOUT...
SUPER NARWHAL !!!
HMMM...CATCHY. BUT WHAT ABOUT A SECRET IDENTITY?

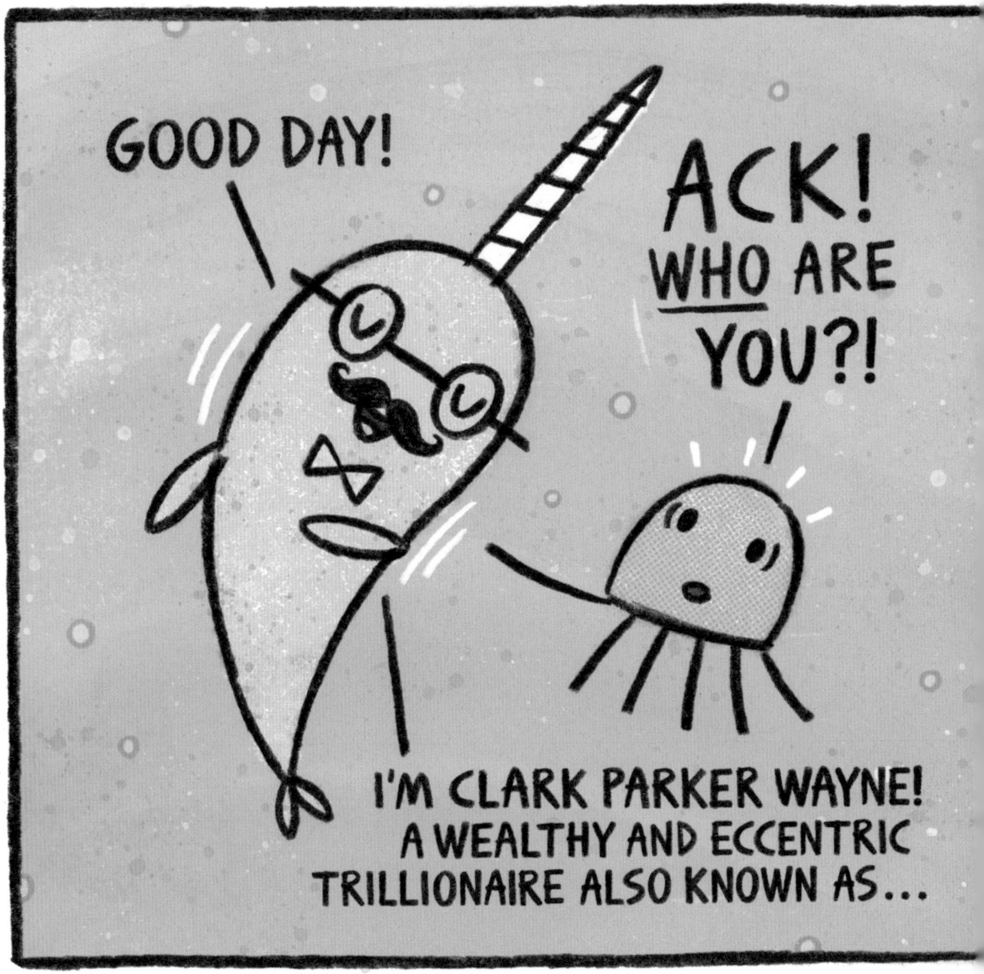
GOOD DAY!
ACK! WHO ARE YOU?!
I'M CLARK PARKER WAYNE! A WEALTHY AND ECCENTRIC TRILLIONAIRE ALSO KNOWN AS...

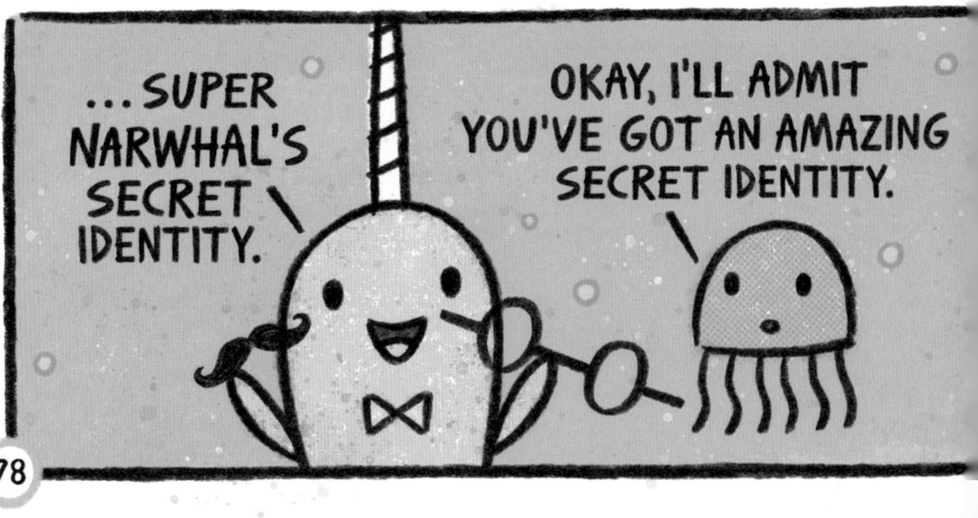
...SUPER NARWHAL'S SECRET IDENTITY.
OKAY, I'LL ADMIT YOU'VE GOT AN AMAZING SECRET IDENTITY.

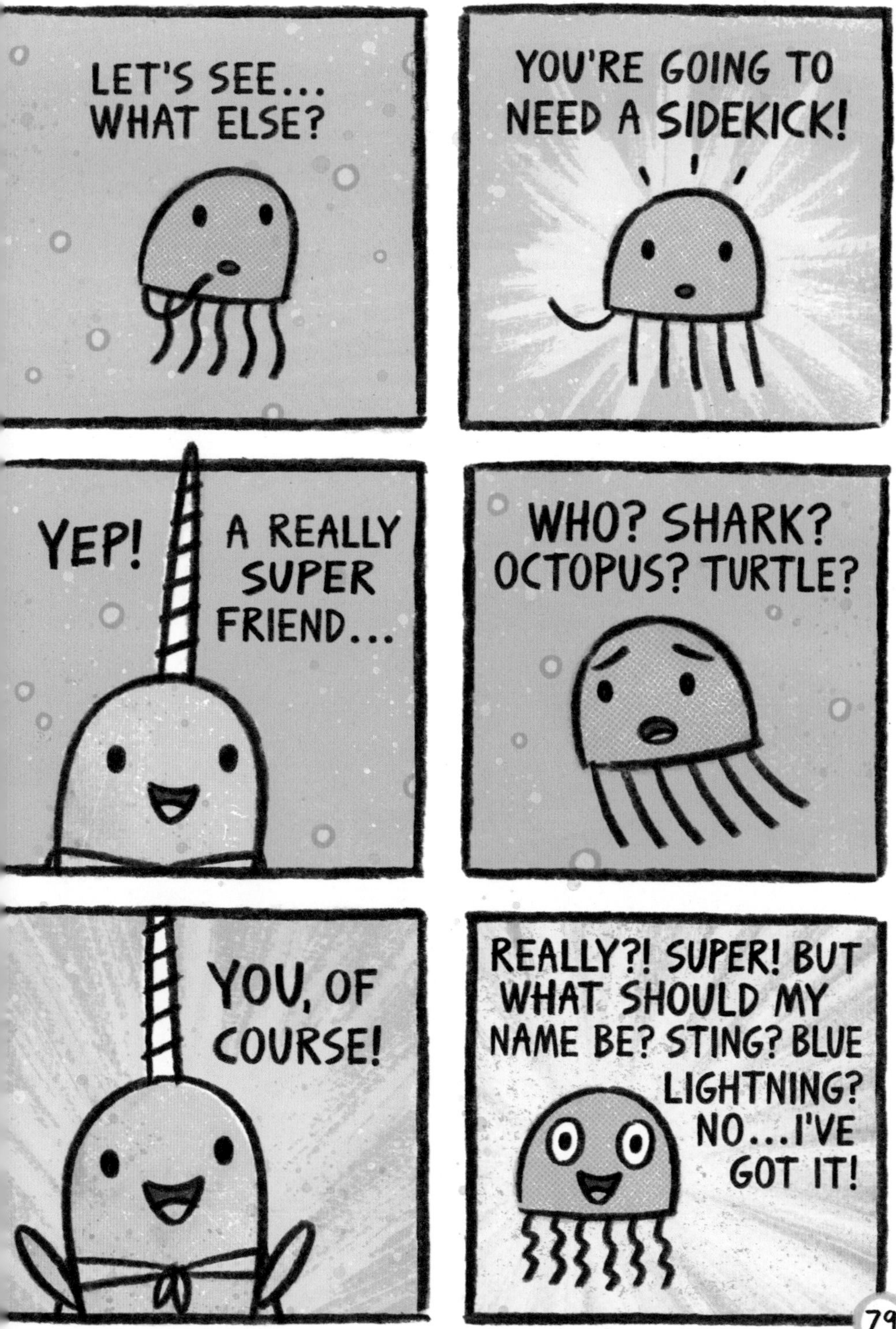
LET'S SEE... WHAT ELSE?
YOU'RE GOING TO NEED A SIDEKICK!
YEP!
A REALLY SUPER FRIEND...
WHO? SHARK? OCTOPUS? TURTLE?
YOU, OF COURSE!
REALLY?! SUPER! BUT WHAT SHOULD MY NAME BE? STING? BLUE LIGHTNING? NO...I'VE GOT IT!

JELLY JOLT THE SUPER SIDEKICK!

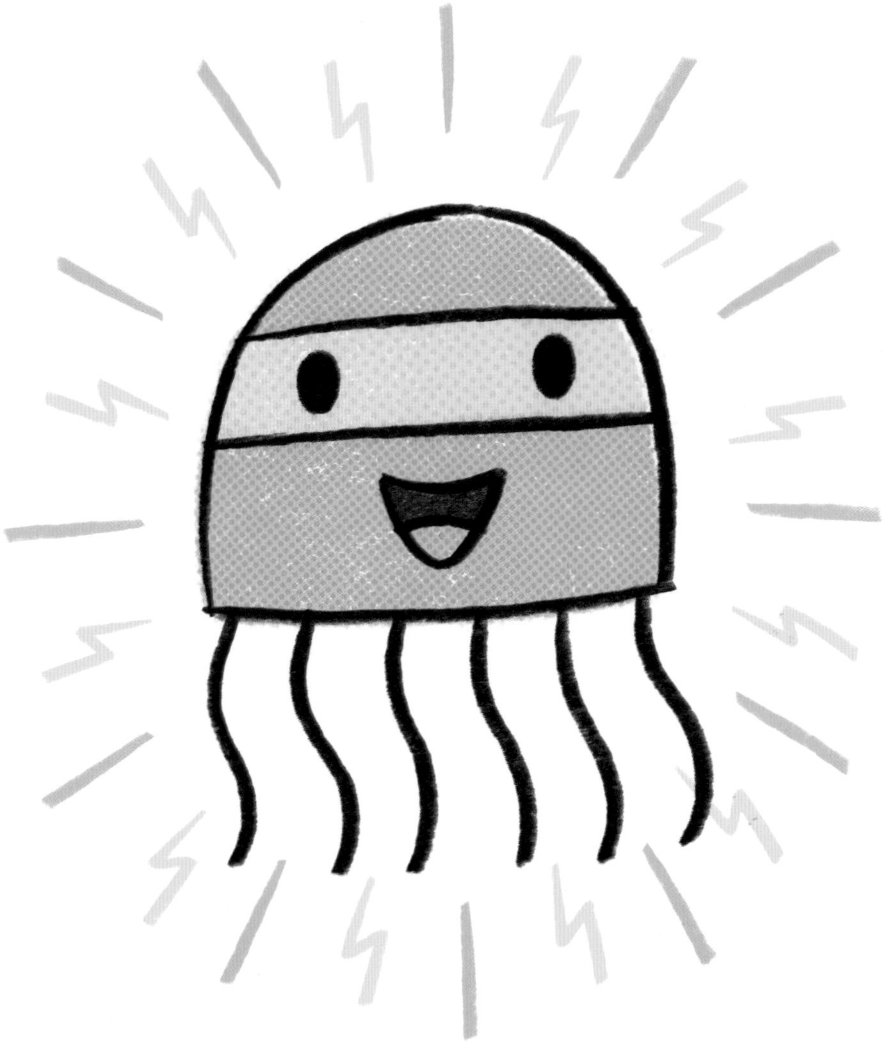

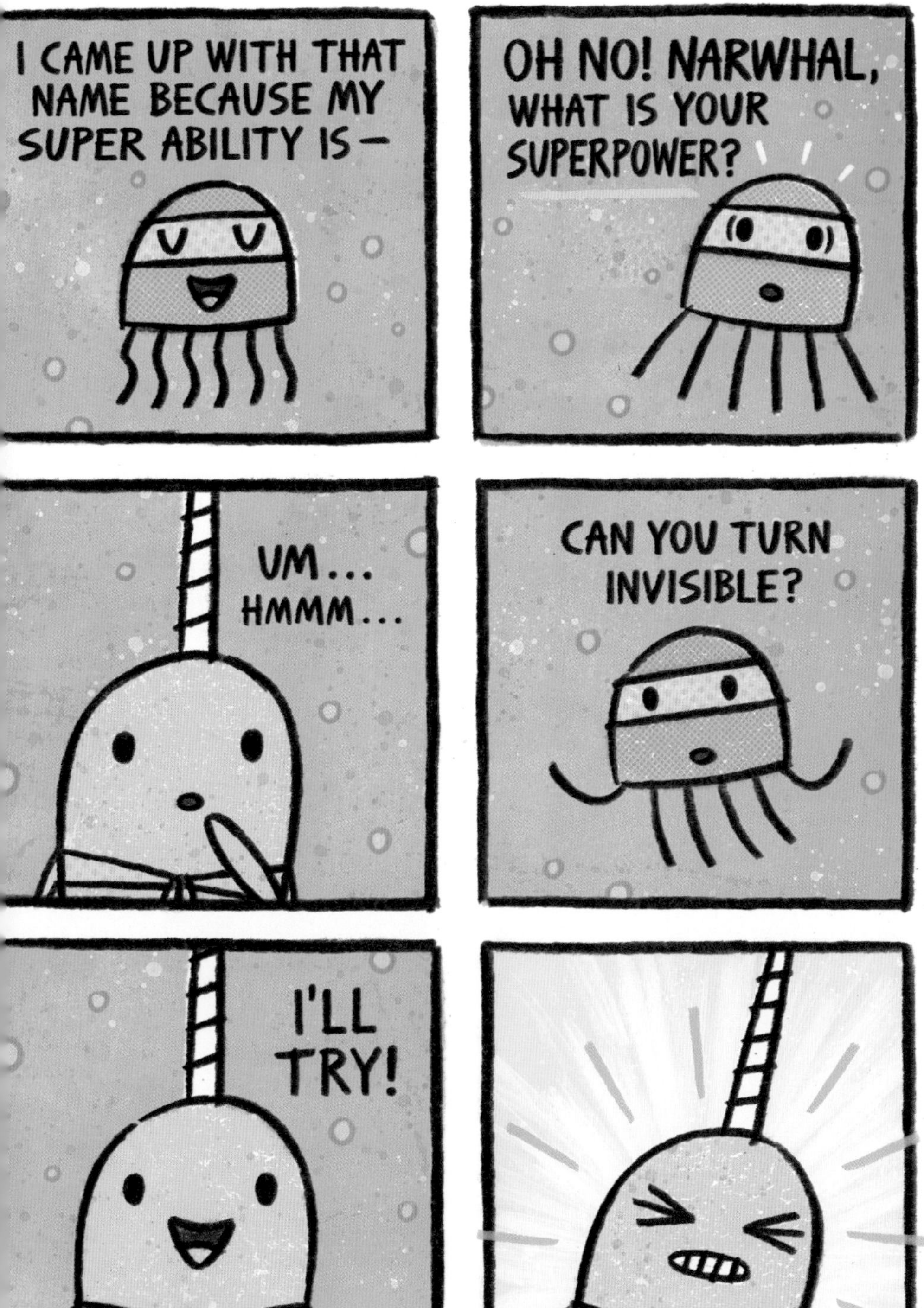

I CAME UP WITH THAT NAME BECAUSE MY SUPER ABILITY IS—
OH NO! NARWHAL, WHAT IS YOUR SUPERPOWER?
UM... HMMM...
CAN YOU TURN INVISIBLE?
I'LL TRY!

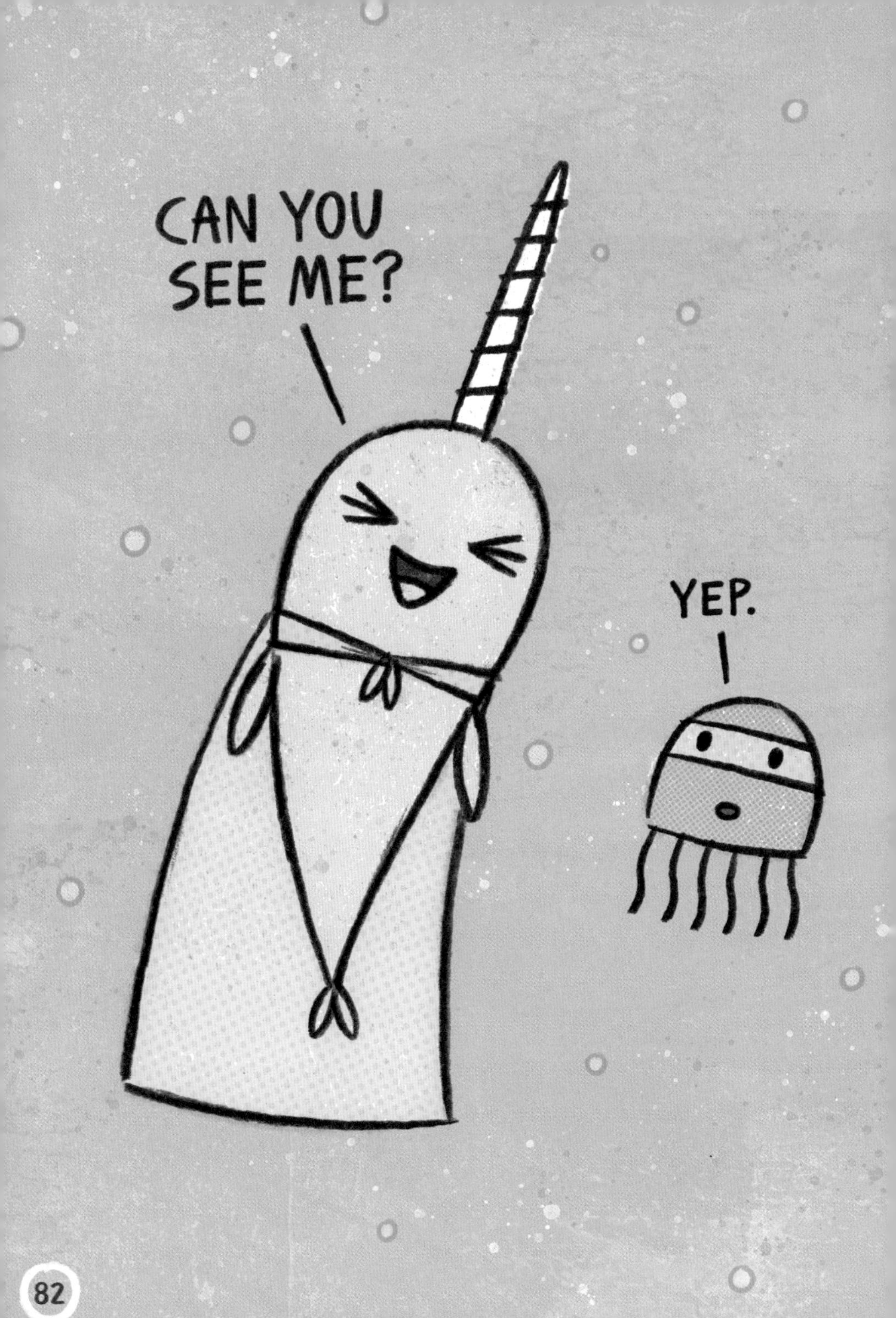
CAN YOU SEE ME?
YEP.

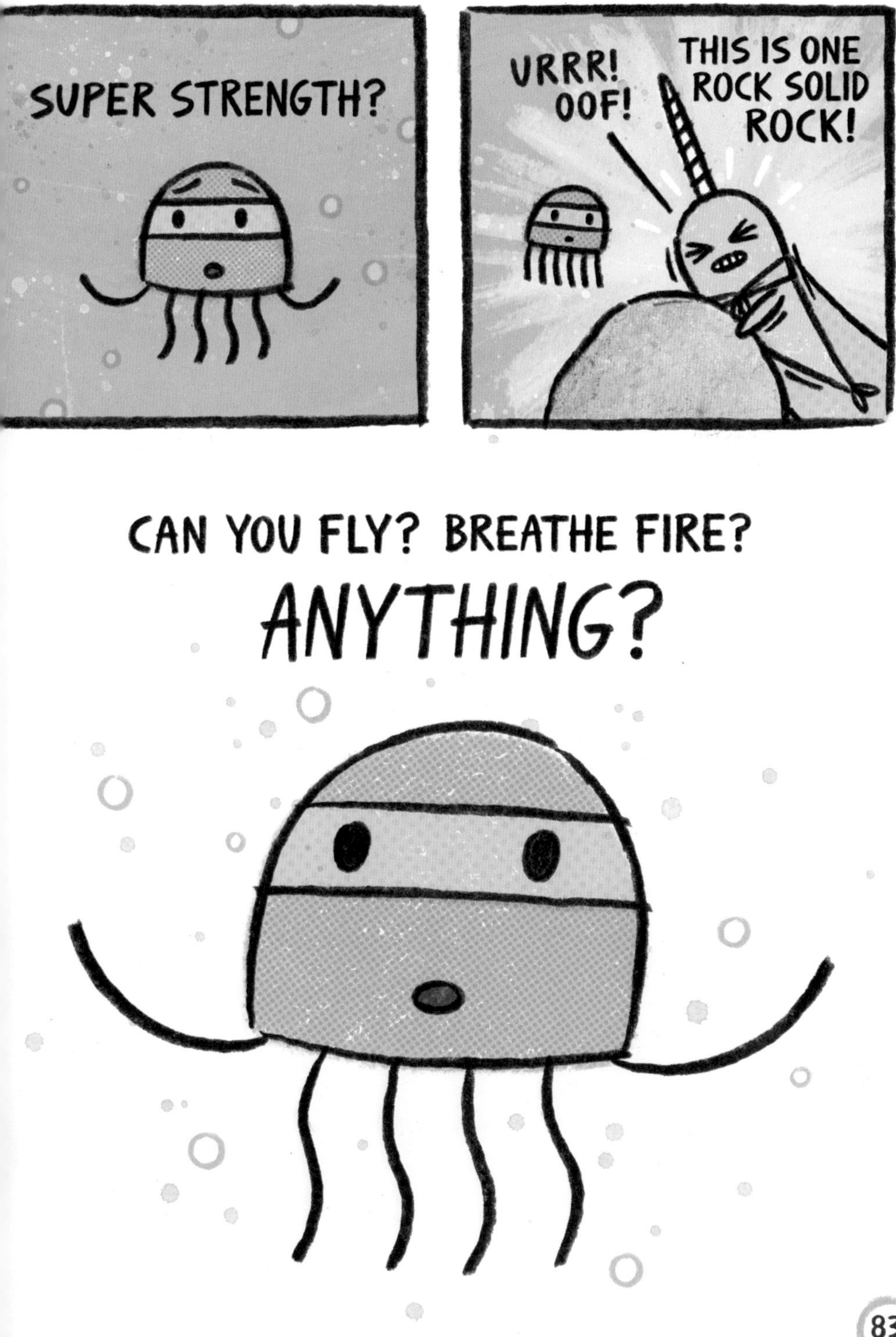
SUPER STRENGTH?
URRR! OOF!
THIS IS ONE ROCK SOLID ROCK!
CAN YOU FLY? BREATHE FIRE?
ANYTHING?

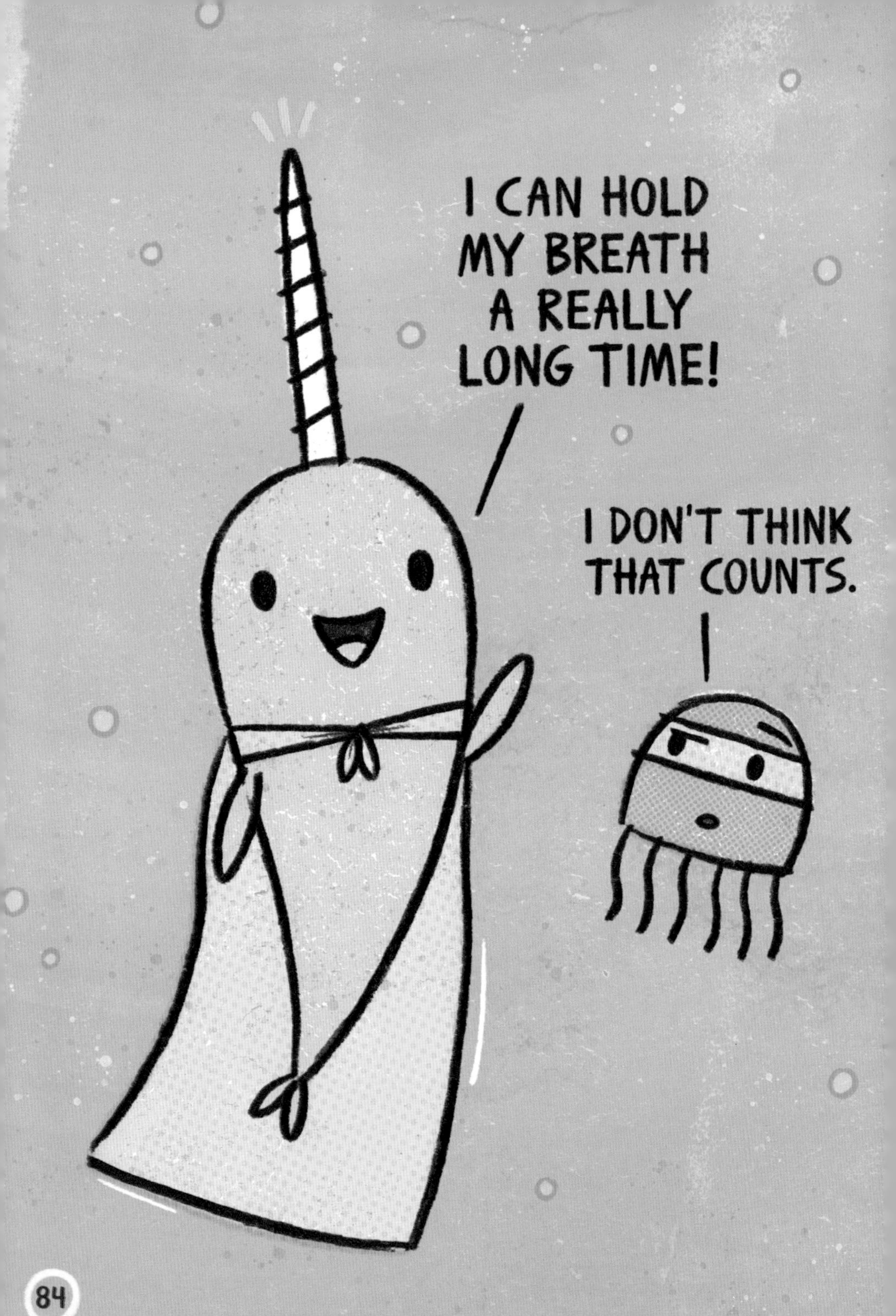
I CAN HOLD MY BREATH A REALLY LONG TIME!
I DON'T THINK THAT COUNTS.

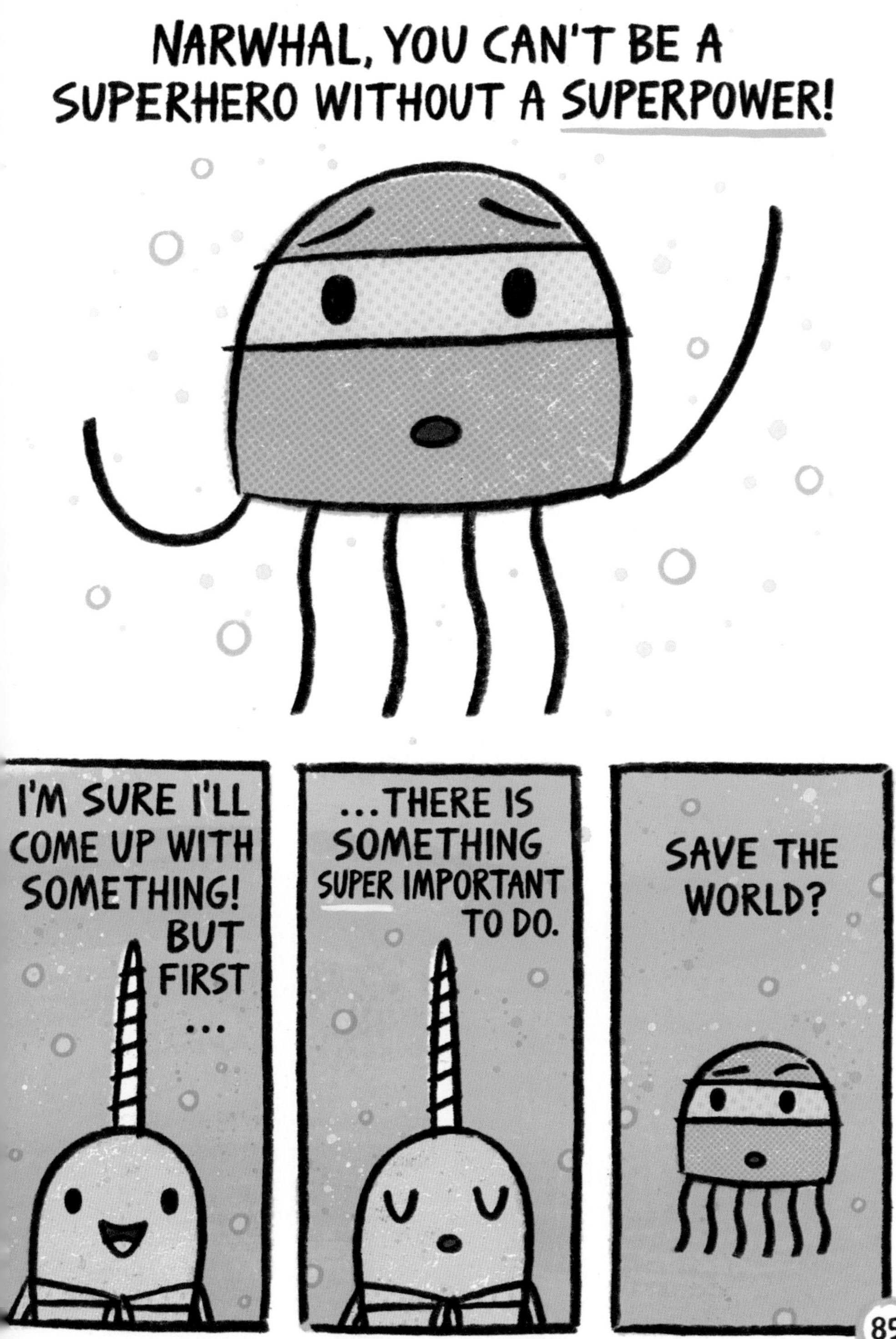

NARWHAL, YOU CAN'T BE A SUPERHERO WITHOUT A SUPERPOWER!
I'M SURE I'LL COME UP WITH SOMETHING! BUT FIRST ...
...THERE IS SOMETHING SUPER IMPORTANT TO DO.
SAVE THE WORLD?

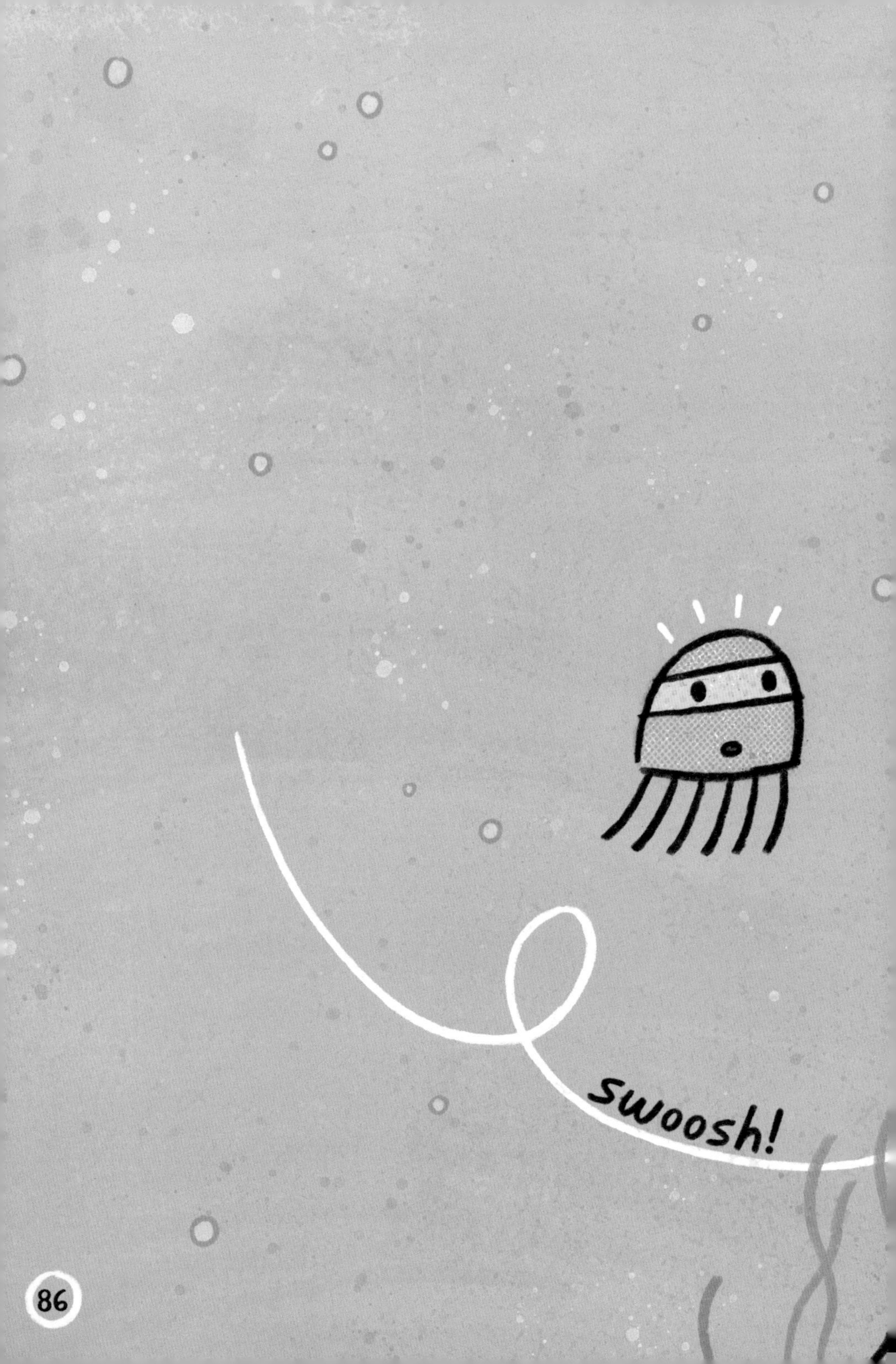
swoosh!

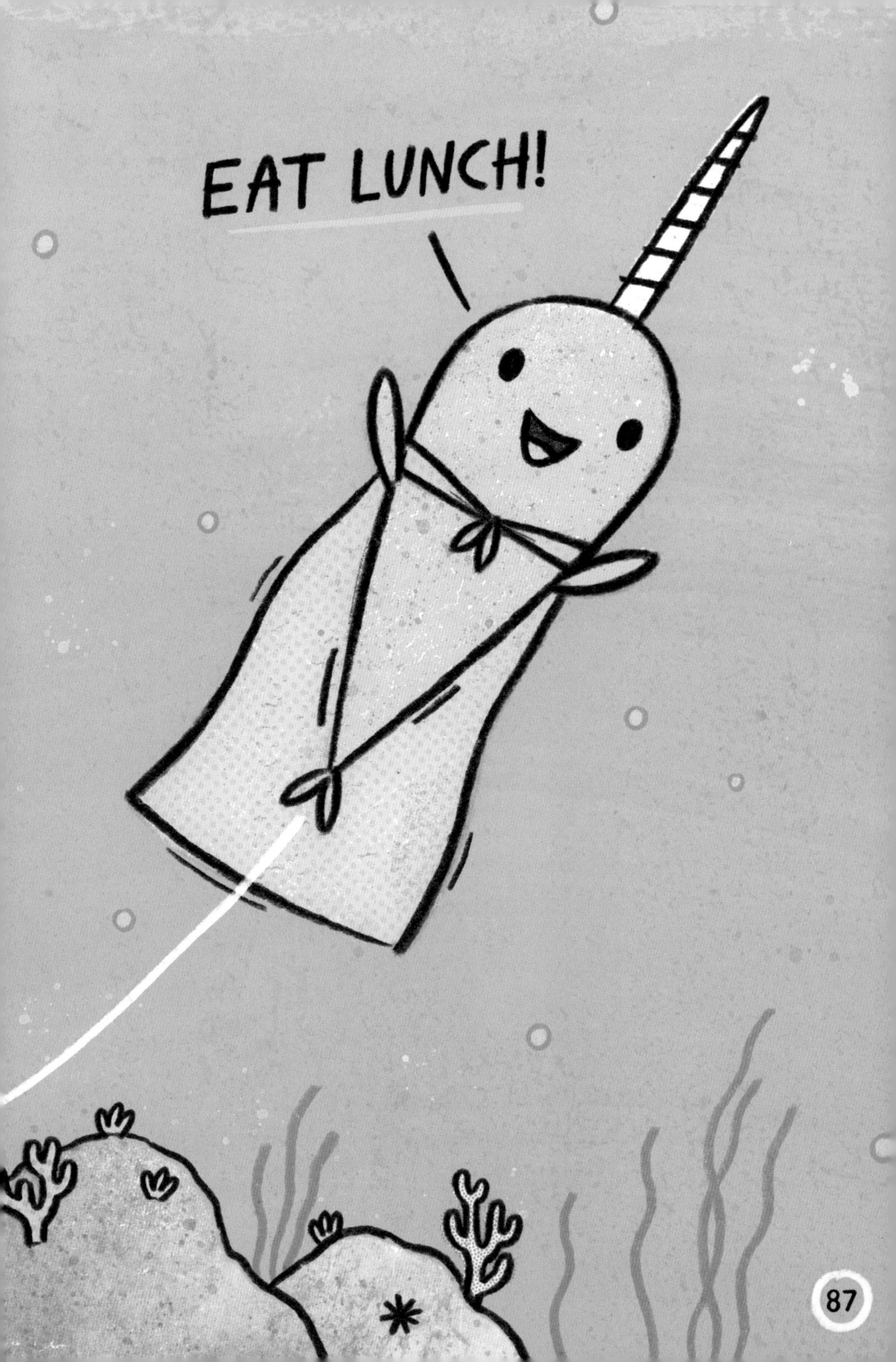
EAT LUNCH!

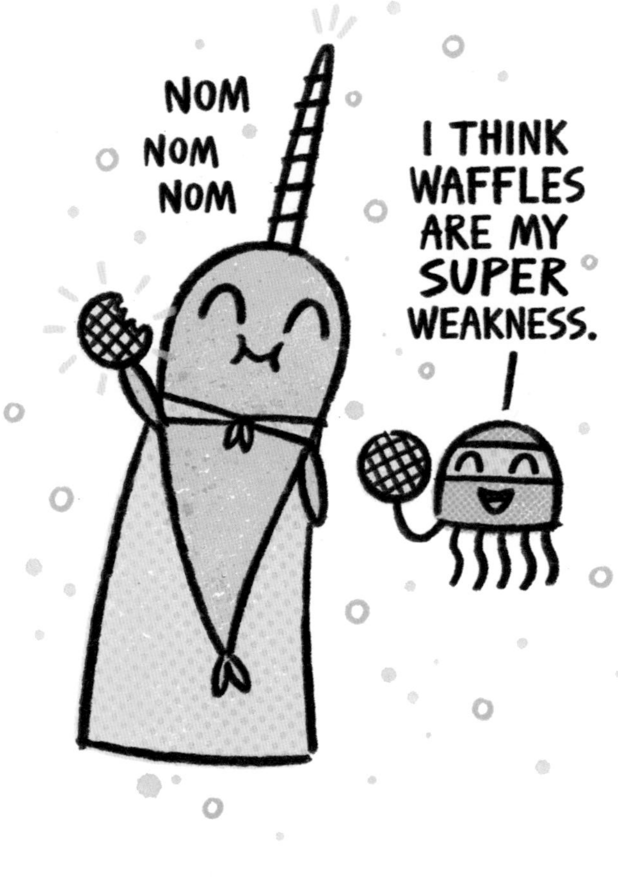
NOM
NOM
NOM
I THINK WAFFLES ARE MY SUPER WEAKNESS.

SUPER SEA CREATURES

REAL SEA CREATURES WITH REAL SUPER-AWESOME ABILITIES

THE MIMIC OCTOPUS CAN CHANGE ITS COLOR, SHAPE AND MOVEMENTS TO LOOK LIKE OTHER SEA LIFE SUCH AS SNAKES, LIONFISH, STINGRAYS AND JELLYFISH.

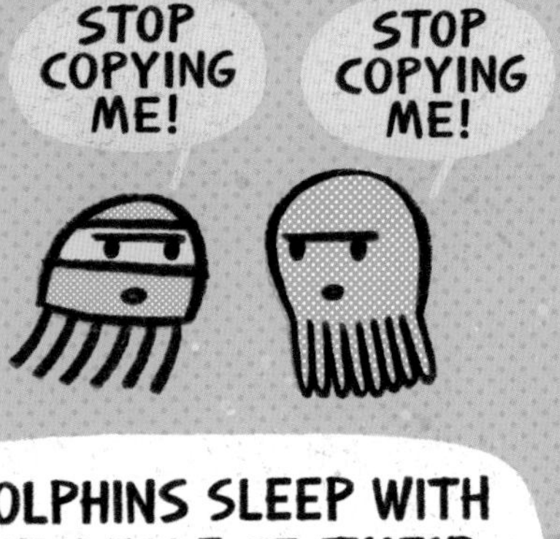
STOP COPYING ME!
STOP COPYING ME!

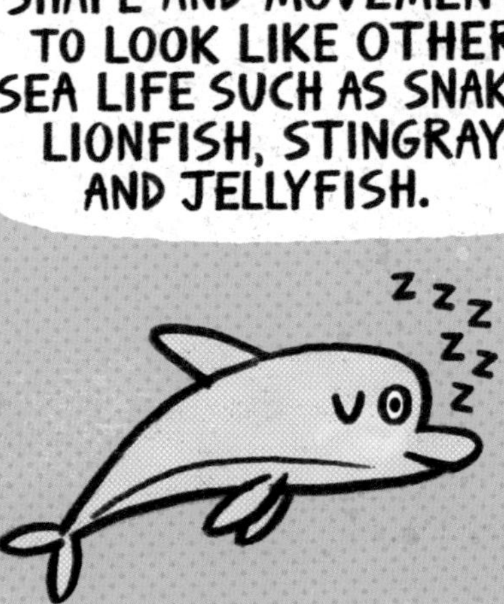
Z Z Z Z Z Z

DOLPHINS SLEEP WITH ONLY HALF OF THEIR BRAIN AND WITH ONE EYE OPEN TO WATCH FOR THREATS.

DOLPHINS CAN ALSO "SEE" INSIDE MANY ANIMALS BY USING SOUND WAVES.

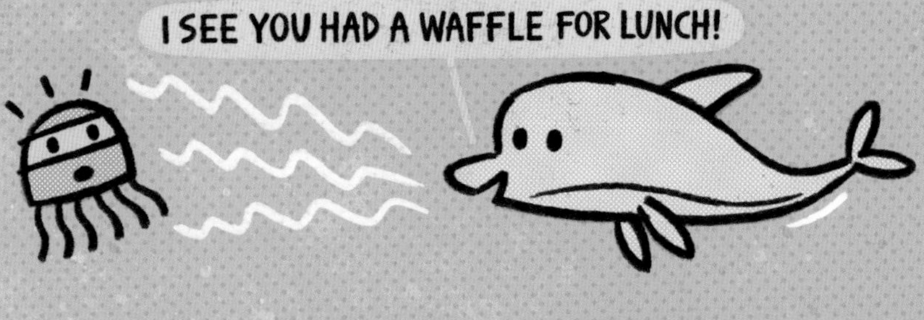
I SEE YOU HAD A WAFFLE FOR LUNCH!

BLUE WHALES ARE ONE OF THE LOUDEST ANIMALS ON EARTH.

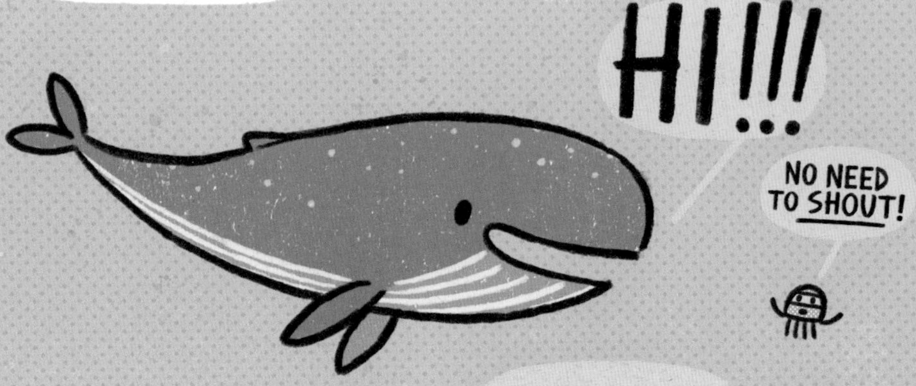
HI!!!...
NO NEED TO SHOUT!

CRABS CAN REGROW CLAWS OR LEGS IF THEY LOSE ONE IN A FIGHT.

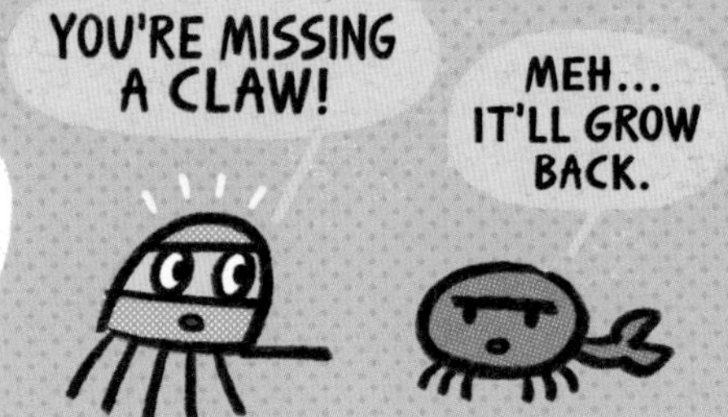
YOU'RE MISSING A CLAW!
MEH... IT'LL GROW BACK.

FLYING FISH CAN GLIDE UP TO 400 m (1,300 ft.) AND TRAVEL AT SPEEDS OF MORE THAN 70 km/h (43 mph). EVEN FASTER, THOUGH, IS THE SAILFISH, WHICH CAN REACH SPEEDS OF UP TO 110 km/h (68 mph).

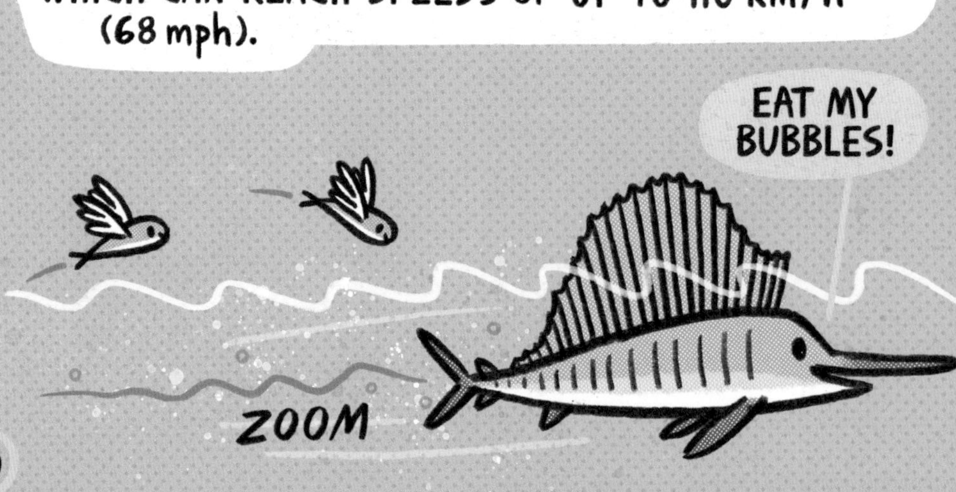
EAT MY BUBBLES!
ZOOM

NARWHAL, YOU'RE

A SUPERSTAR!

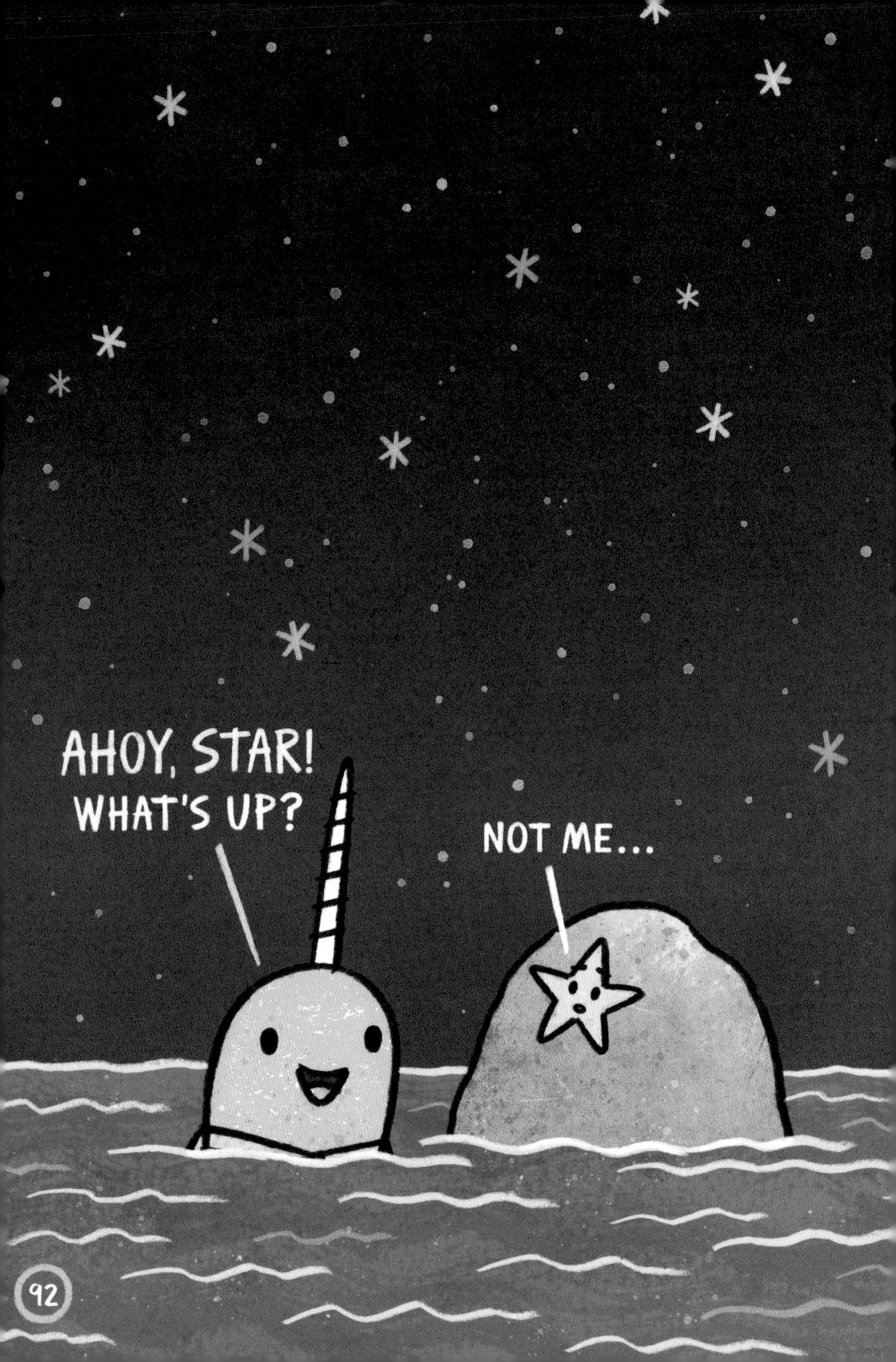
AHOY, STAR! WHAT'S UP?
NOT ME...

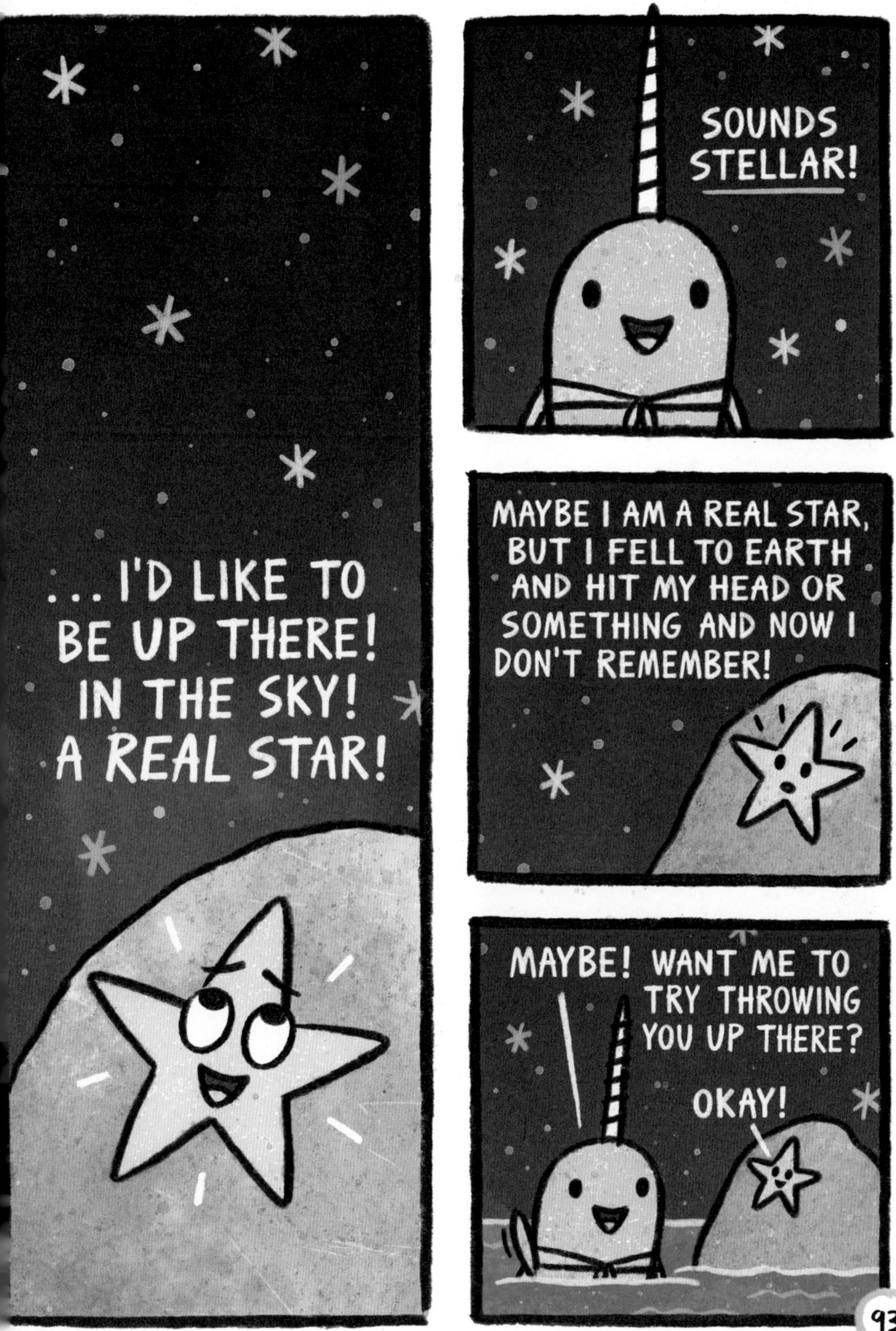

...I'D LIKE TO BE UP THERE! IN THE SKY! A REAL STAR!
SOUNDS STELLAR!
MAYBE I AM A REAL STAR, BUT I FELL TO EARTH AND HIT MY HEAD OR SOMETHING AND NOW I DON'T REMEMBER!
MAYBE! WANT ME TO TRY THROWING YOU UP THERE?
OKAY!

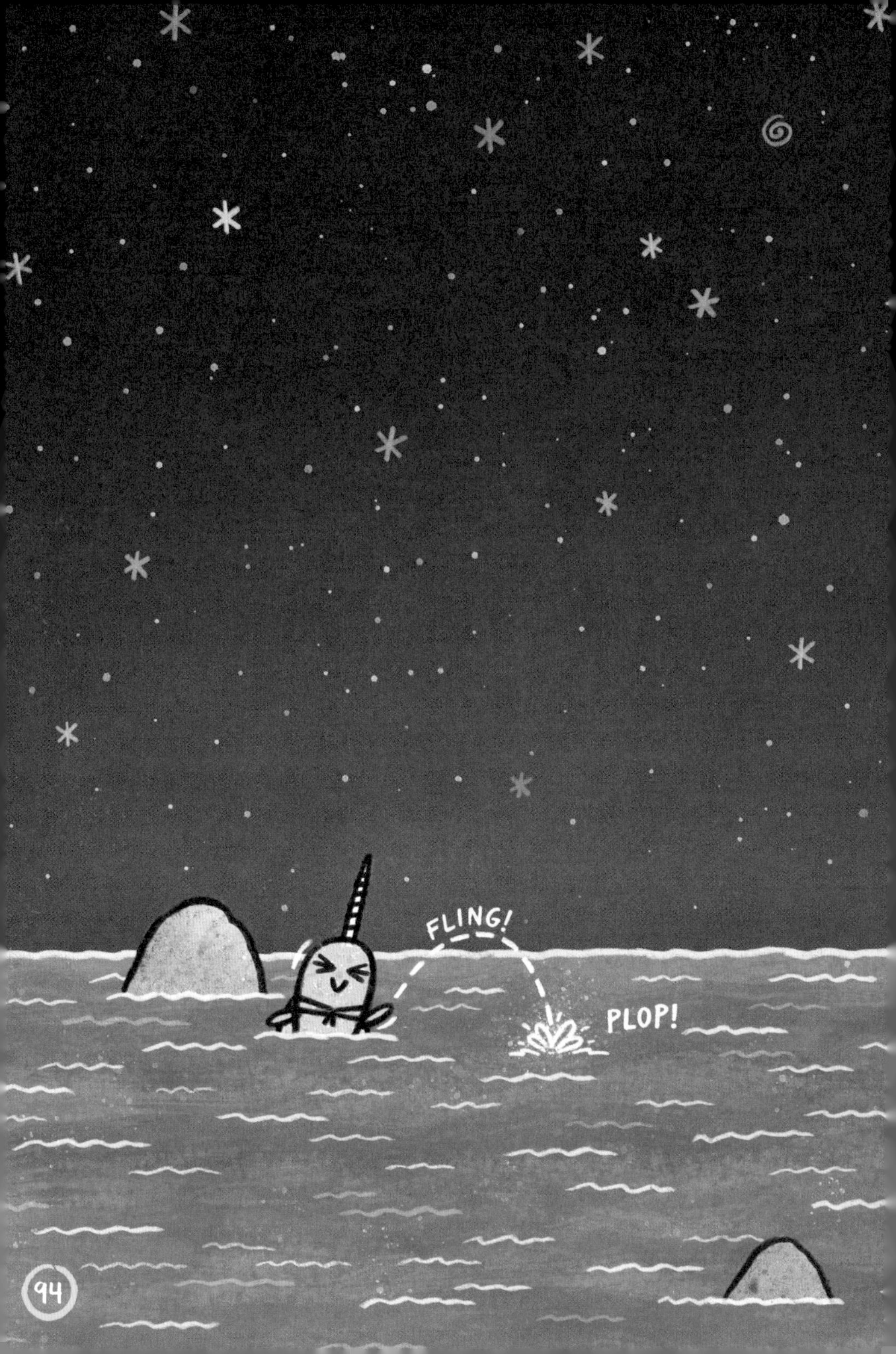
FLING!
PLOP!

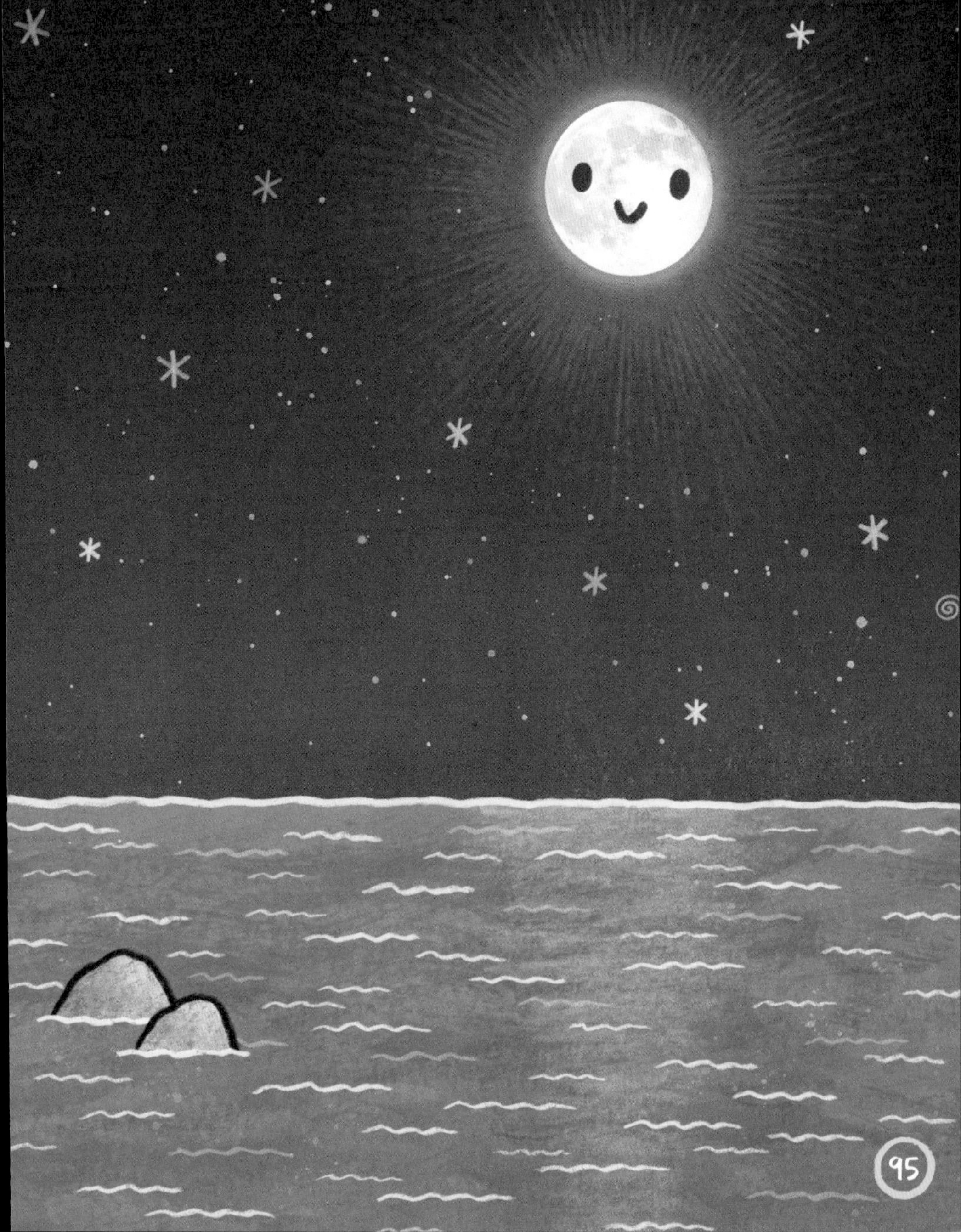

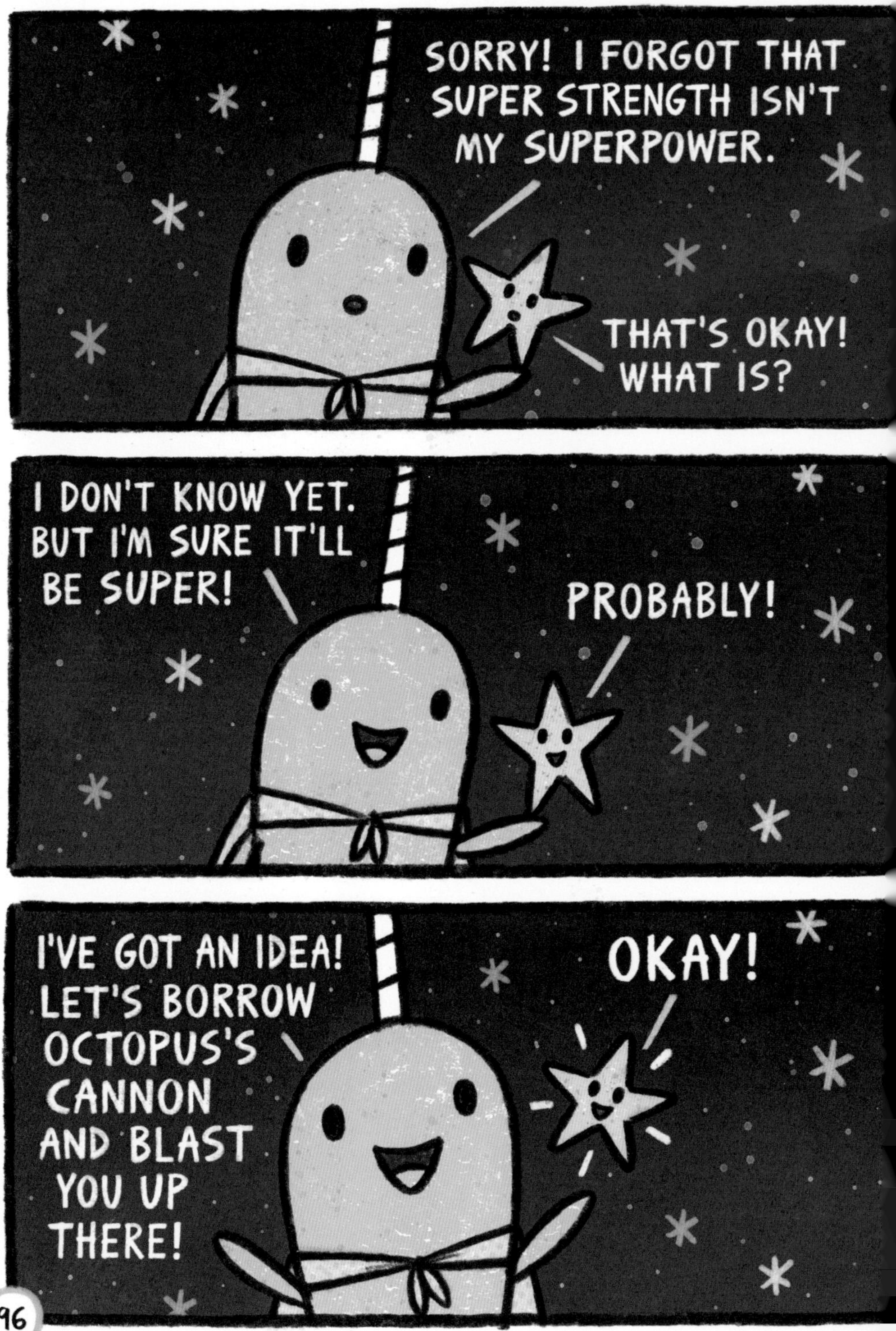
SORRY! I FORGOT THAT SUPER STRENGTH ISN'T MY SUPERPOWER.
THAT'S OKAY! WHAT IS?
I DON'T KNOW YET. BUT I'M SURE IT'LL BE SUPER!
PROBABLY!
I'VE GOT AN IDEA! LET'S BORROW OCTOPUS'S CANNON AND BLAST YOU UP THERE!
OKAY!

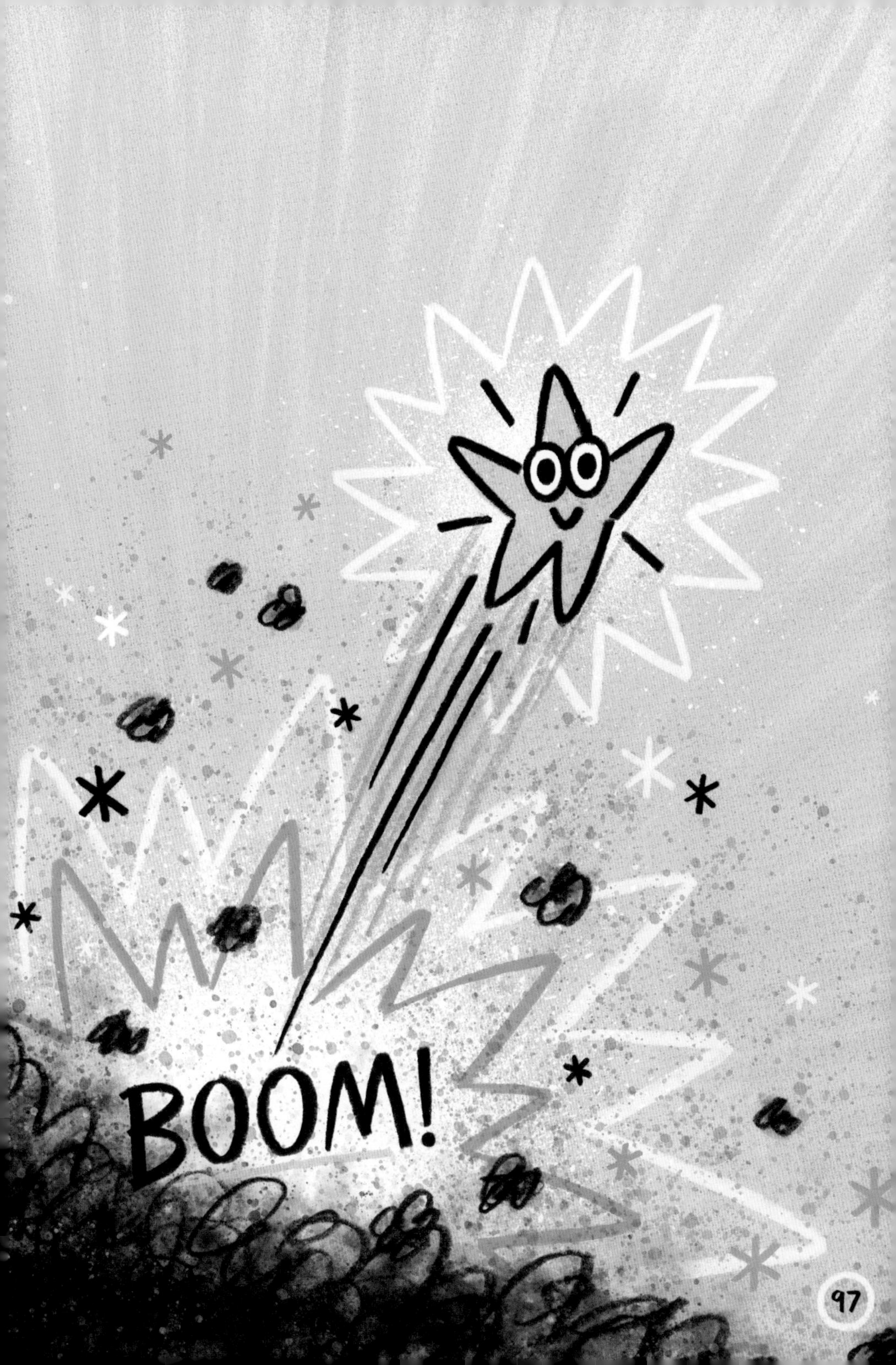
BOOM!

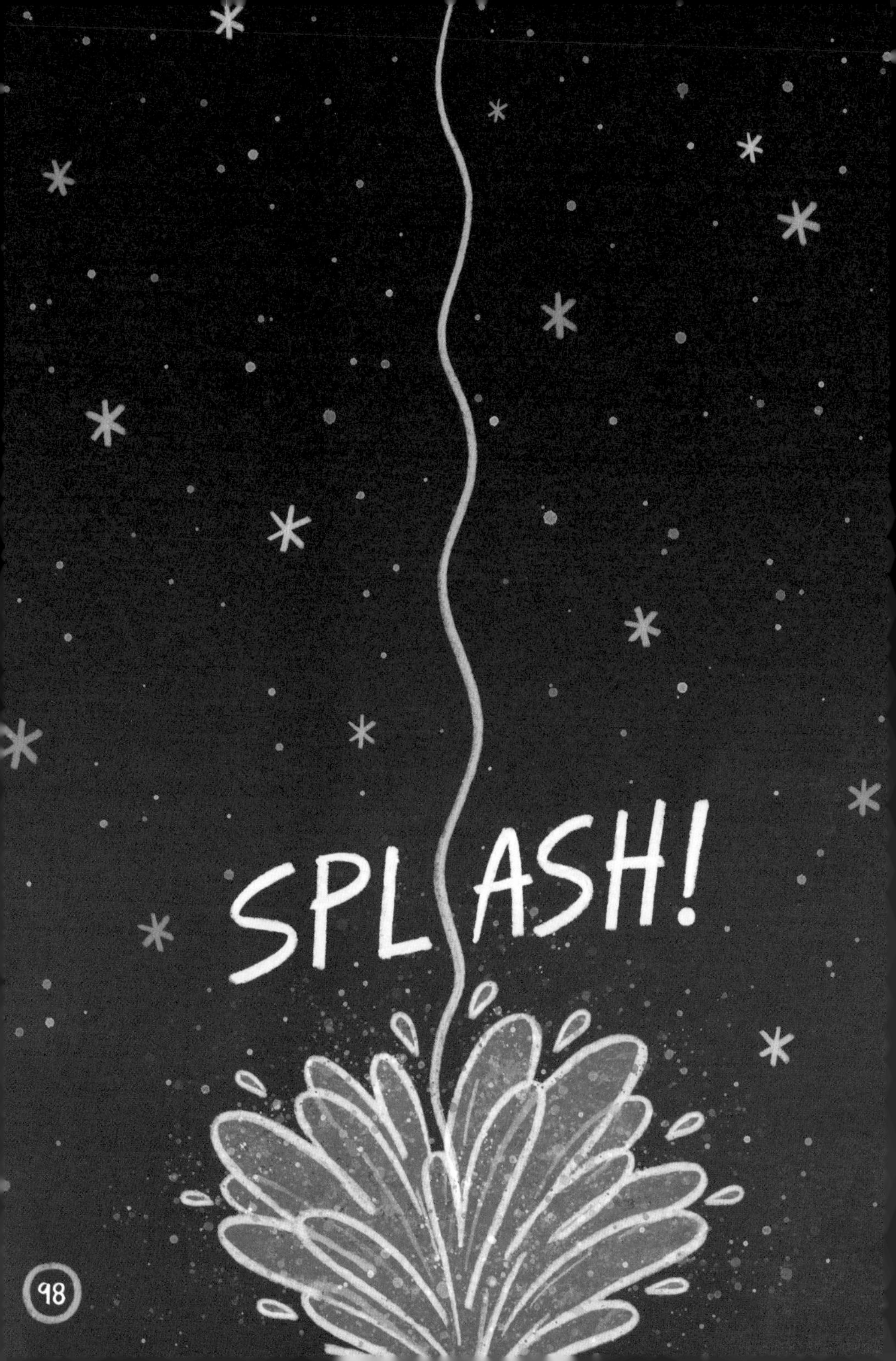
SPLASH!

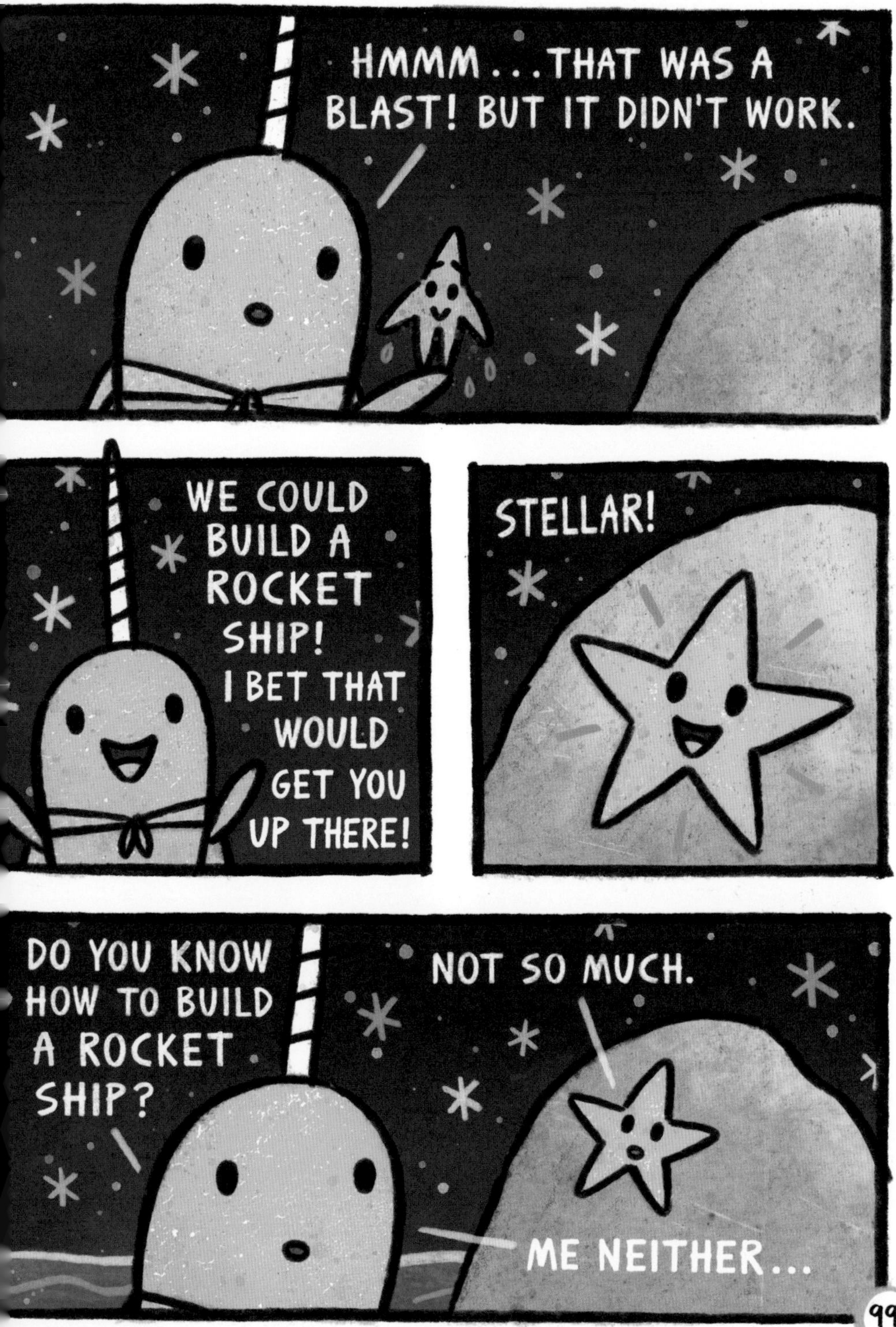
HMMM...THAT WAS A BLAST! BUT IT DIDN'T WORK.
WE COULD BUILD A ROCKET SHIP! I BET THAT WOULD GET YOU UP THERE!
STELLAR!
DO YOU KNOW HOW TO BUILD A ROCKET SHIP?
NOT SO MUCH.
ME NEITHER...

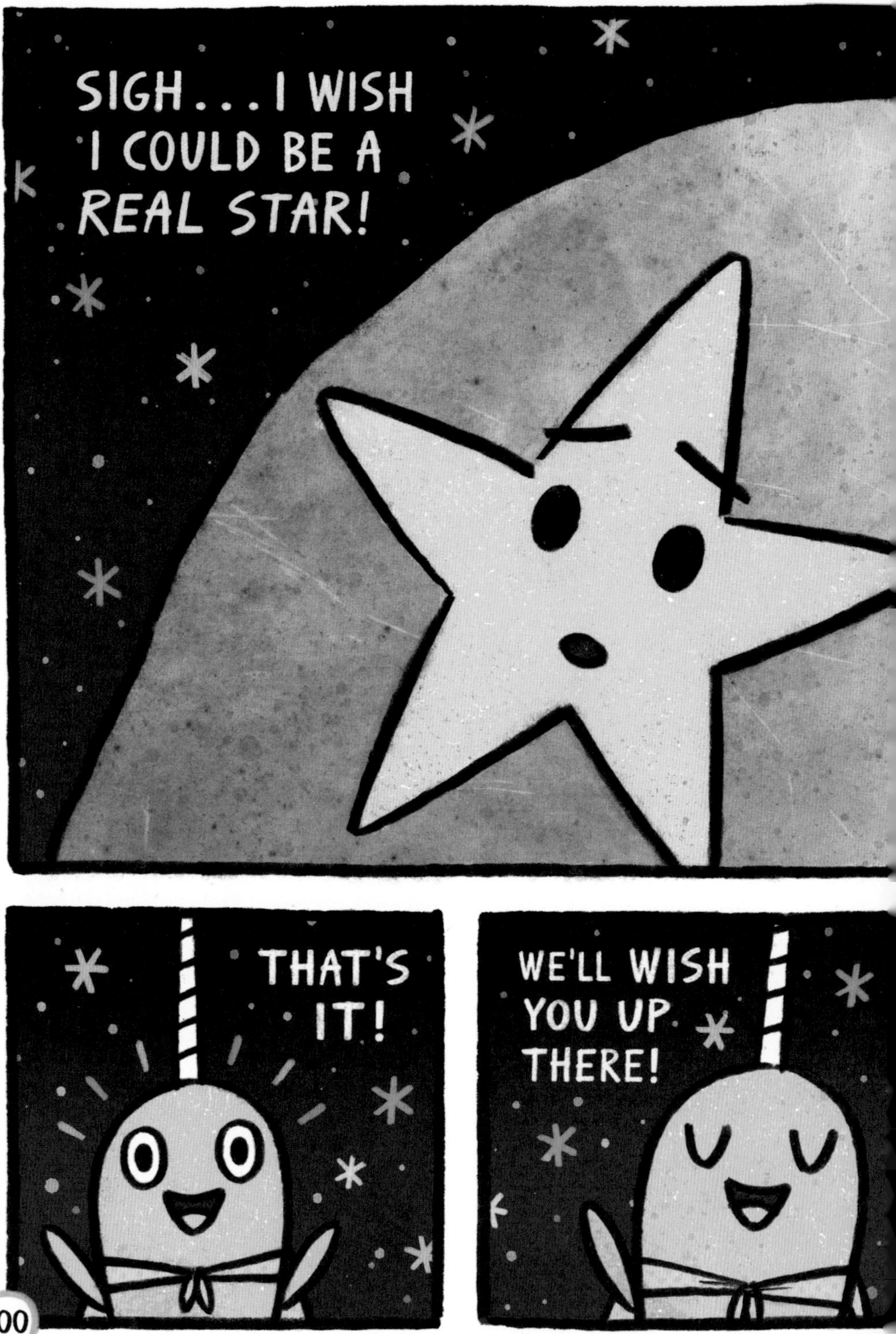
SIGH...I WISH I COULD BE A *REAL* STAR!
THAT'S IT!
WE'LL WISH YOU UP THERE!

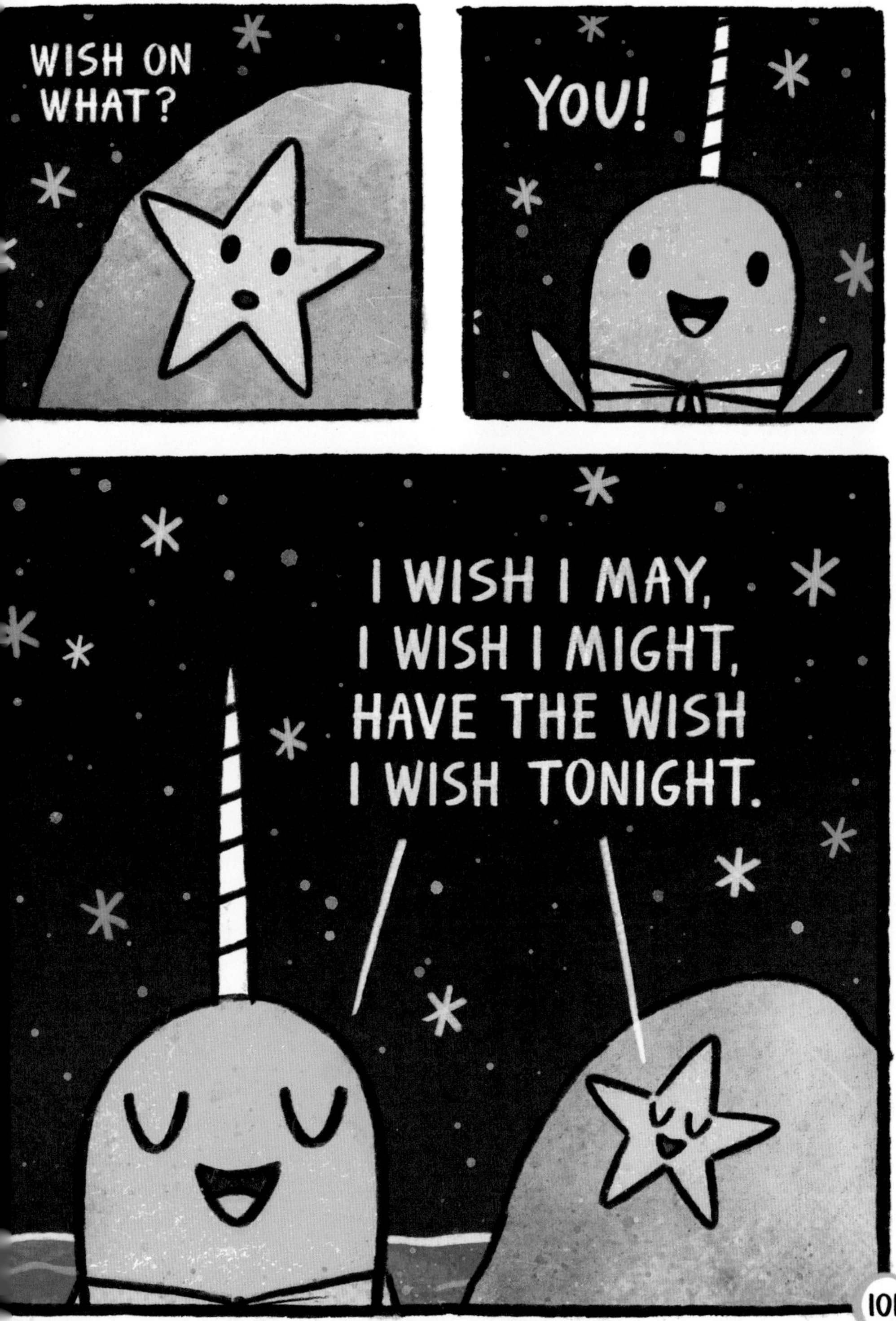
WISH ON WHAT?
YOU!
I WISH I MAY, I WISH I MIGHT, HAVE THE WISH I WISH TONIGHT.

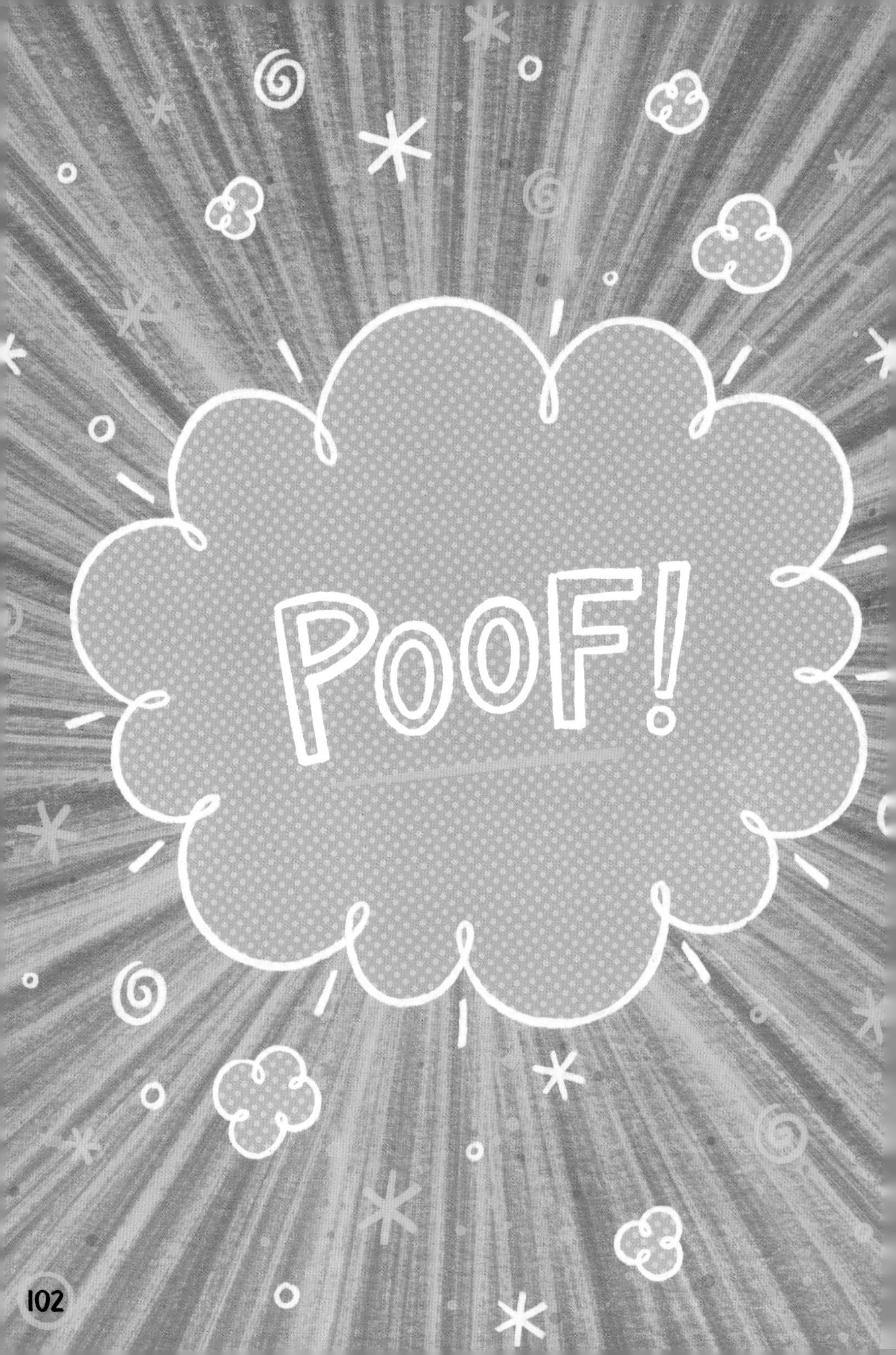
POOF!

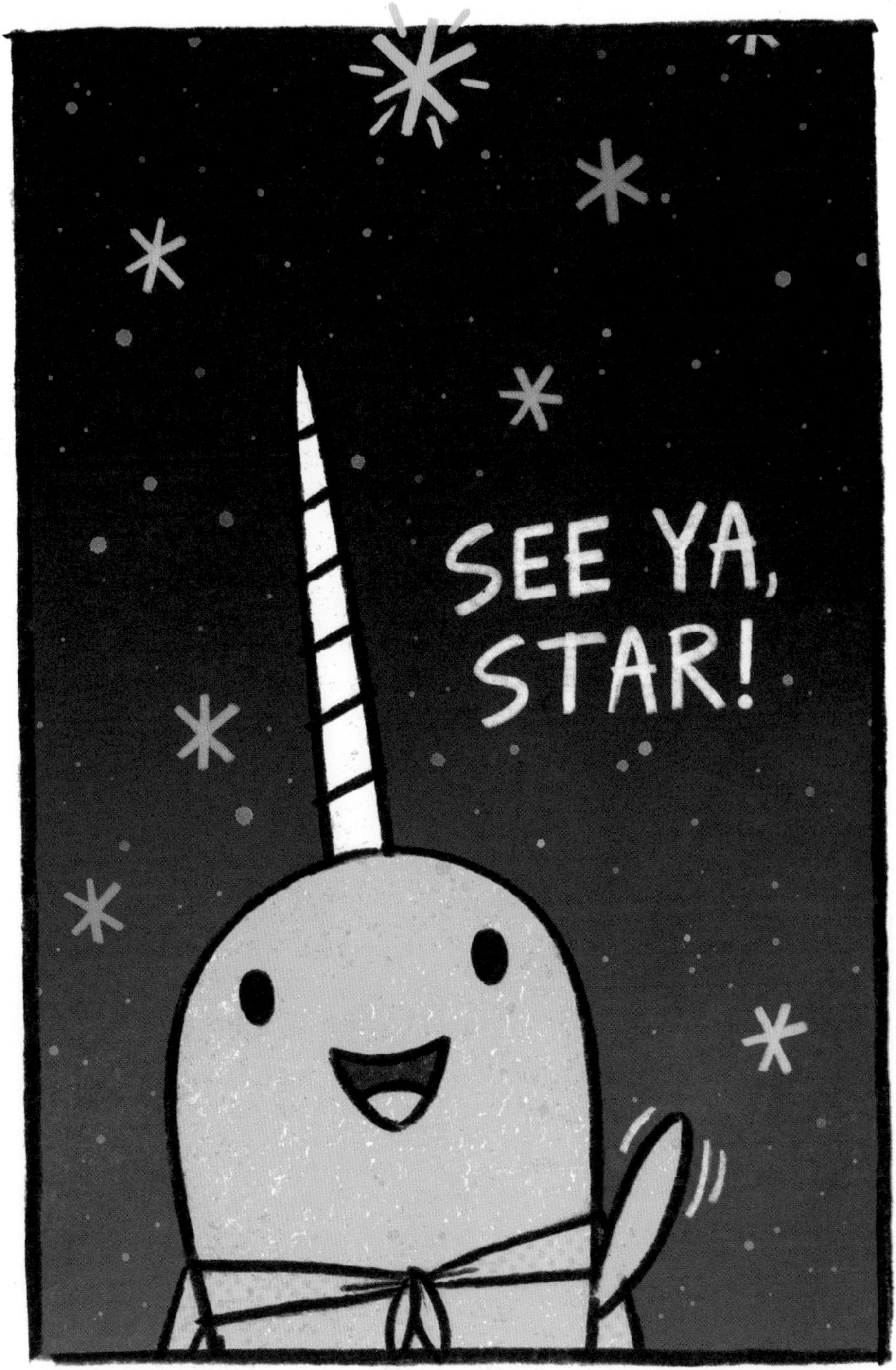
SEE YA, STAR!

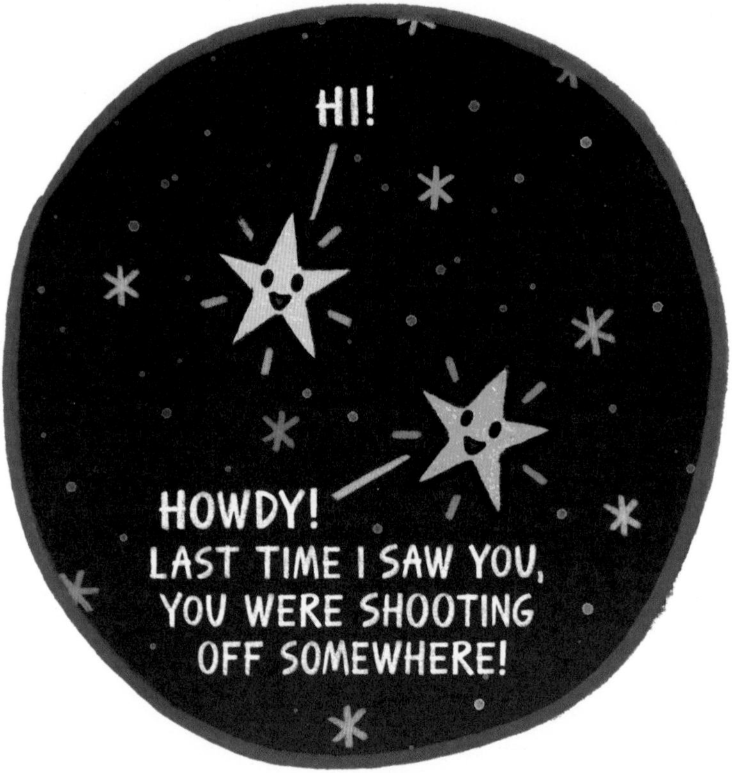
HI!
HOWDY!
LAST TIME I SAW YOU, YOU WERE SHOOTING OFF SOMEWHERE!

SUPER WAFFLE
AND STRAWBERRY SIDEKICK!

by Narwhal and Jelly

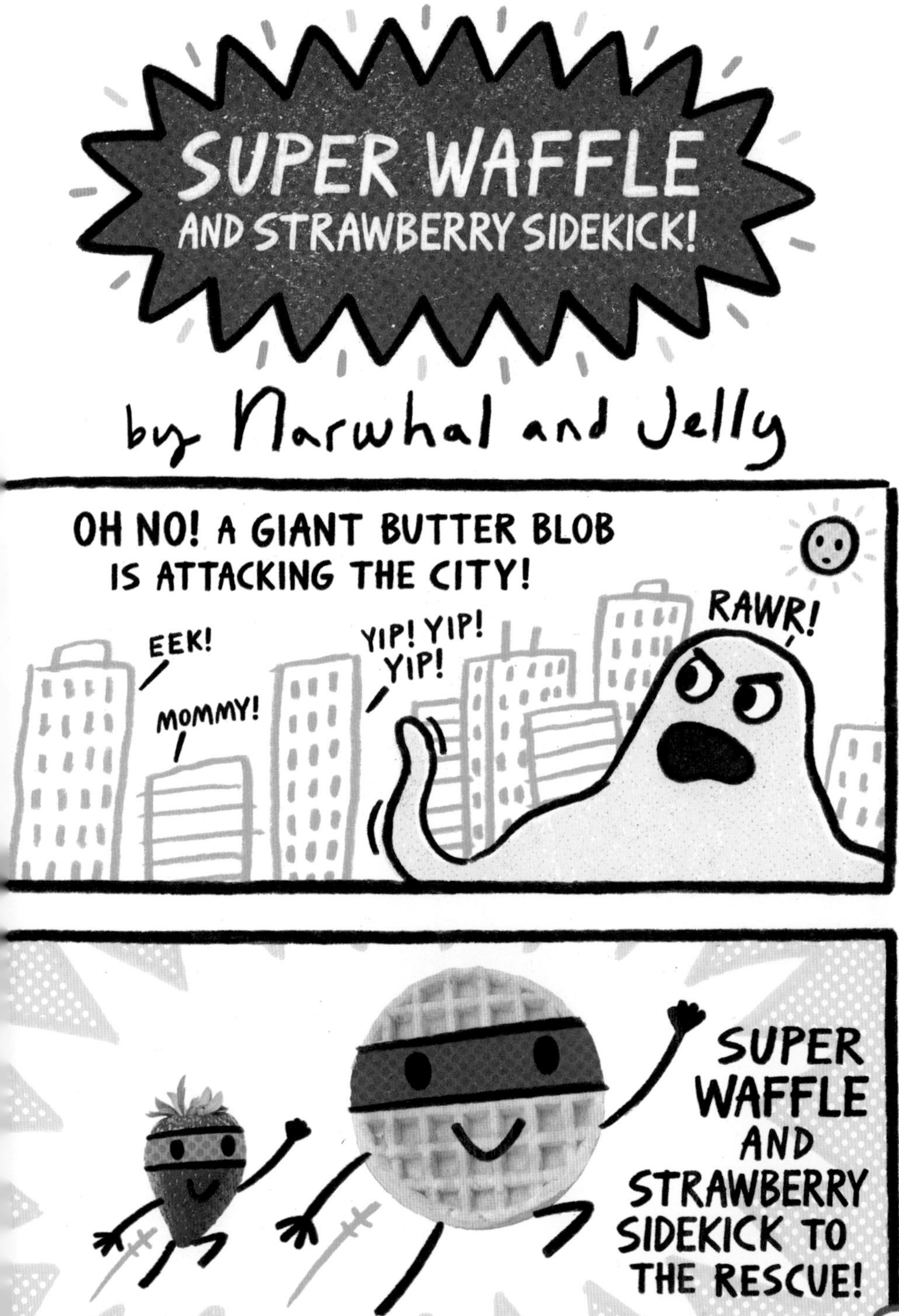
OH NO! A GIANT BUTTER BLOB IS ATTACKING THE CITY!
EEK!
MOMMY!
YIP! YIP! YIP!
RAWR!
SUPER WAFFLE AND STRAWBERRY SIDEKICK TO THE RESCUE!

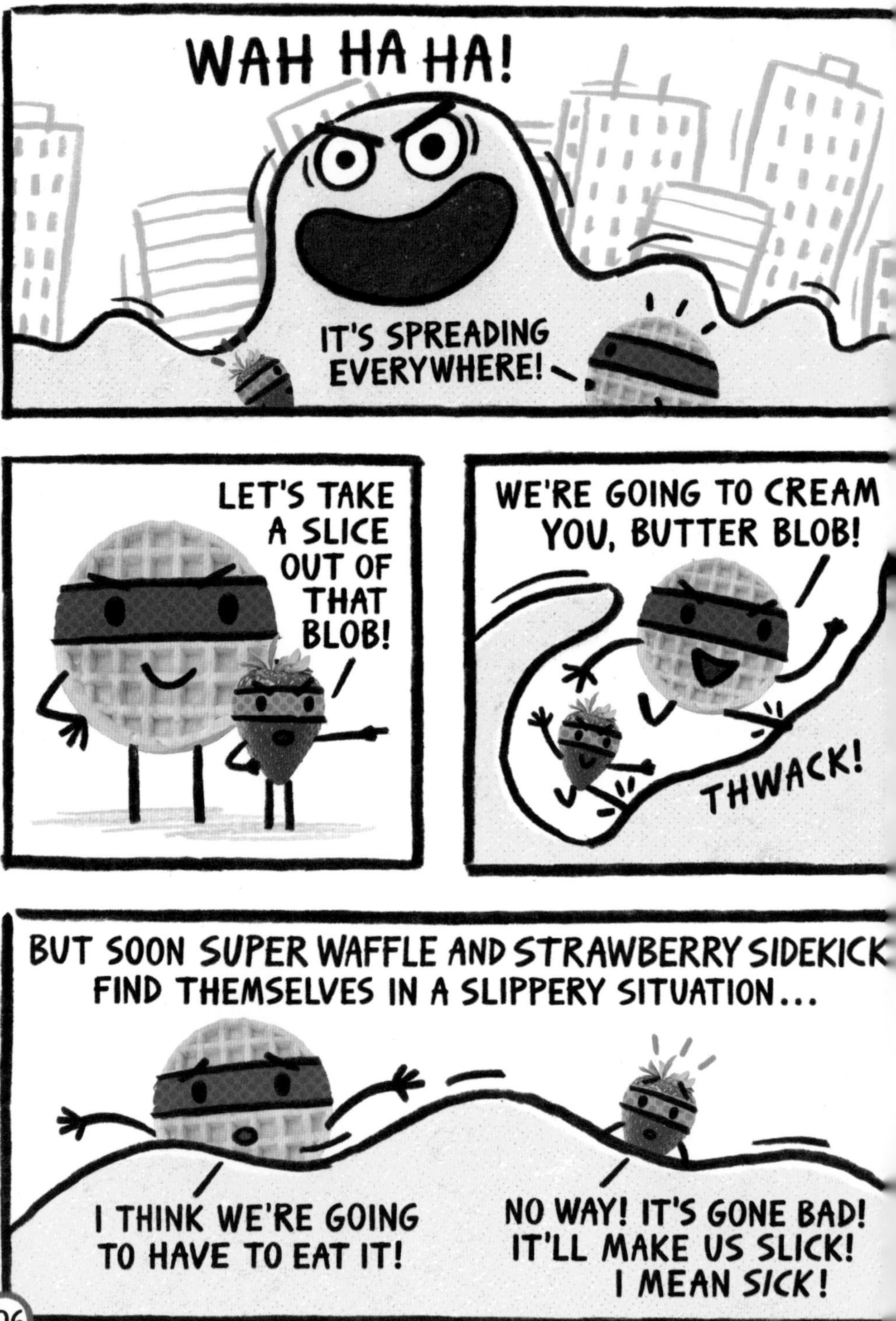
WAH HA HA!
IT'S SPREADING EVERYWHERE!
LET'S TAKE A SLICE OUT OF THAT BLOB!
WE'RE GOING TO CREAM YOU, BUTTER BLOB!
THWACK!
BUT SOON SUPER WAFFLE AND STRAWBERRY SIDEKICK FIND THEMSELVES IN A SLIPPERY SITUATION...
I THINK WE'RE GOING TO HAVE TO EAT IT!
NO WAY! IT'S GONE BAD! IT'LL MAKE US SLICK! I MEAN SICK!

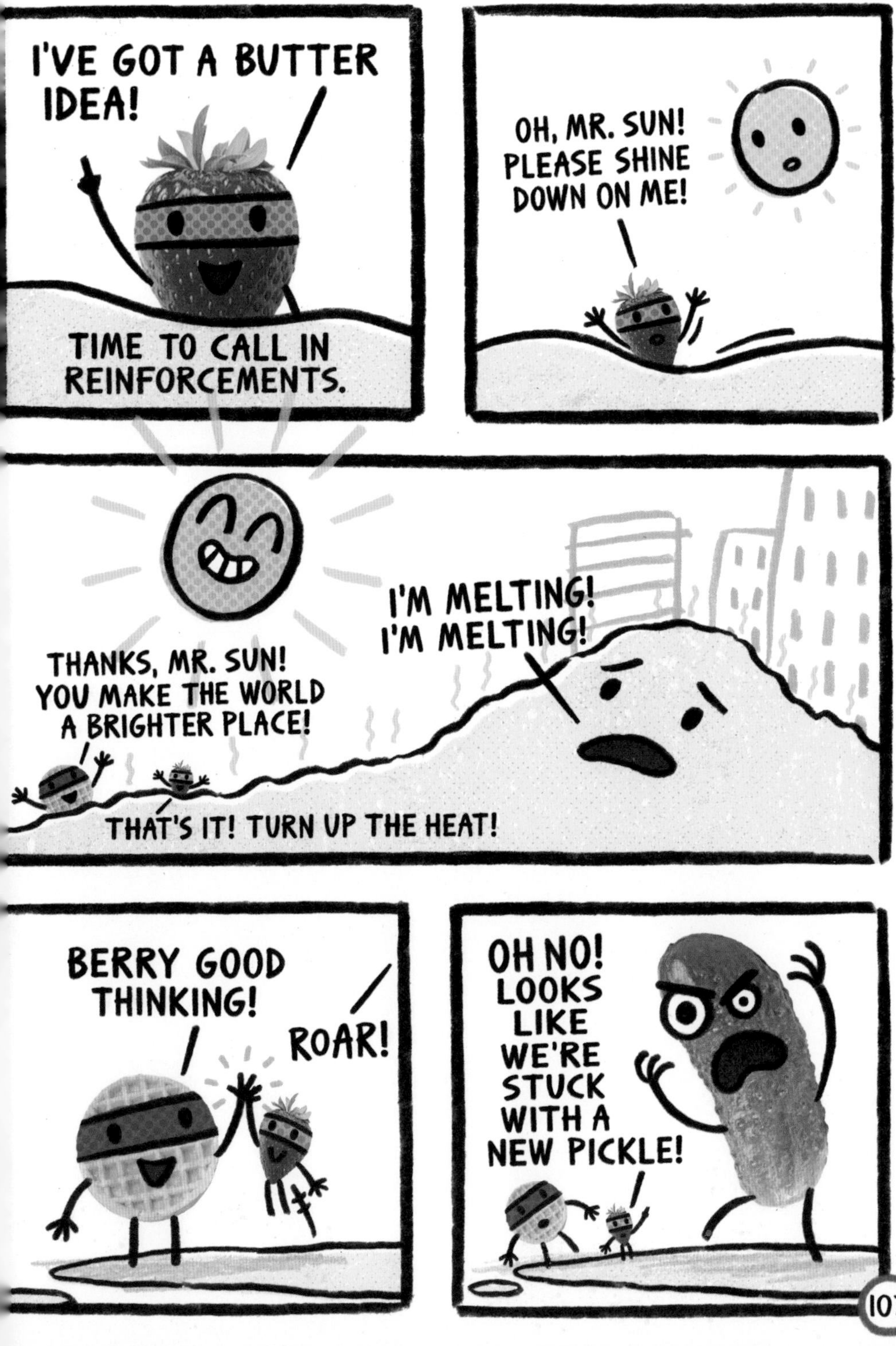
I'VE GOT A BUTTER IDEA!
TIME TO CALL IN REINFORCEMENTS.
OH, MR. SUN! PLEASE SHINE DOWN ON ME!
THANKS, MR. SUN! YOU MAKE THE WORLD A BRIGHTER PLACE!
I'M MELTING! I'M MELTING!
THAT'S IT! TURN UP THE HEAT!
BERRY GOOD THINKING!
ROAR!
OH NO! LOOKS LIKE WE'RE STUCK WITH A NEW PICKLE!

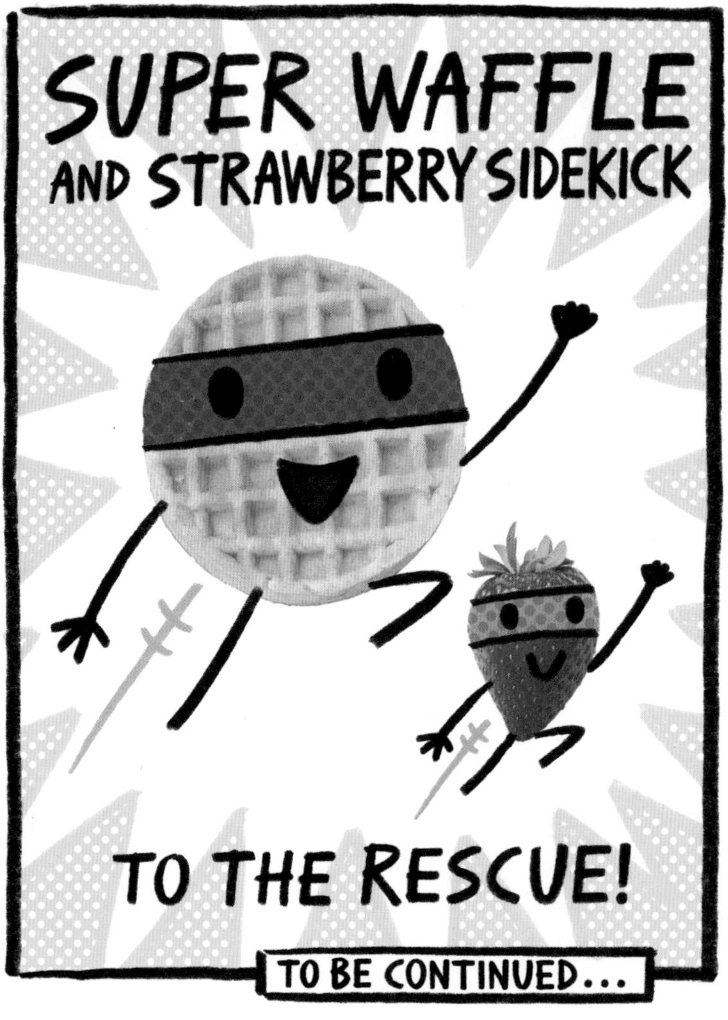
SUPER WAFFLE
AND STRAWBERRY SIDEKICK
TO THE RESCUE!
TO BE CONTINUED...

SUPER NARWHAL VS. BLUE JELLY

A.K.A.

THE SUPER SUPERPOWER!

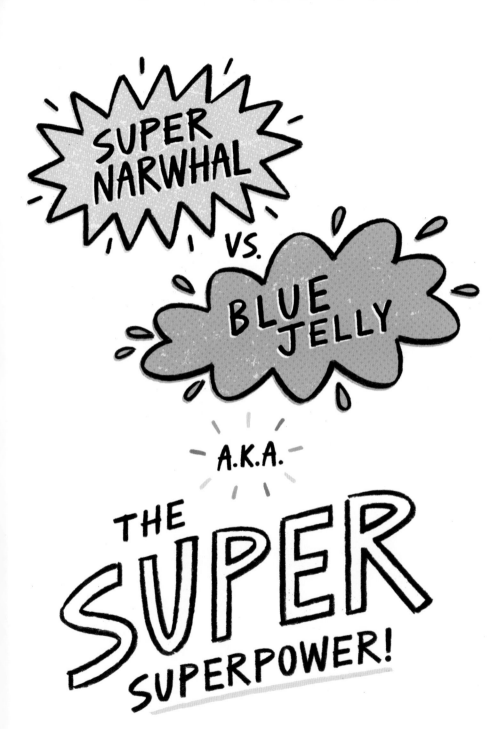

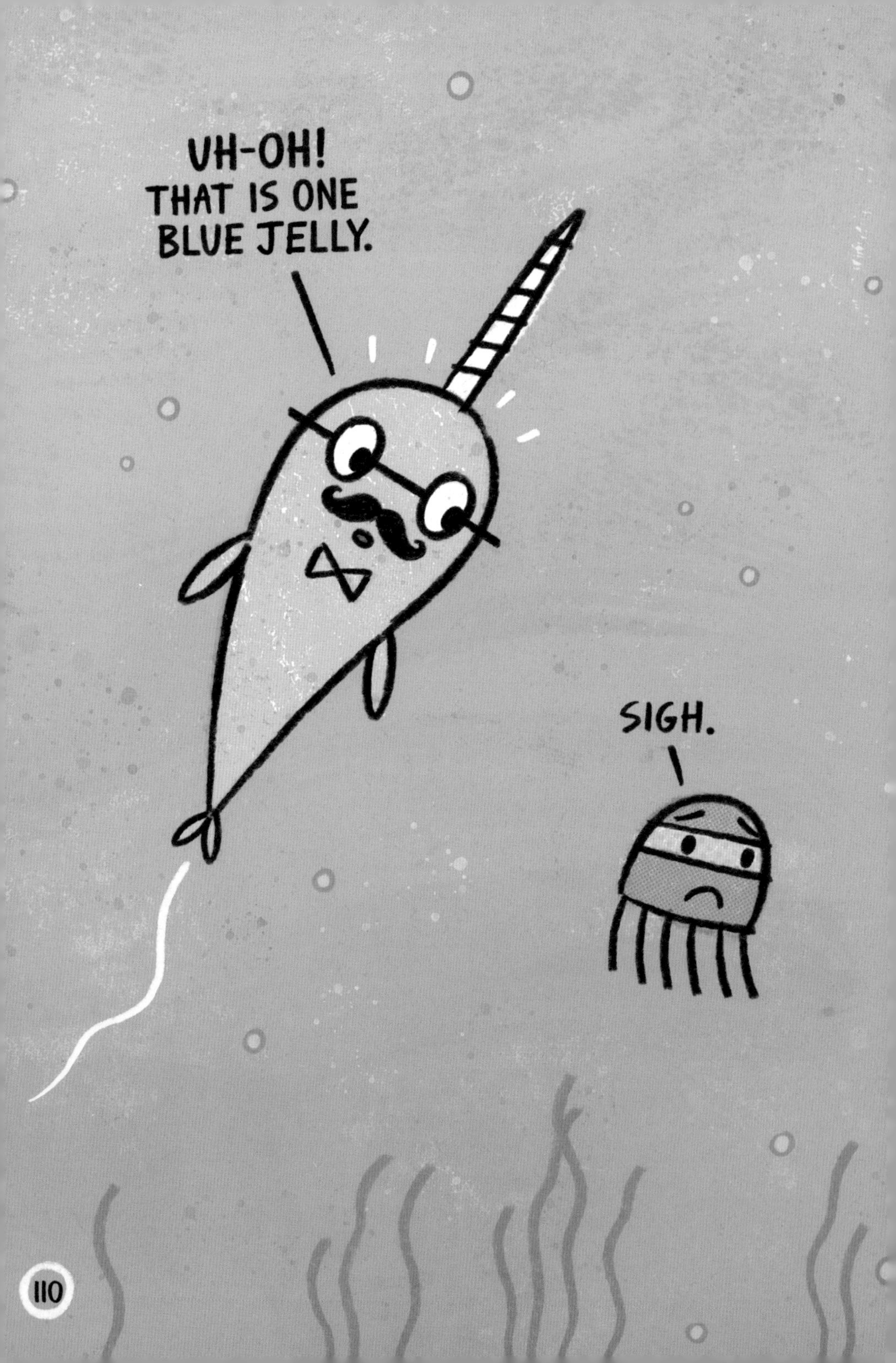
UH-OH! THAT IS ONE BLUE JELLY.
SIGH.

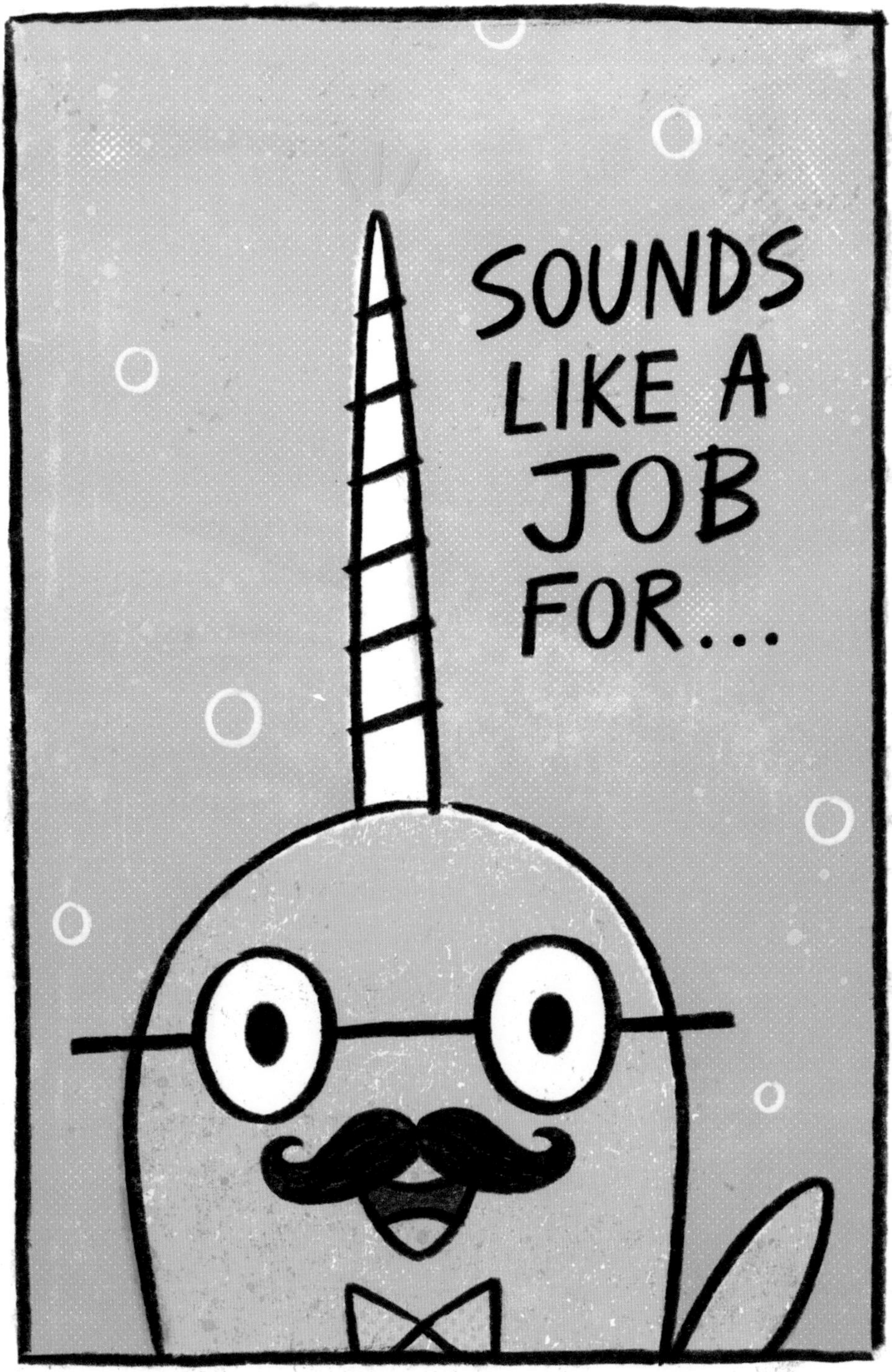
SOUNDS LIKE A JOB FOR...

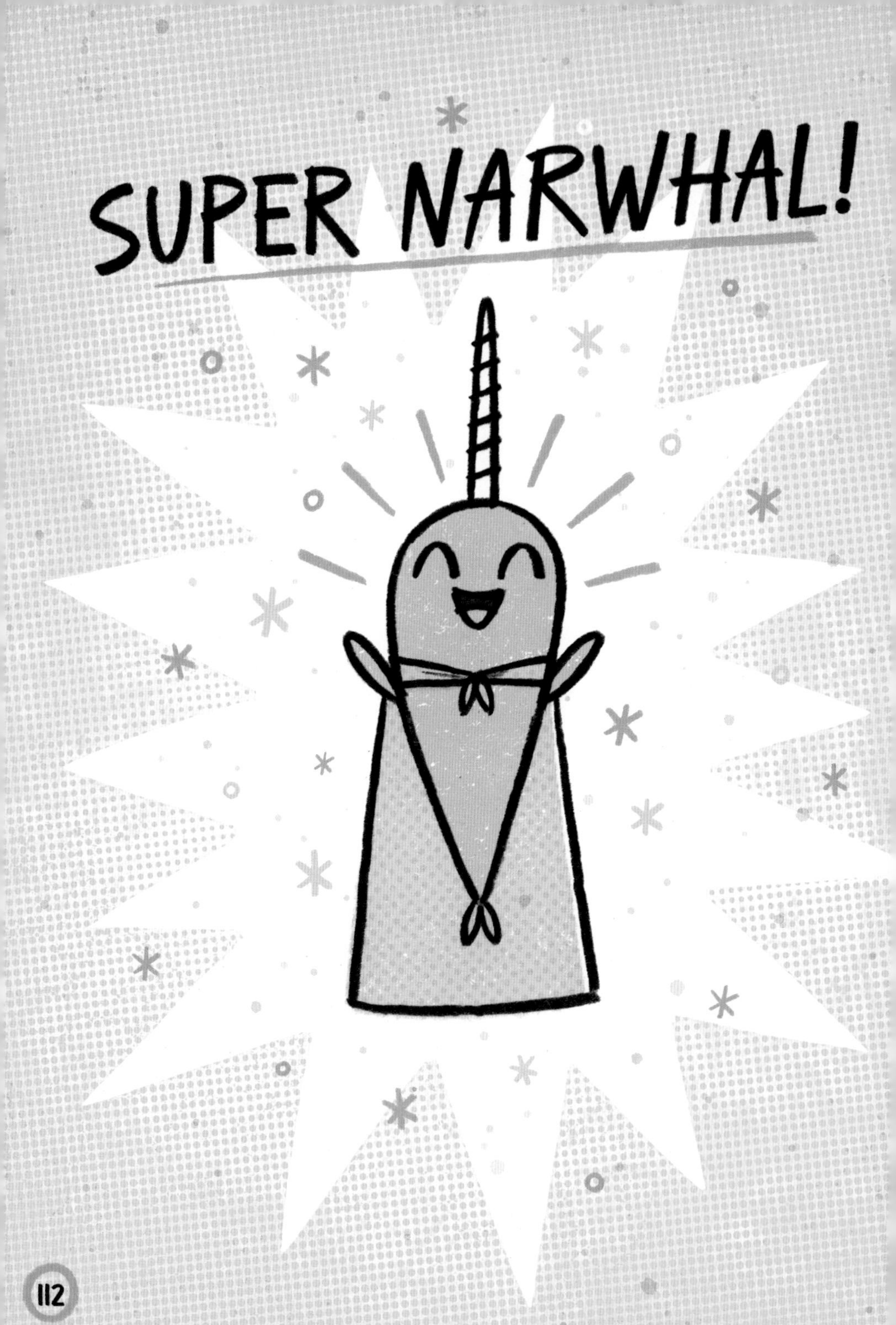
SUPER NARWHAL!

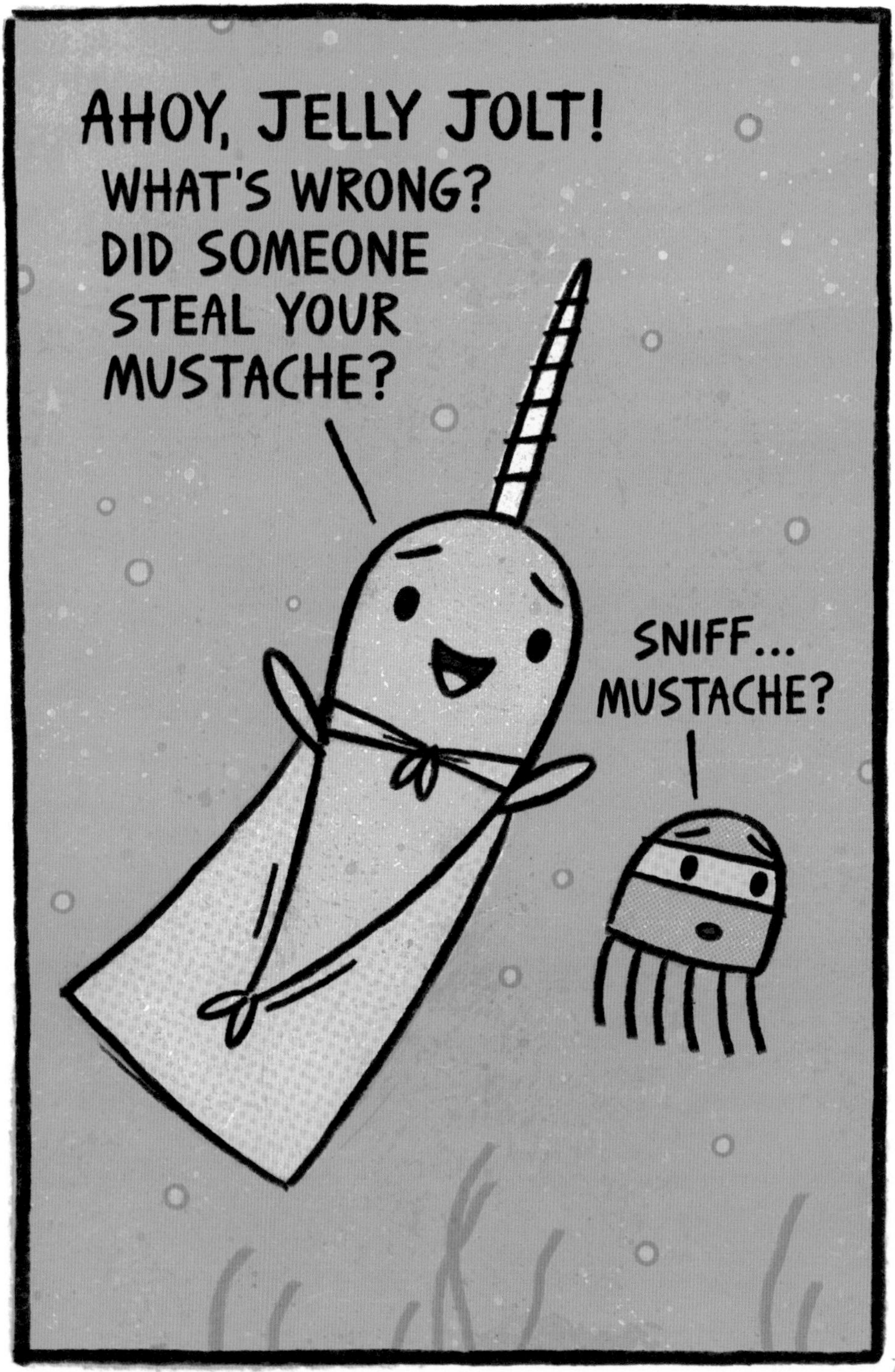
AHOY, JELLY JOLT!
WHAT'S WRONG? DID SOMEONE STEAL YOUR MUSTACHE?
SNIFF... MUSTACHE?

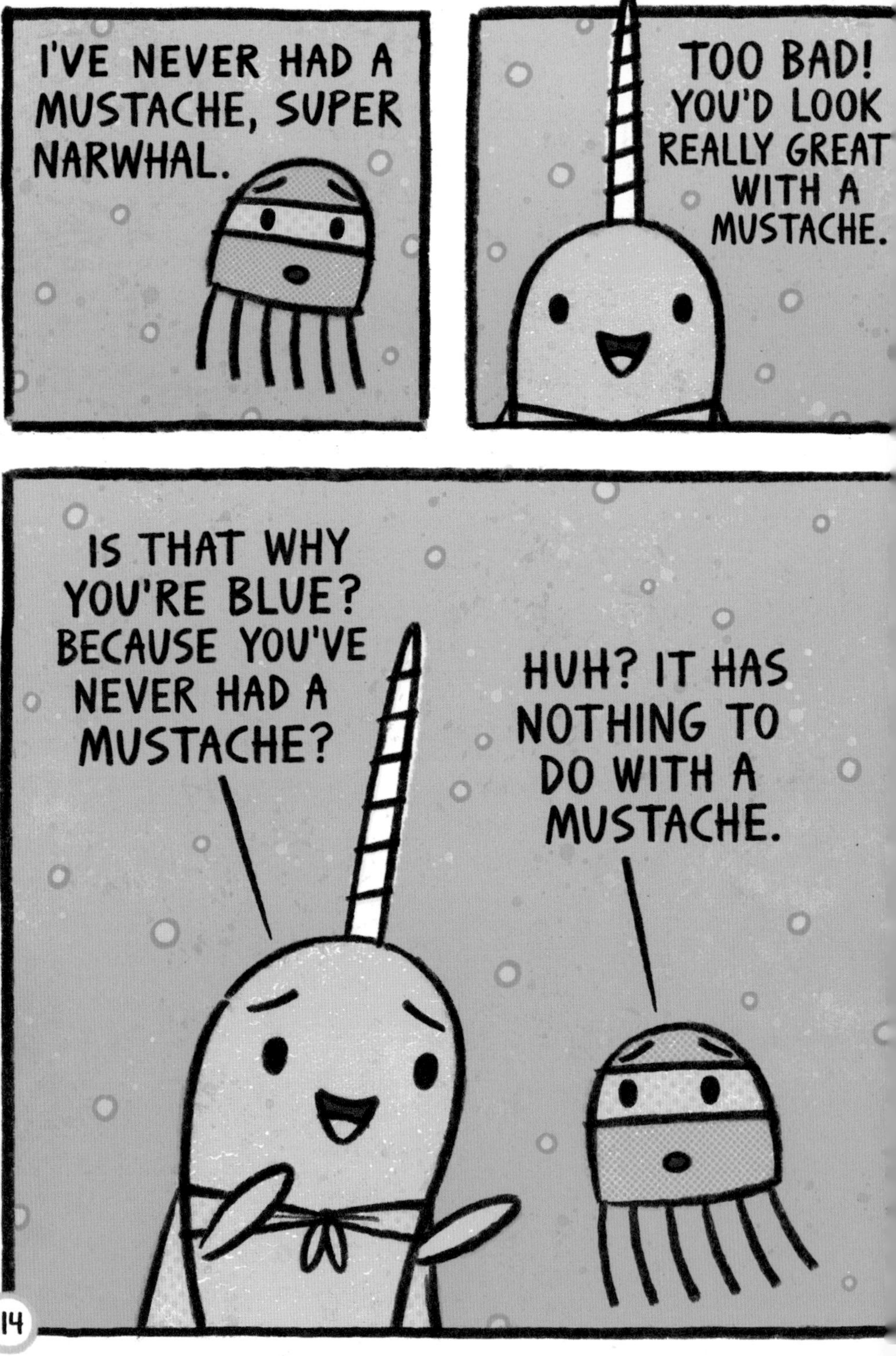
I'VE NEVER HAD A MUSTACHE, SUPER NARWHAL.
TOO BAD! YOU'D LOOK REALLY GREAT WITH A MUSTACHE.
IS THAT WHY YOU'RE BLUE? BECAUSE YOU'VE NEVER HAD A MUSTACHE?
HUH? IT HAS NOTHING TO DO WITH A MUSTACHE.

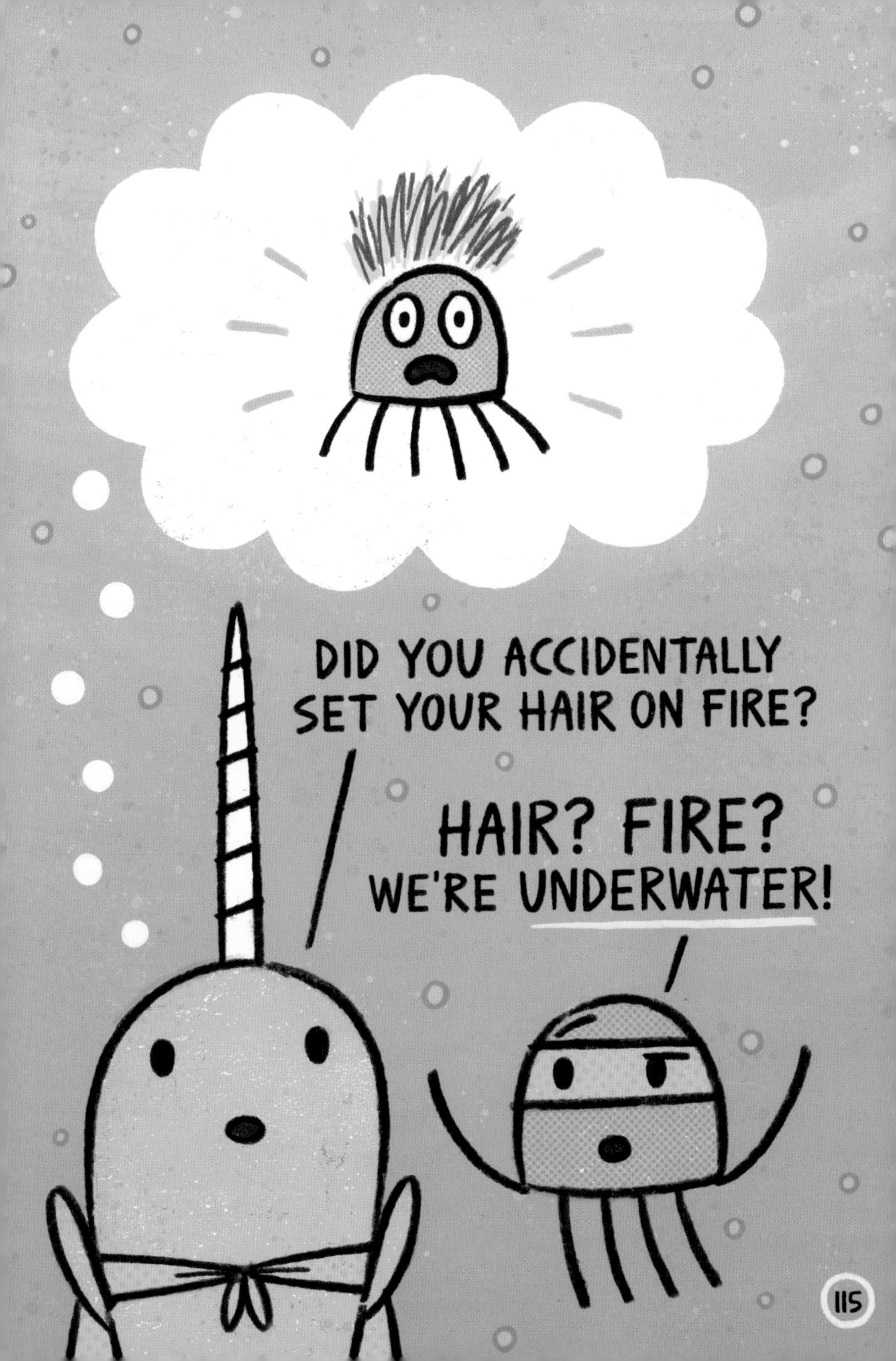
DID YOU ACCIDENTALLY SET YOUR HAIR ON FIRE?
HAIR? FIRE? WE'RE UNDERWATER!

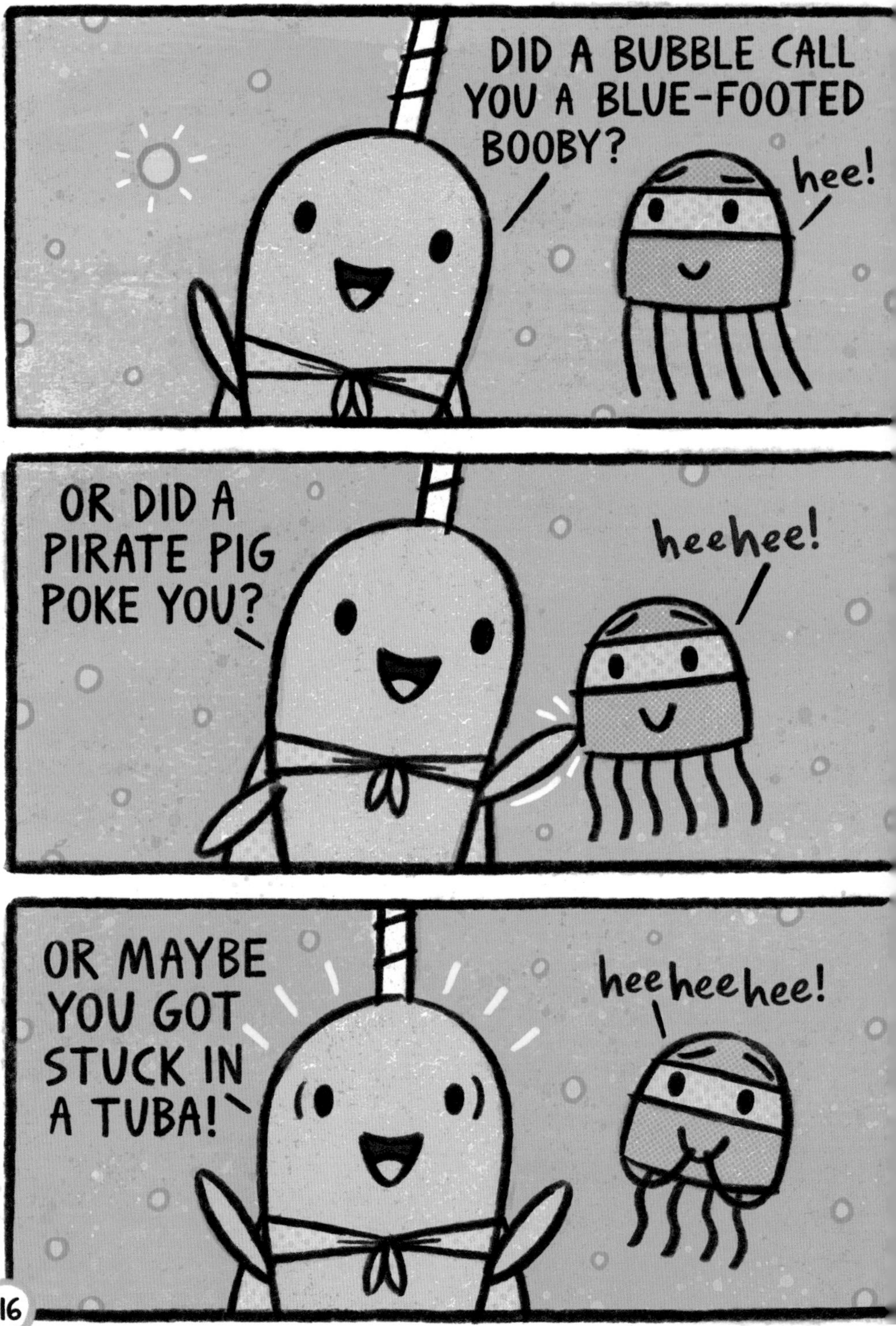
DID A BUBBLE CALL YOU A BLUE-FOOTED BOOBY?
hee!
OR DID A PIRATE PIG POKE YOU?
heehee!
OR MAYBE YOU GOT STUCK IN A TUBA!
heeheehee!

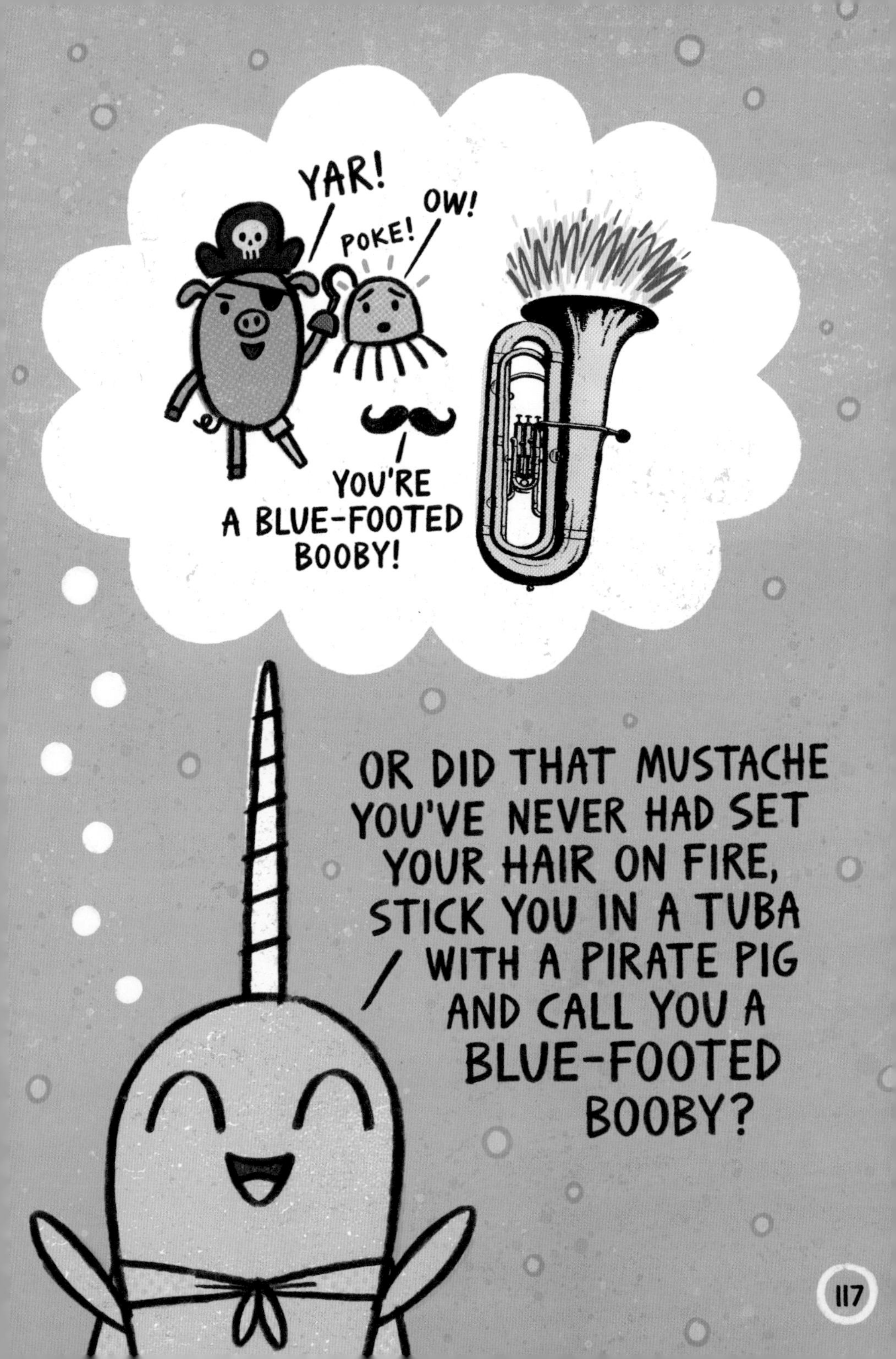
YAR!
POKE!
OW!
YOU'RE A BLUE-FOOTED BOOBY!
OR DID THAT MUSTACHE YOU'VE NEVER HAD SET YOUR HAIR ON FIRE, STICK YOU IN A TUBA WITH A PIRATE PIG AND CALL YOU A BLUE-FOOTED BOOBY?

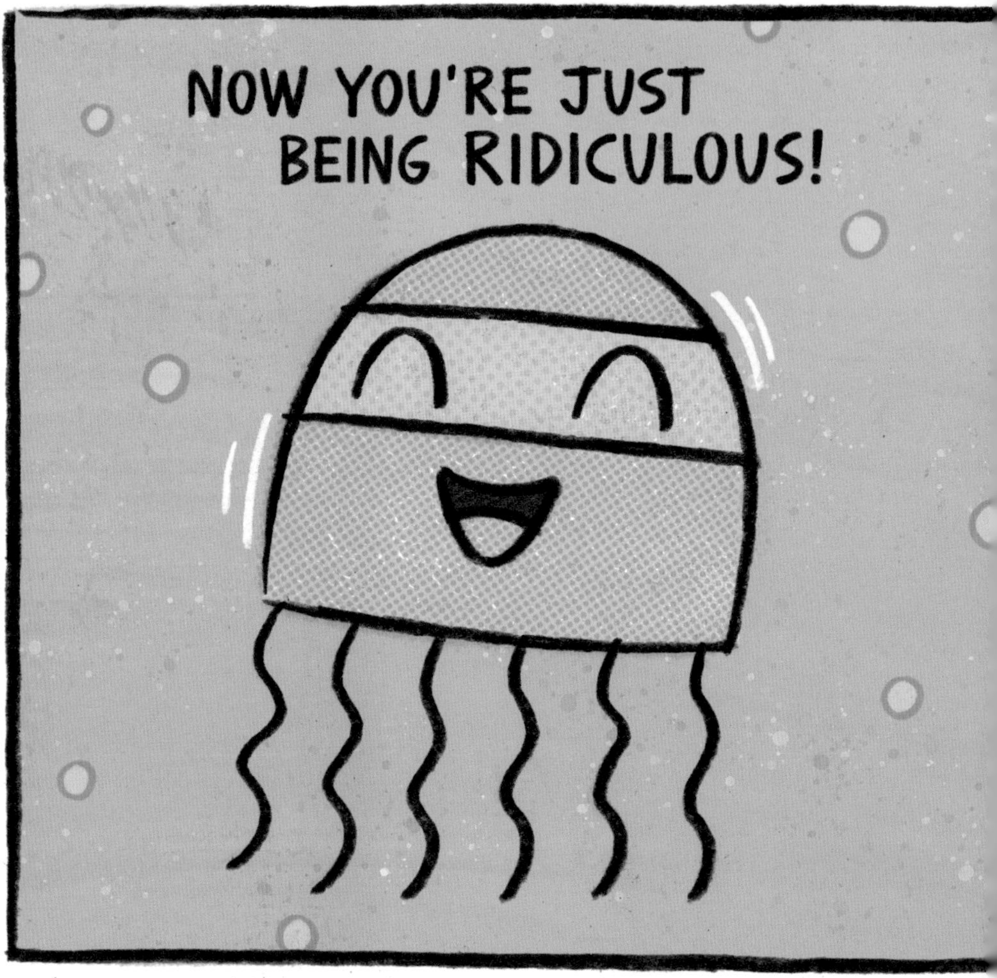
NOW YOU'RE JUST BEING RIDICULOUS!

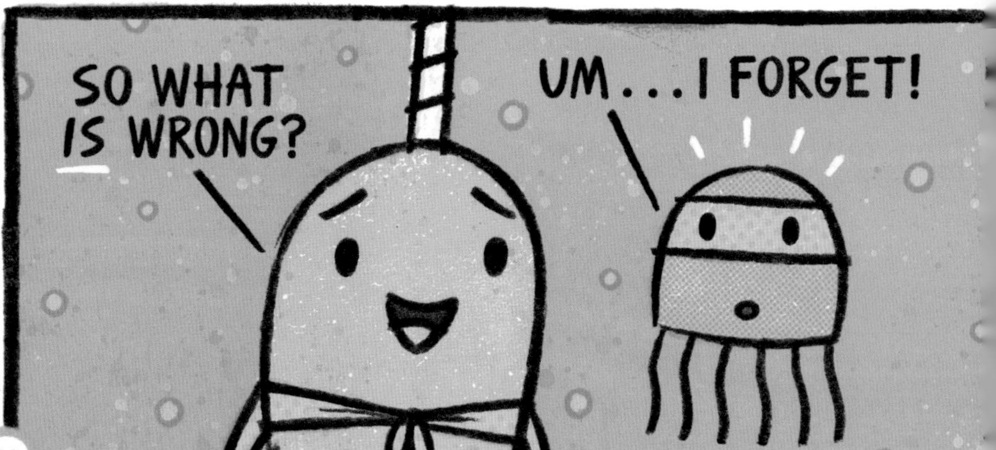
SO WHAT IS WRONG?
UM...I FORGET!

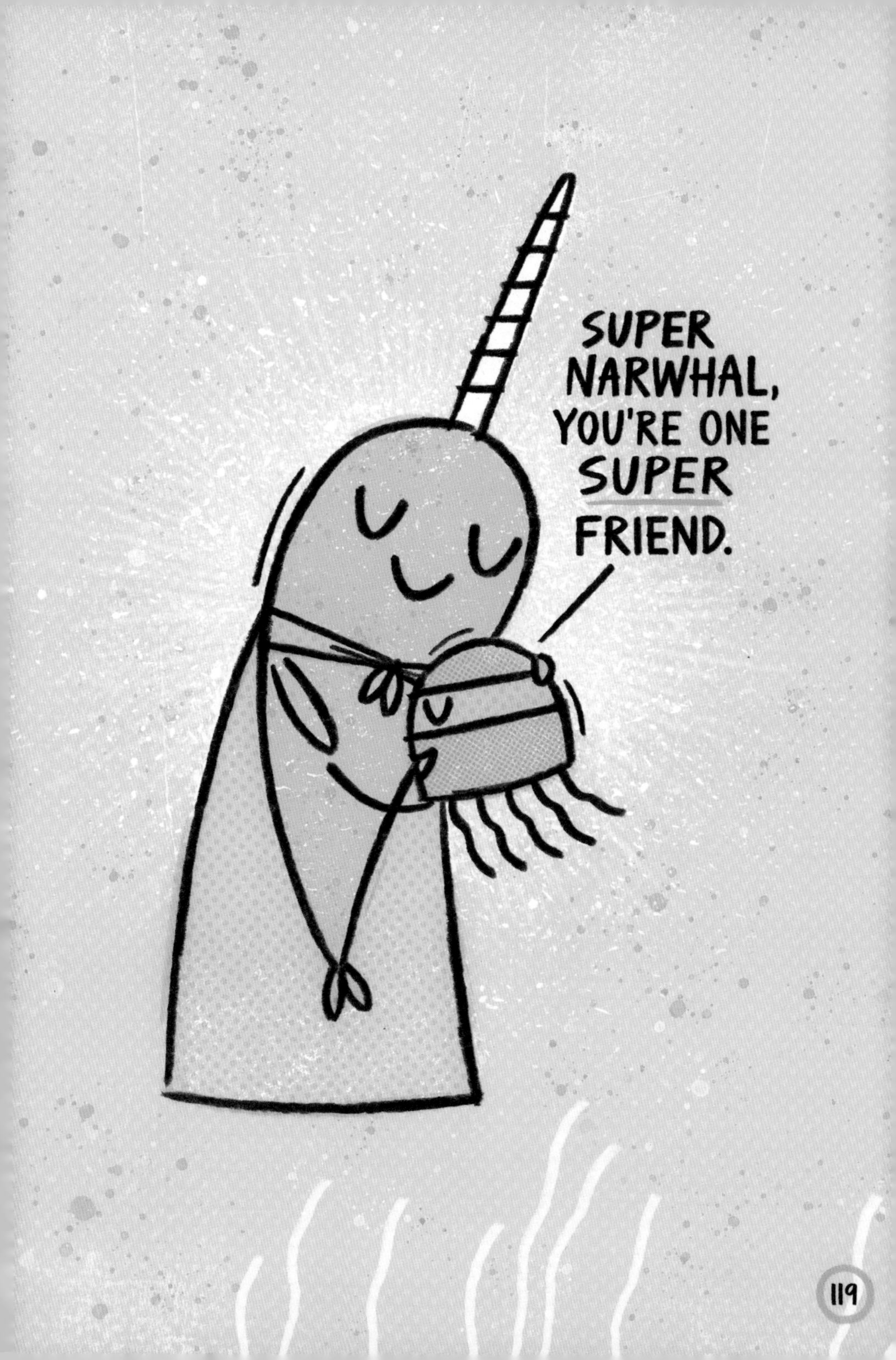
SUPER NARWHAL, YOU'RE ONE SUPER FRIEND.

OH, WAIT, NOW I REMEMBER...

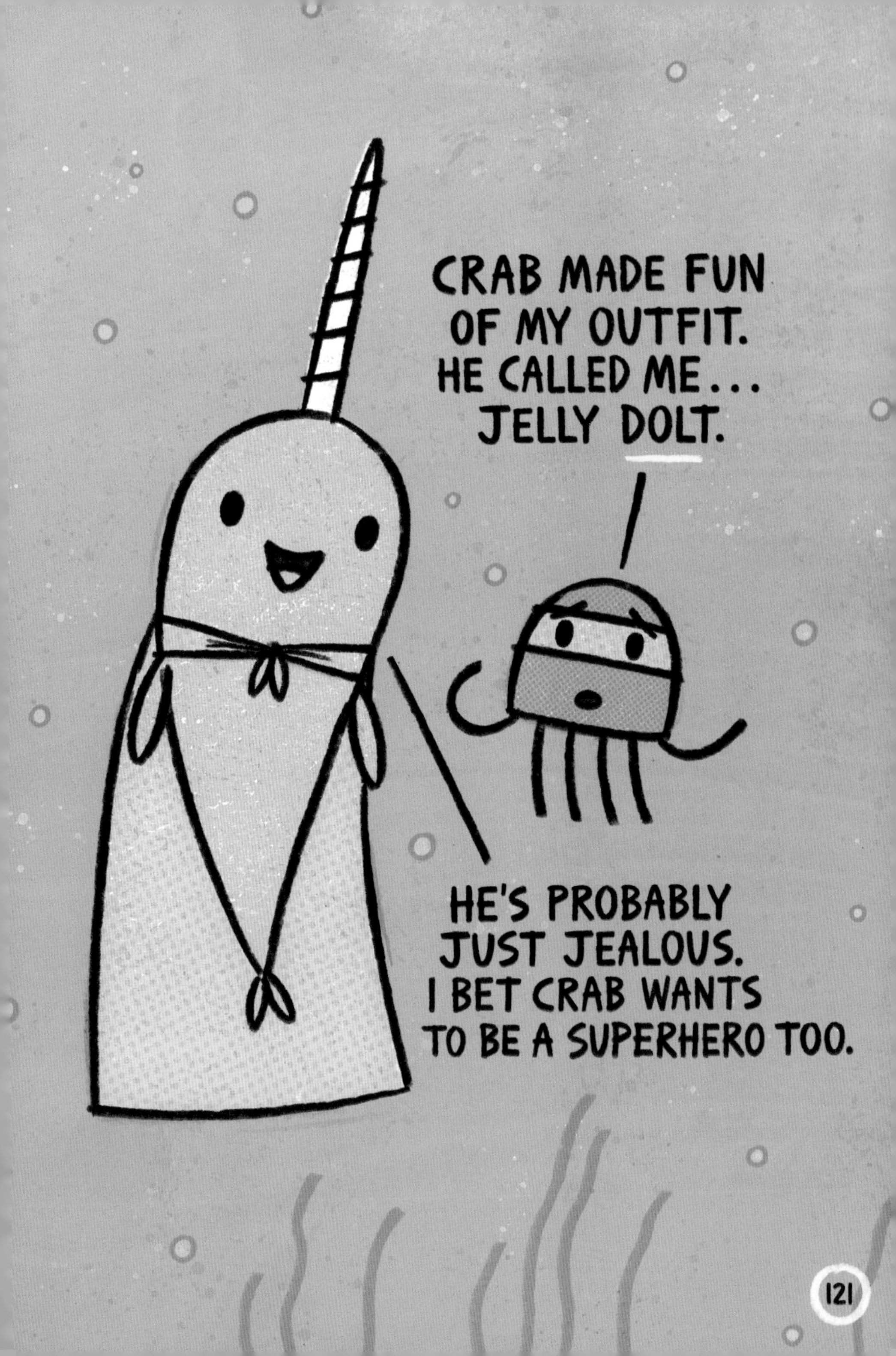
CRAB MADE FUN OF MY OUTFIT. HE CALLED ME... JELLY DOLT.
HE'S PROBABLY JUST JEALOUS. I BET CRAB WANTS TO BE A SUPERHERO TOO.

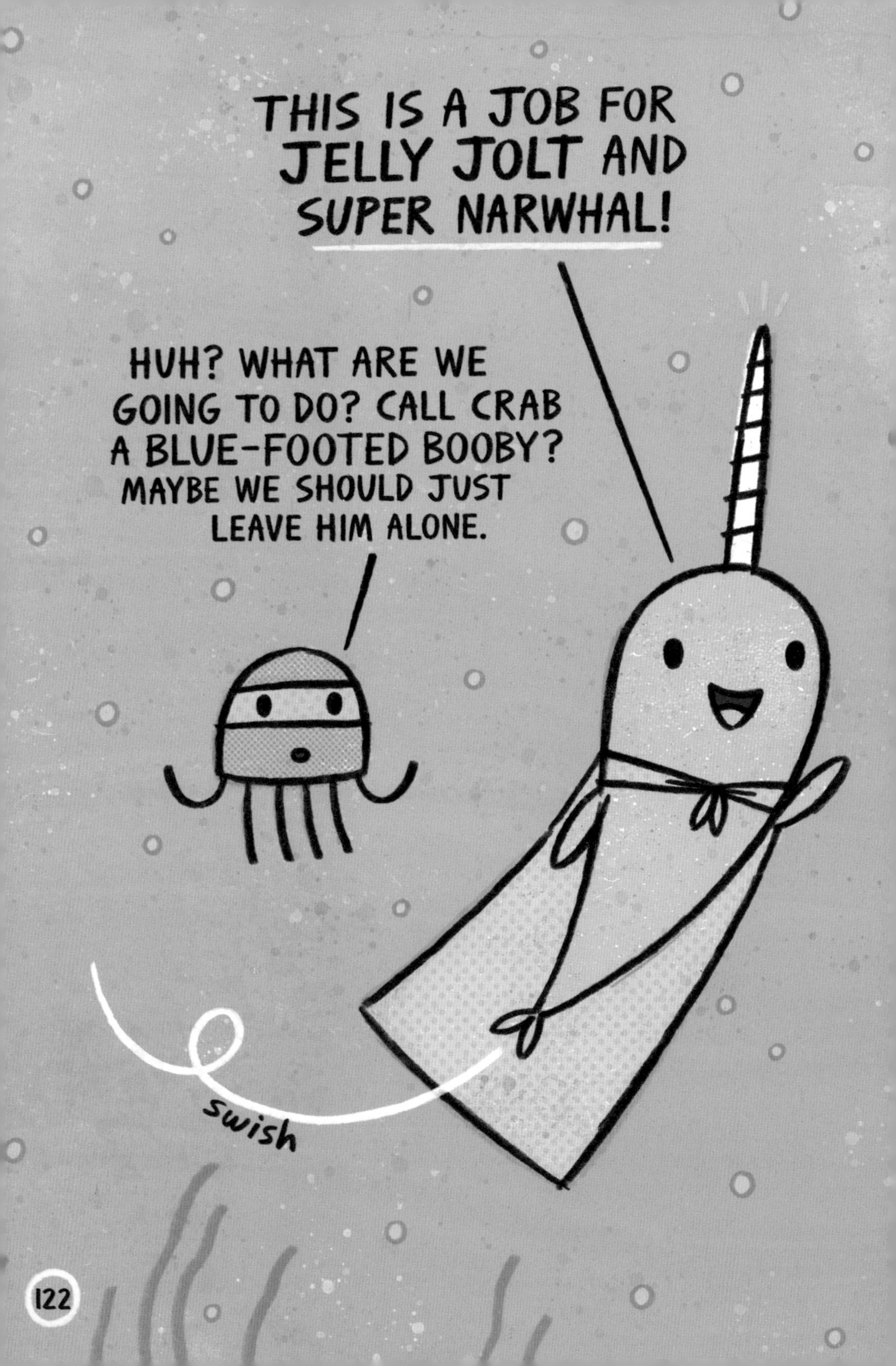
THIS IS A JOB FOR JELLY JOLT AND SUPER NARWHAL!
HUH? WHAT ARE WE GOING TO DO? CALL CRAB A BLUE-FOOTED BOOBY? MAYBE WE SHOULD JUST LEAVE HIM ALONE.
swish

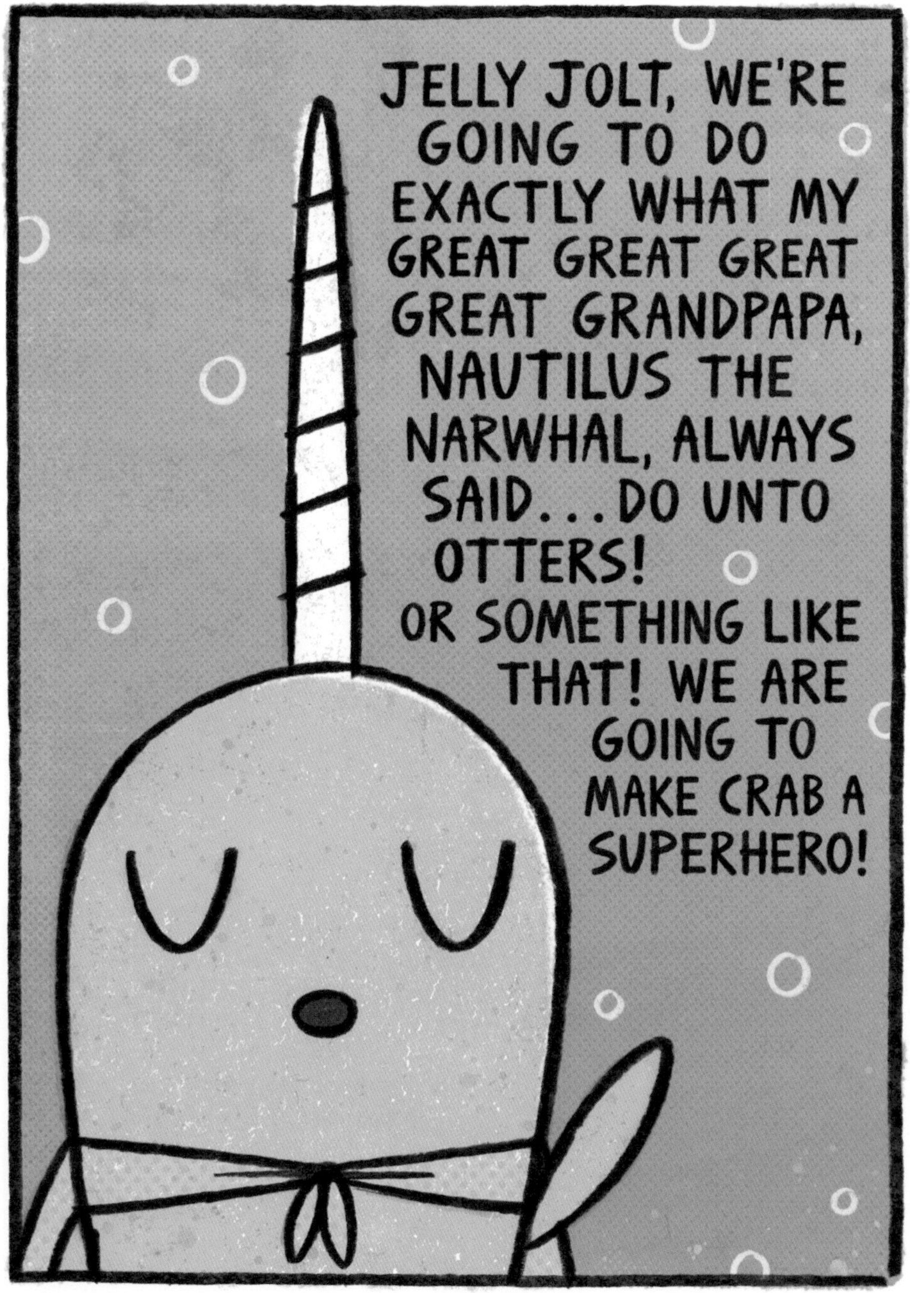
JELLY JOLT, WE'RE GOING TO DO EXACTLY WHAT MY GREAT GREAT GREAT GREAT GRANDPAPA, NAUTILUS THE NARWHAL, ALWAYS SAID...DO UNTO OTTERS! OR SOMETHING LIKE THAT! WE ARE GOING TO MAKE CRAB A SUPERHERO!

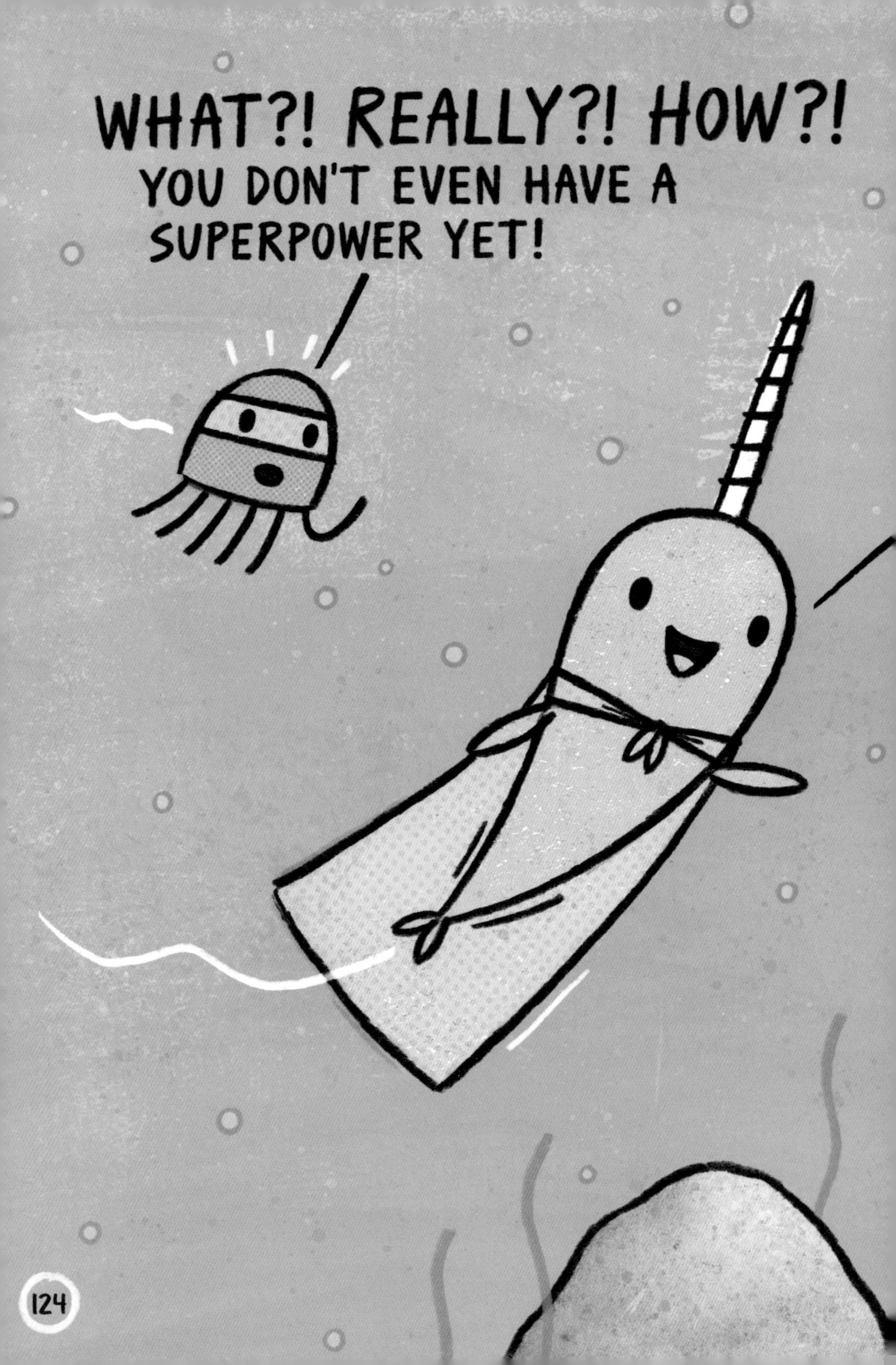
WHAT?! REALLY?! HOW?!
YOU DON'T EVEN HAVE A SUPERPOWER YET!

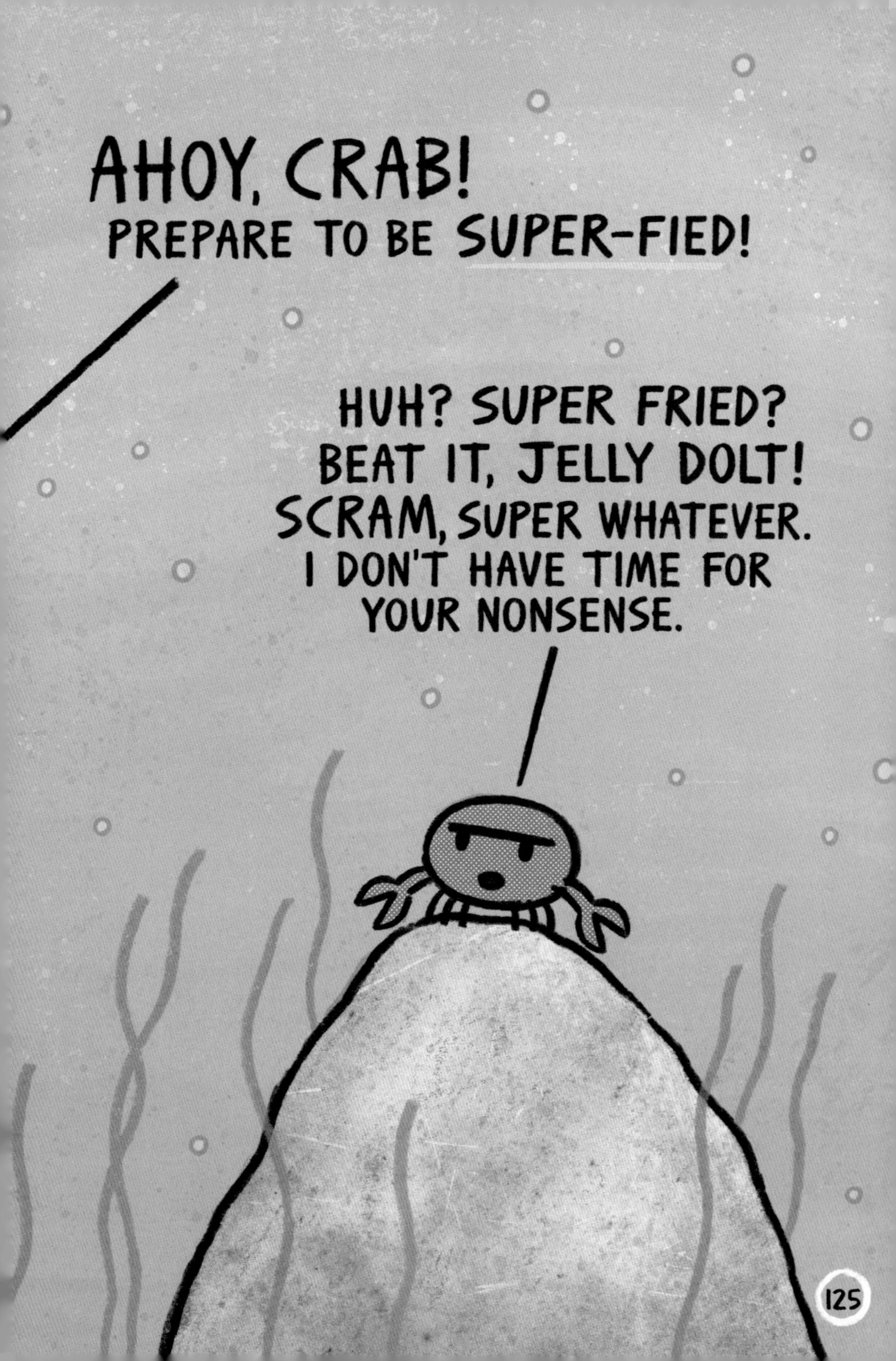
AHOY, CRAB! PREPARE TO BE SUPER-FIED!
HUH? SUPER FRIED? BEAT IT, JELLY DOLT! SCRAM, SUPER WHATEVER. I DON'T HAVE TIME FOR YOUR NONSENSE.

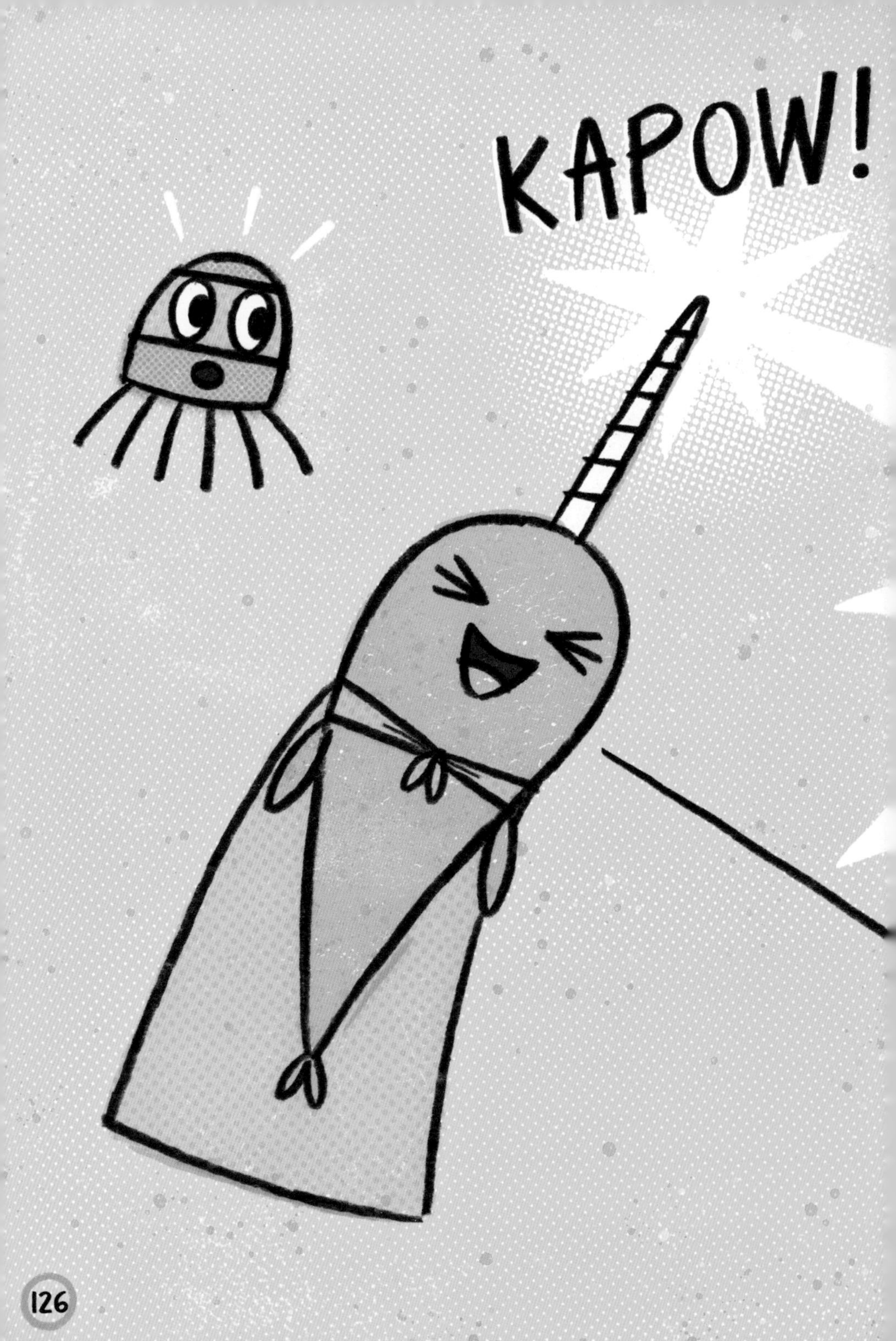
KAPOW!

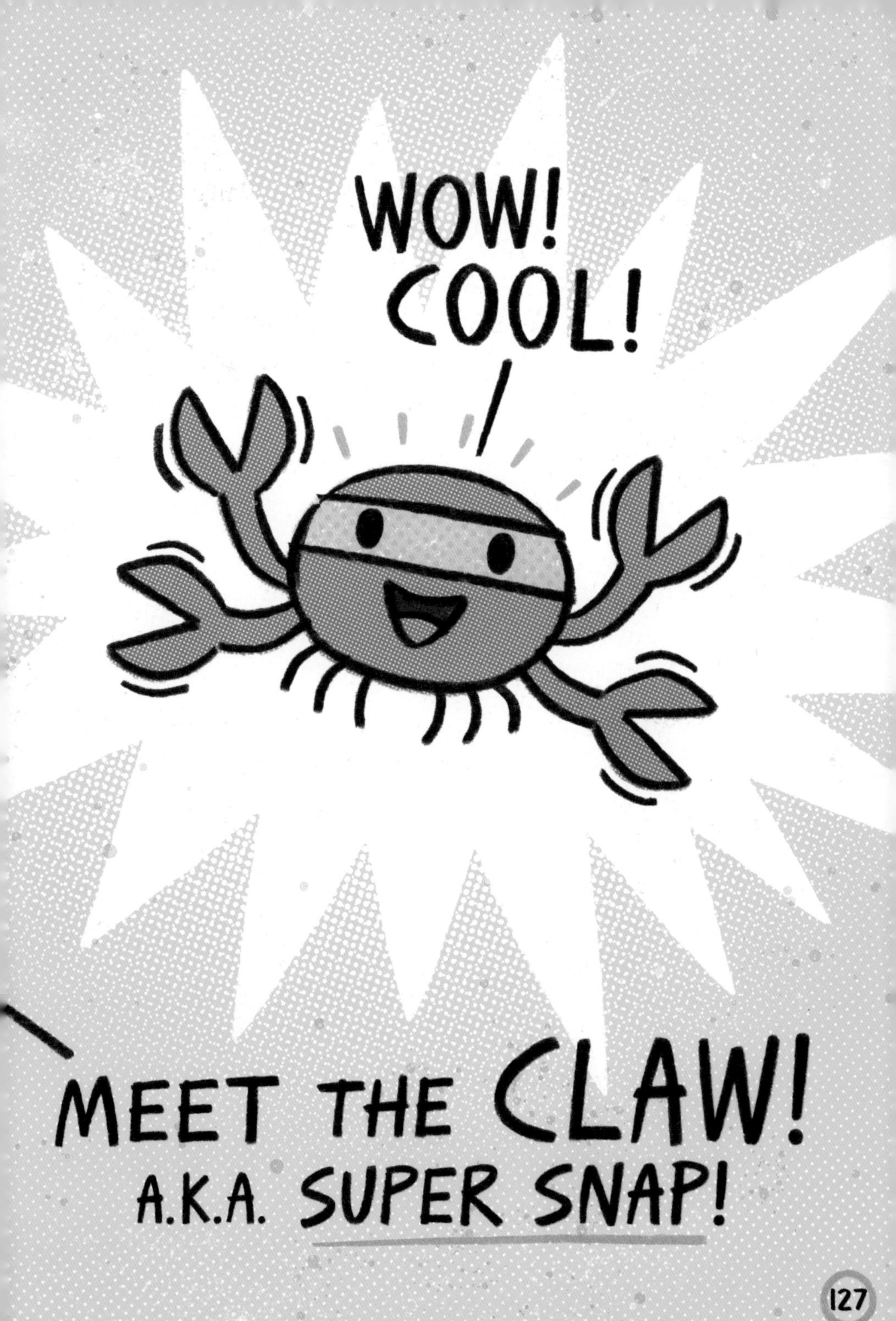
WOW! COOL!
MEET THE CLAW!
A.K.A. SUPER SNAP!

WHOA! I CAN'T BELIEVE IT! YOUR SUPERPOWER IS THE POWER TO BRING OUT THE SUPER IN OTHERS!

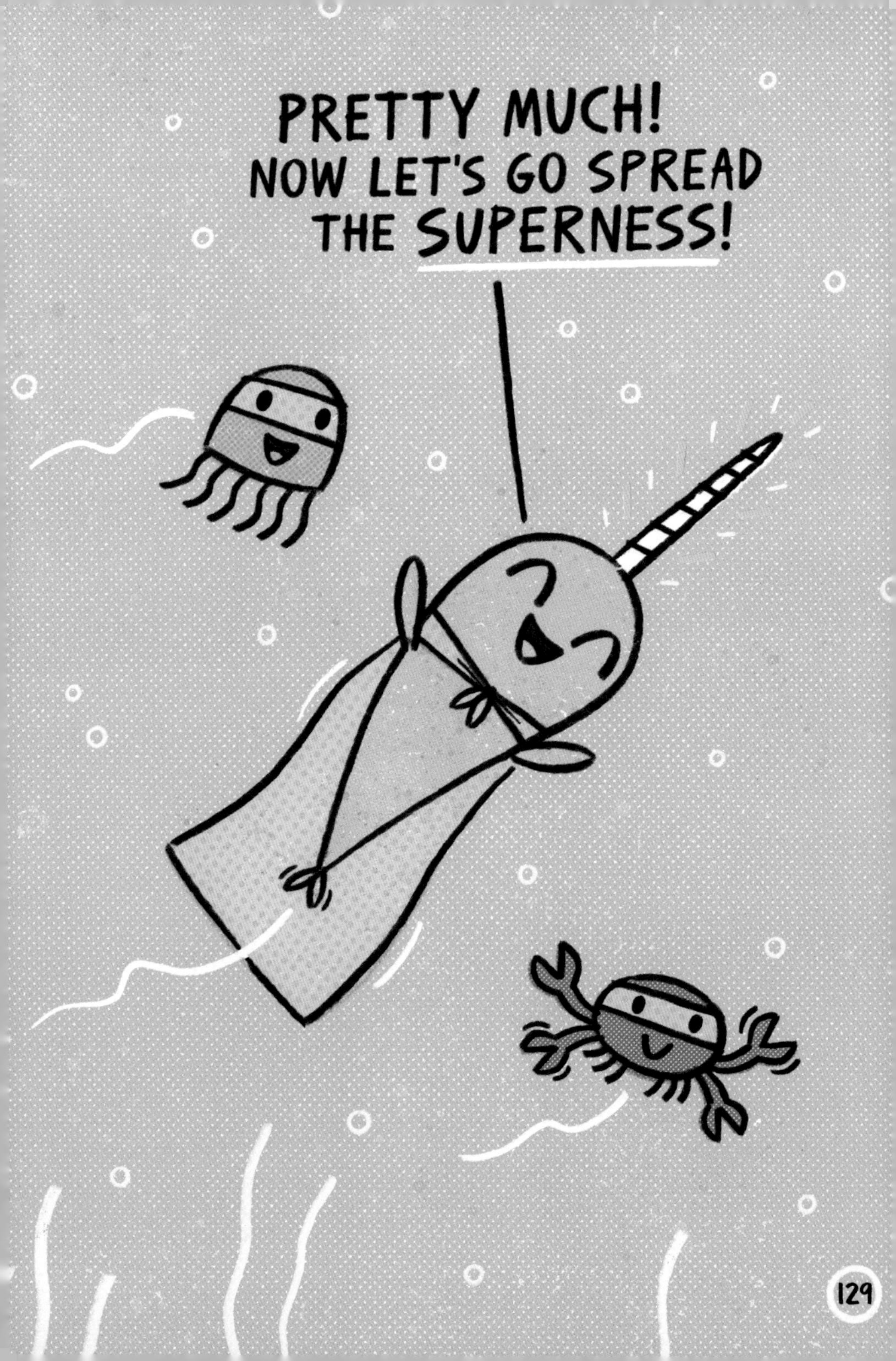
PRETTY MUCH! NOW LET'S GO SPREAD THE SUPERNESS!

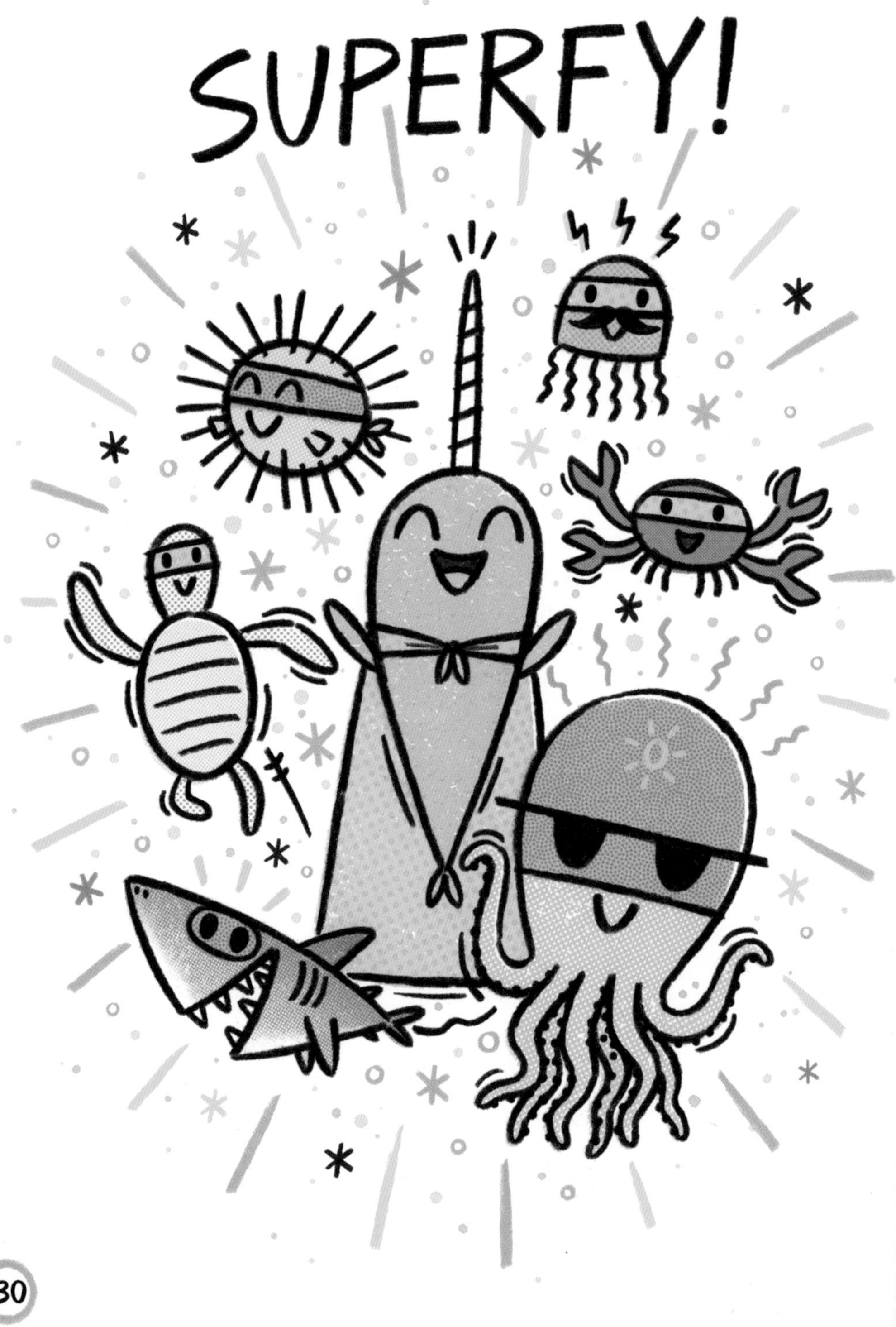
SUPERFY!

READ ON FOR SOME
SUPER PODTASTIC
NARWHAL AND JELLY
ACTIVITIES!

HOW TO DRAW NARWHAL!

1 DRAW AN UPSIDE-DOWN RAINDROP.

2 DRAW TWO TALL DOTS FOR EYES A BIT ABOVE THE WIDEST POINT OF THE RAINDROP.

3 LOOKS LIKE NARWHAL IS HAPPY TO SEE YOU!

4 DRAW TWO SUNFLOWER PETAL SHAPES FOR FLIPPERS — JUST ABOUT HALFWAY UP THE RAINDROP.

5 TWO MORE OF THOSE SHAPES AT THE TIP FOR THE TAIL.

6 AT THE VERY TOP, ADD A TALL TRIANGLE AND SLANTED STRIPES FOR A TUSK.*

7 ADD COLOR AND ACCESSORIZE (NARWHAL LOVES TO DRESS UP)!

*ON AN ACTUAL NARWHAL, THE TUSK COMES OUT OF THE UPPER LIP!

HOW TO DRAW JELLY JOLT!

1

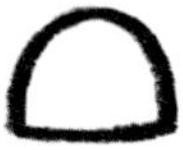

DRAW HALF
AN OVAL . . .

2

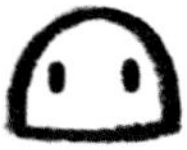

TWO LITTLE DOTS
IN THE MIDDLE
FOR EYES . . .

3

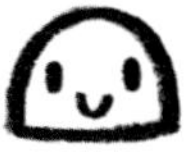

A "U" FOR A SMILE
A BIT BELOW THE
EYES . . .

4

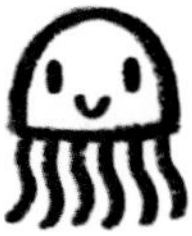

AND SIX WIGGLY LINES
FOR TENTACLES.

5

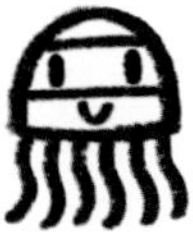

NOW TWO LINES
FOR A MASK . . .

6

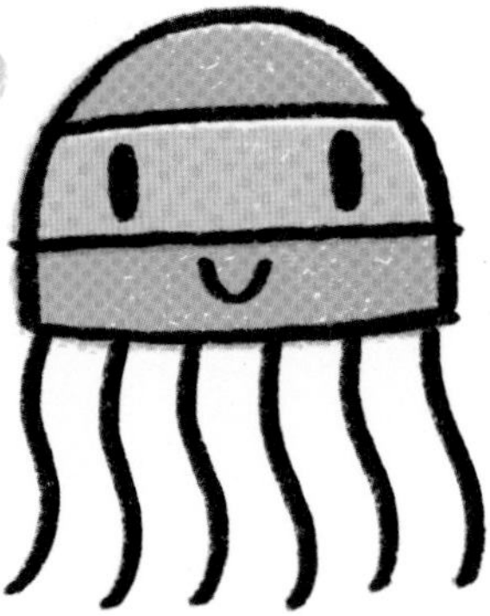

ADD SOME BLUE
AND YELLOW TOO!
THAT'LL DO!
LOOKS SUPER!

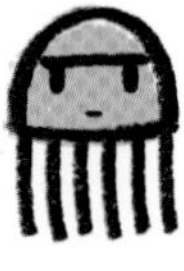

OR GO WITH SOME
STRAIGHT LINES
FOR BROW, MOUTH
AND TENTACLES FOR
A GRUMPY JELLY.

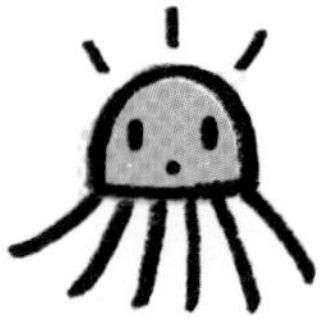

OR A DOT MOUTH AND
TENTACLES GOING
EVERY WHICH WAY FOR
A SURPRISED JELLY.

SUPERHERO
NAME GENERATOR

WHAT IS YOUR SUPERHERO NAME?

USE THE FIRST LETTER OF YOUR FIRST NAME . . .

A – AWESOME	J – JET	S – SUPER
B – BRILLIANT	K – KNIGHT	T – TOTAL
C – CAPTAIN	L – LEGENDARY	U – ULTIMATE
D – DAZZLING	M – MERVELOUS	V – VALIANT
E – ELECTRIC	N – NOBLE	W – WONDER
F – FINTASTIC	O – OUTSTANDING	X – XTRA
G – GOLDEN	P – POWTASTIC	Y – YONDER
H – HERO	Q – QUICK	Z – ZIPPY
I – INCREDIBLE	R – RADIANT	

AND THE FIRST LETTER OF YOUR LAST NAME!

A – AQUA	J – JOLT	S – SPARKLE
B – BUBBLES	K – KICK	T – TIDE
C – CRUNCH	L – LIGHTNING	U – UNIVERSE
D – DEEP	M – MASH	V – VICTORY
E – ECHO	N – NIGHT	W – WAFFLE
F – FLAVOR	O – OOMPH	X – X
G – GLOW	P – POP	Y – YEAH
H – HEART	Q – QUEST	Z – ZAP
I – INK	R – RAIN	

JOIN NARWHAL'S POD!
TAKE THIS PLEDGE TO O-FISH-ALLY BECOME A POD PAL.

THE POD PLEDGE!

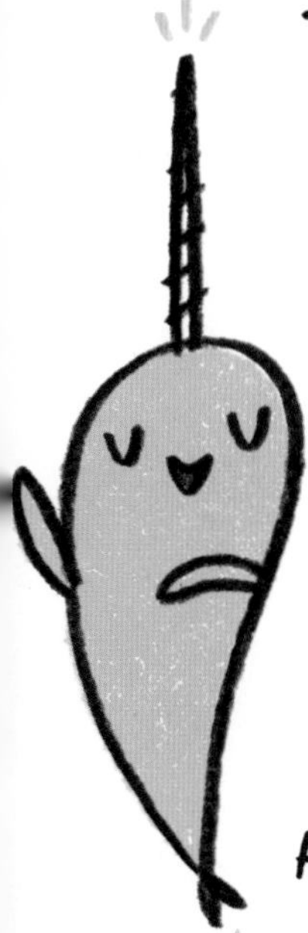

I PLEDGE TO BE PODTASTIC.

TO BE SWEET AND AWESOME
LIKE A WAFFLE!

TO BUOY UP MY POD PALS
AND ALL THOSE I MEET.

TO IMAGINE THE UNIMAGINABLE
AND MAKE MY DREAMS COME TRUE.
(OR AT LEAST TRY!)

YEP, I SOLEMNLY SWEAR TO BE SUPER
AND TO SUPERFY
THIS WATERFUL WORLD.

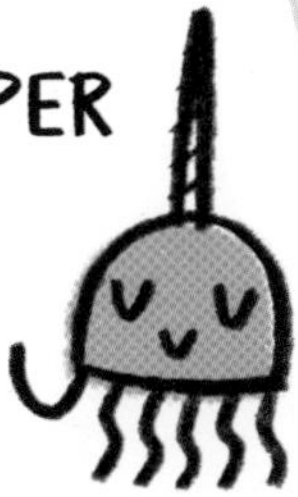

BECAUSE LIKE A NARWHAL . . .
I AM FINTASTIC, MER-VELOUS
AND UNFATHOMABLY AMAZING.

I AM A POD PAL.

NOW LET'S EAT WAFFLES!

HAVE YOU READ THESE NARWHAL AND JELLY BOOKS?

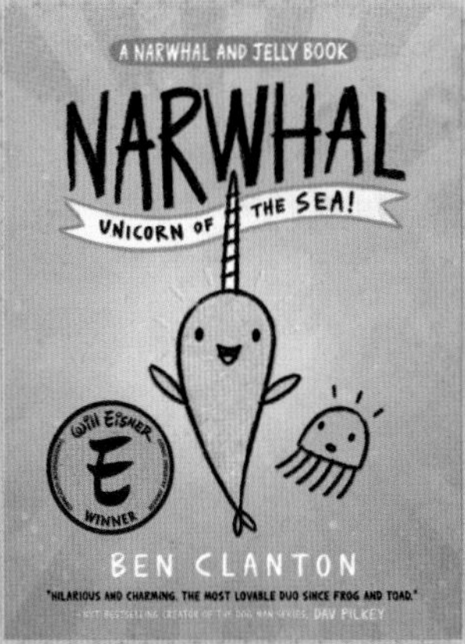
A NARWHAL AND JELLY BOOK
NARWHAL
UNICORN OF THE SEA!
WILL EISNER
E
WINNER
BEN CLANTON
"HILARIOUS AND CHARMING. THE MOST LOVABLE DUO SINCE FROG AND TOAD."
—NYT BESTSELLING CREATOR OF THE DOG MAN SERIES, DAV PILKEY

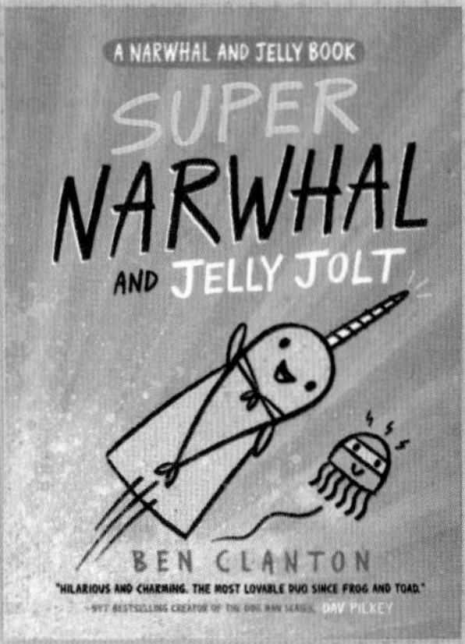
A NARWHAL AND JELLY BOOK
SUPER NARWHAL
AND JELLY JOLT
BEN CLANTON
"HILARIOUS AND CHARMING. THE MOST LOVABLE DUO SINCE FROG AND TOAD."
—NYT BESTSELLING CREATOR OF THE DOG MAN SERIES, DAV PILKEY

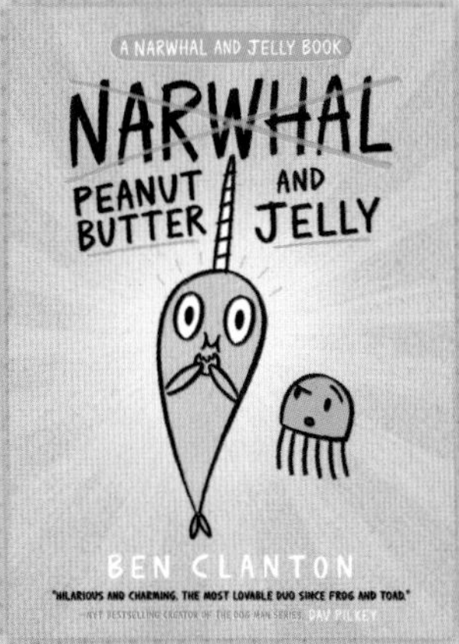
A NARWHAL AND JELLY BOOK
NARWHAL
PEANUT BUTTER AND JELLY
BEN CLANTON
"HILARIOUS AND CHARMING. THE MOST LOVABLE DUO SINCE FROG AND TOAD."
—NYT BESTSELLING CREATOR OF THE DOG MAN SERIES, DAV PILKEY

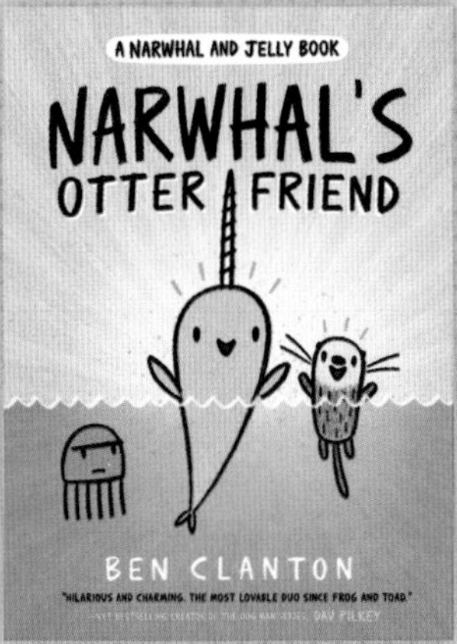
A NARWHAL AND JELLY BOOK
NARWHAL'S OTTER FRIEND
BEN CLANTON
"HILARIOUS AND CHARMING. THE MOST LOVABLE DUO SINCE FROG AND TOAD."
—NYT BESTSELLING CREATOR OF THE DOG MAN SERIES, DAV PILKEY

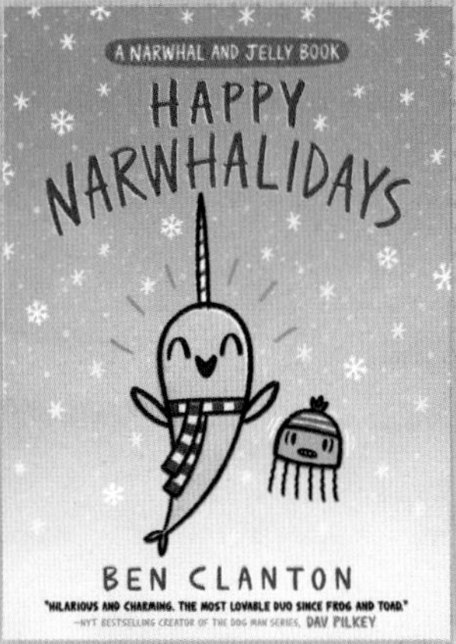
A NARWHAL AND JELLY BOOK
HAPPY NARWHALIDAYS
BEN CLANTON
"HILARIOUS AND CHARMING. THE MOST LOVABLE DUO SINCE FROG AND TOAD."
—NYT BESTSELLING CREATOR OF THE DOG MAN SERIES, DAV PILKEY

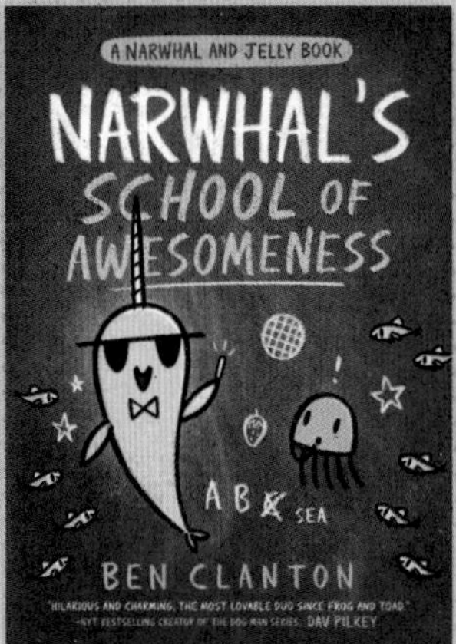
A NARWHAL AND JELLY BOOK
NARWHAL'S SCHOOL OF AWESOMENESS
A B SEA
BEN CLANTON
"HILARIOUS AND CHARMING. THE MOST LOVABLE DUO SINCE FROG AND TOAD."
—NYT BESTSELLING CREATOR OF THE DOG MAN SERIES, DAV PILKEY

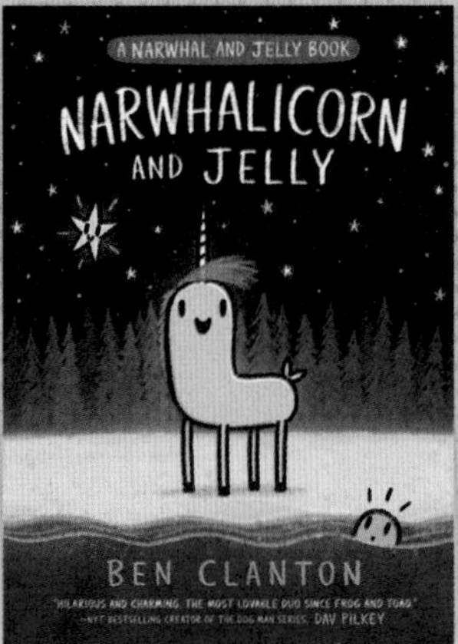
A NARWHAL AND JELLY BOOK
NARWHALICORN AND JELLY
BEN CLANTON
"HILARIOUS AND CHARMING. THE MOST LOVABLE DUO SINCE FROG AND TOAD."
—NYT BESTSELLING CREATOR OF THE DOG MAN SERIES, DAV PILKEY

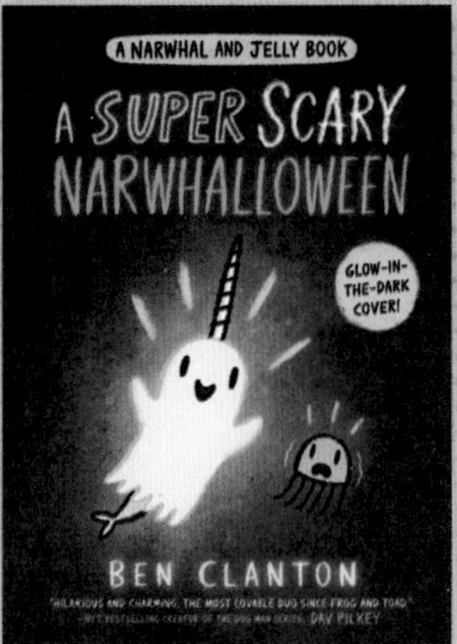
A NARWHAL AND JELLY BOOK
A SUPER SCARY NARWHALLOWEEN
GLOW-IN-THE-DARK COVER!
BEN CLANTON
"HILARIOUS AND CHARMING. THE MOST LOVABLE DUO SINCE FROG AND TOAD."
—NYT BESTSELLING CREATOR OF THE DOG MAN SERIES, DAV PILKEY